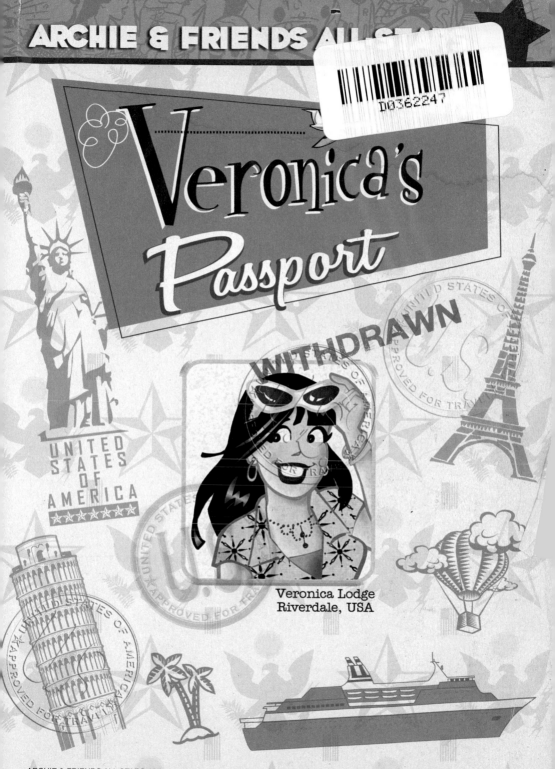

ARCHIE & FRIENDS ALL STARS

Veronica's Passport

Veronica Lodge
Riverdale, USA

ARCHIE & FRIENDS ALL STARS, Volume 1, 2009 Veronica's Passport. Printed in Canada. Published by Archie Comic Publications, Inc., 325 Fayette Avenue, Mamaroneck, New York 10543-2318. Archie characters created by John L. Goldwater; the likenesses of the Archie characters were drawn by Bob Montana. The individual characters' names and likenesses are the exclusive trademarks of Archie Comic Publications, Inc. All stories previously published and copyrighted by Archie Comic Publications, Inc. (or its predecessors) in magazine form in 1989-1991. This compilation copyright © 2009 Archie Comic Publications, Inc. All rights reserved. Nothing may be reprinted in whole or part without written permission from Archie Comic Publications, Inc.

ISBN-13: 978-1-879794-43-6 ISBN-10: 1-879794-43-8

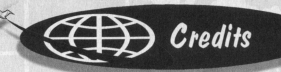

Credits

Co-CEO:
Jonathan Goldwater

Co-CEO:
Nancy Silberkleit

Co-President/Editor-in-Chief:
Victor Gorelick

Co-President/Director of Circulation:
Fred Mausser

Vice President/Managing Editor:
Michael Pellerito

Cover Art: **Dan Parent**
Art Director: **Joe Pepitone**
Production: **Stephen Oswald, Carlos Antunes, Paul Kaminski, Joe Morciglio, Rosario "Tito" Peña, Suzannah Rowntree**

COOLER THAN EVER!
R
ARCHIECOMICS.COM
TM & © Archie Comic Publications, Inc

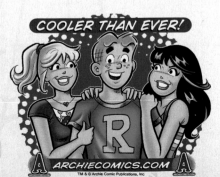

Table of Contents

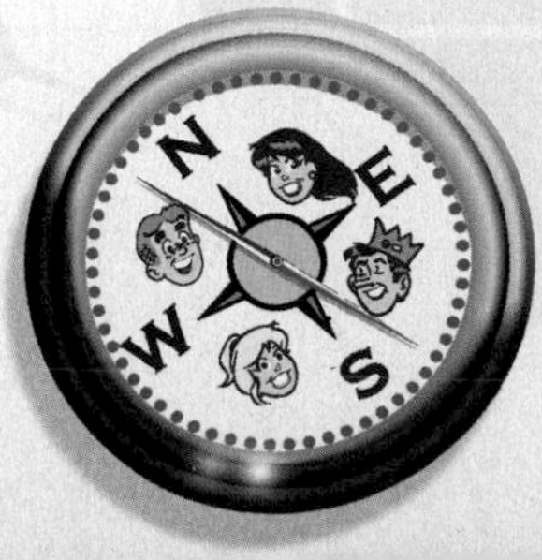

N
E
S
W

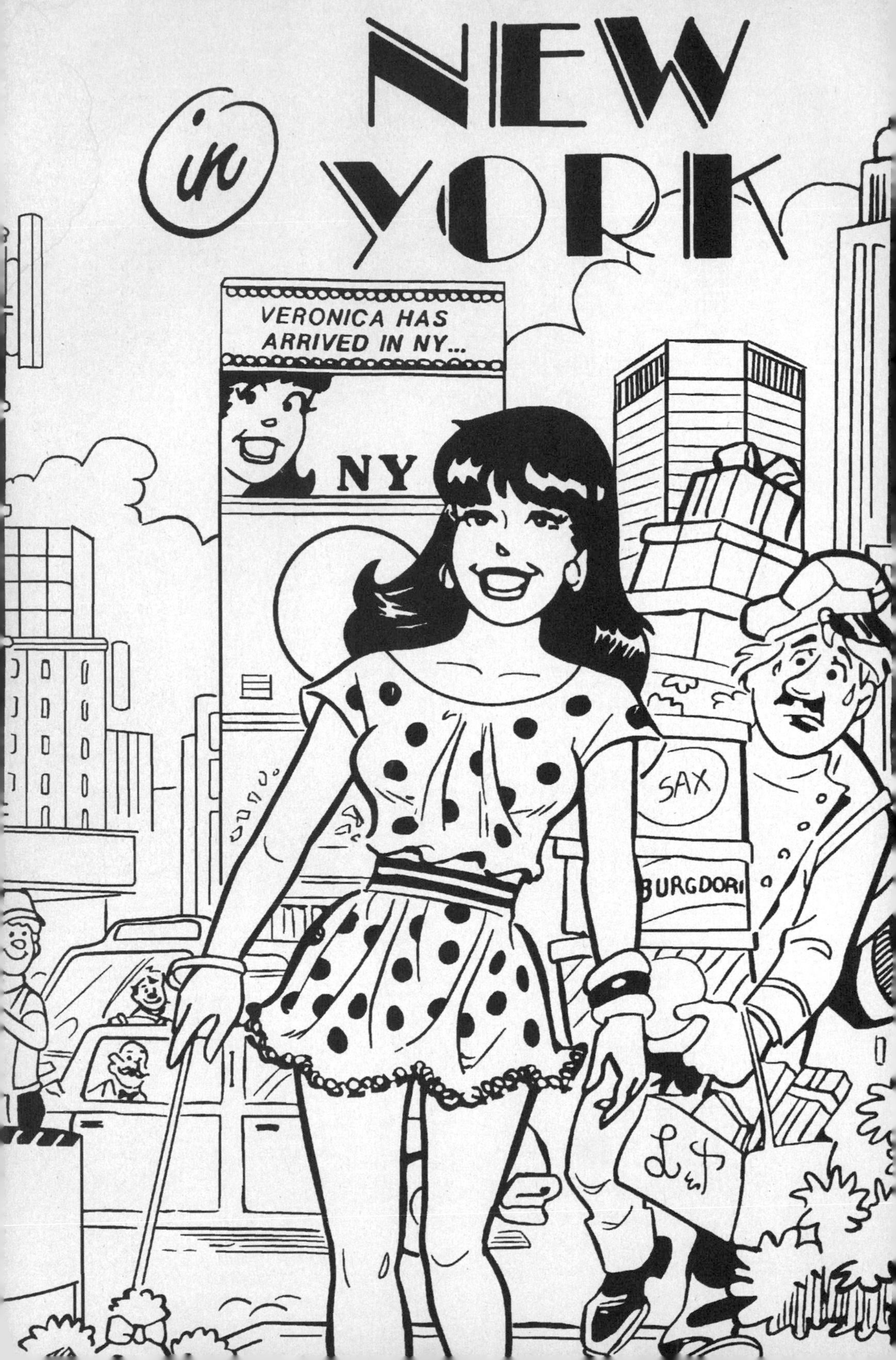
NEW
in
YORK
VERONICA HAS ARRIVED IN NY...
NY
SAX
BURGDORI

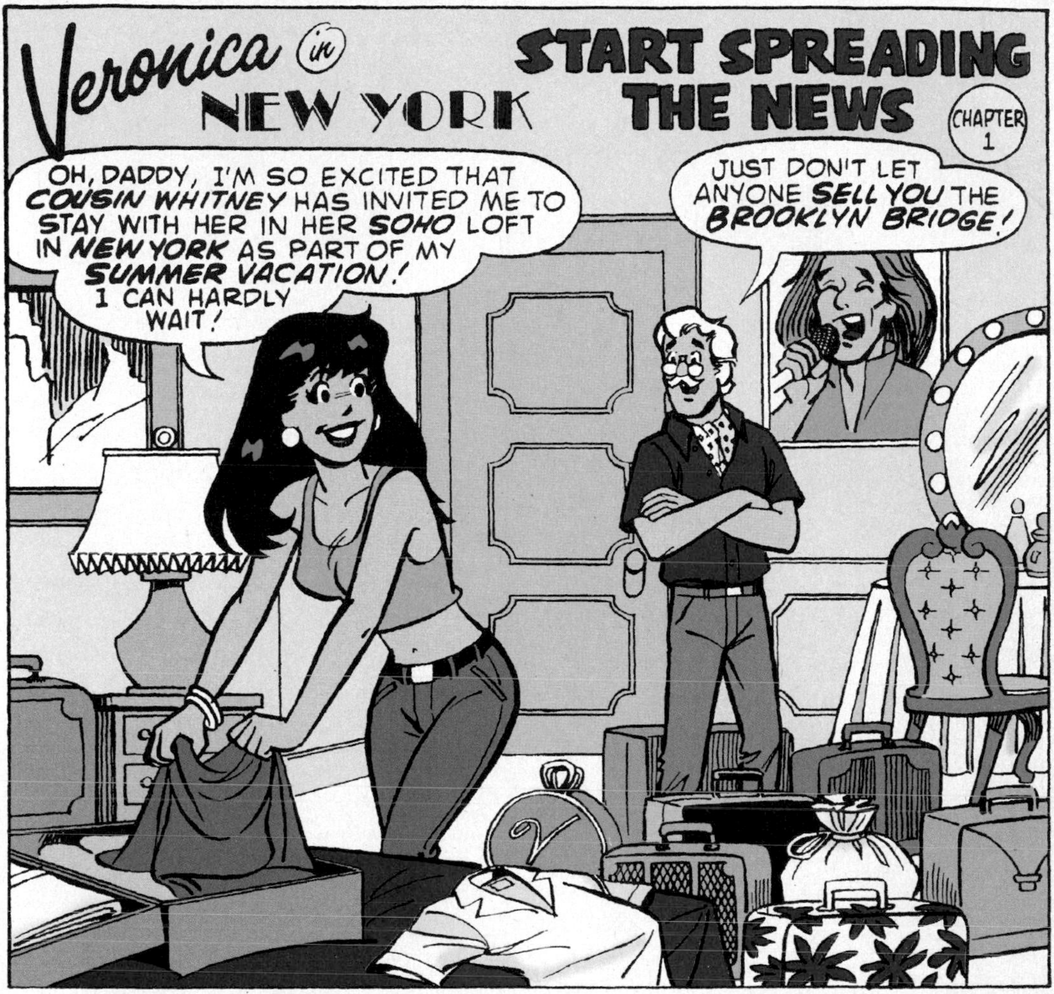
Veronica in NEW YORK
START SPREADING THE NEWS
CHAPTER 1
OH, DADDY, I'M SO EXCITED THAT COUSIN WHITNEY HAS INVITED ME TO STAY WITH HER IN HER SOHO LOFT IN NEW YORK AS PART OF MY SUMMER VACATION! I CAN HARDLY WAIT!
JUST DON'T LET ANYONE SELL YOU THE BROOKLYN BRIDGE!

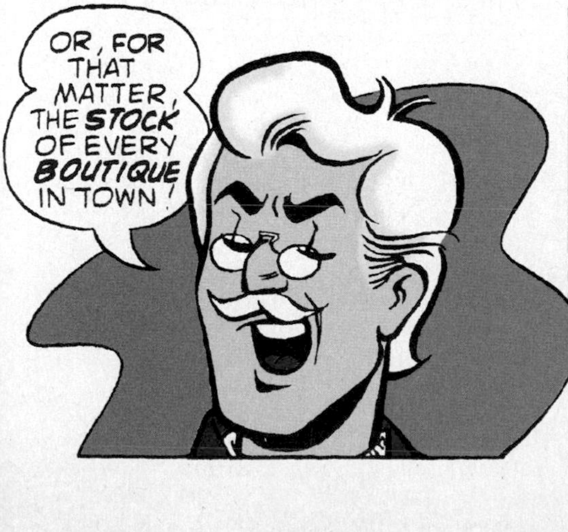
OR, FOR THAT MATTER, THE STOCK OF EVERY BOUTIQUE IN TOWN!

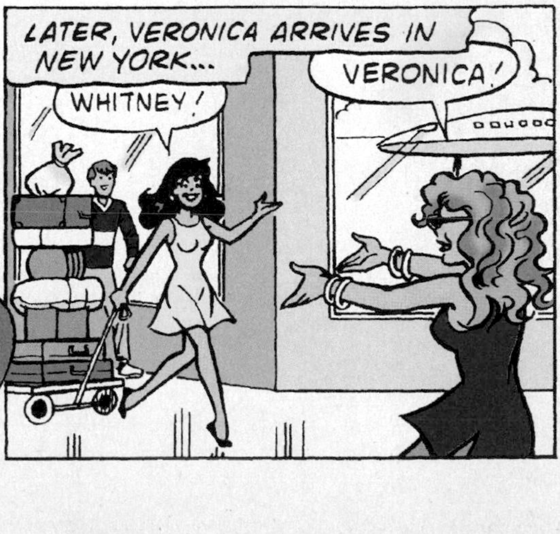
LATER, VERONICA ARRIVES IN NEW YORK...
WHITNEY!
VERONICA!

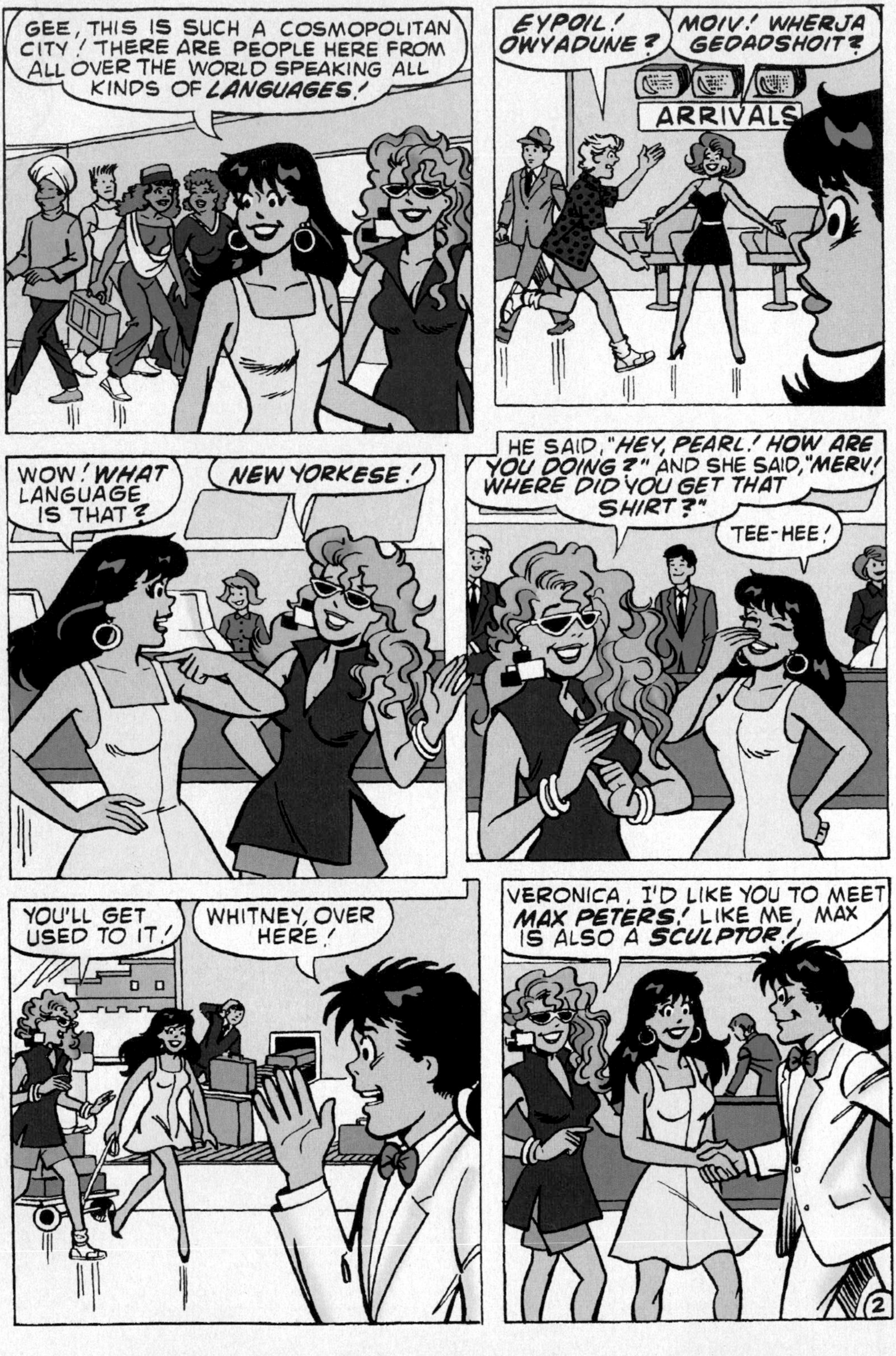
GEE, THIS IS SUCH A COSMOPOLITAN CITY! THERE ARE PEOPLE HERE FROM ALL OVER THE WORLD SPEAKING ALL KINDS OF LANGUAGES!
EYPOIL! OWYADUNE?
MOIV! WHERJA GEDADSHOIT?
ARRIVALS
WOW! WHAT LANGUAGE IS THAT?
NEW YORKESE!
HE SAID, "HEY, PEARL! HOW ARE YOU DOING?" AND SHE SAID, "MERV! WHERE DID YOU GET THAT SHIRT?"
TEE-HEE!
YOU'LL GET USED TO IT!
WHITNEY, OVER HERE!
VERONICA, I'D LIKE YOU TO MEET MAX PETERS! LIKE ME, MAX IS ALSO A SCULPTOR!
2

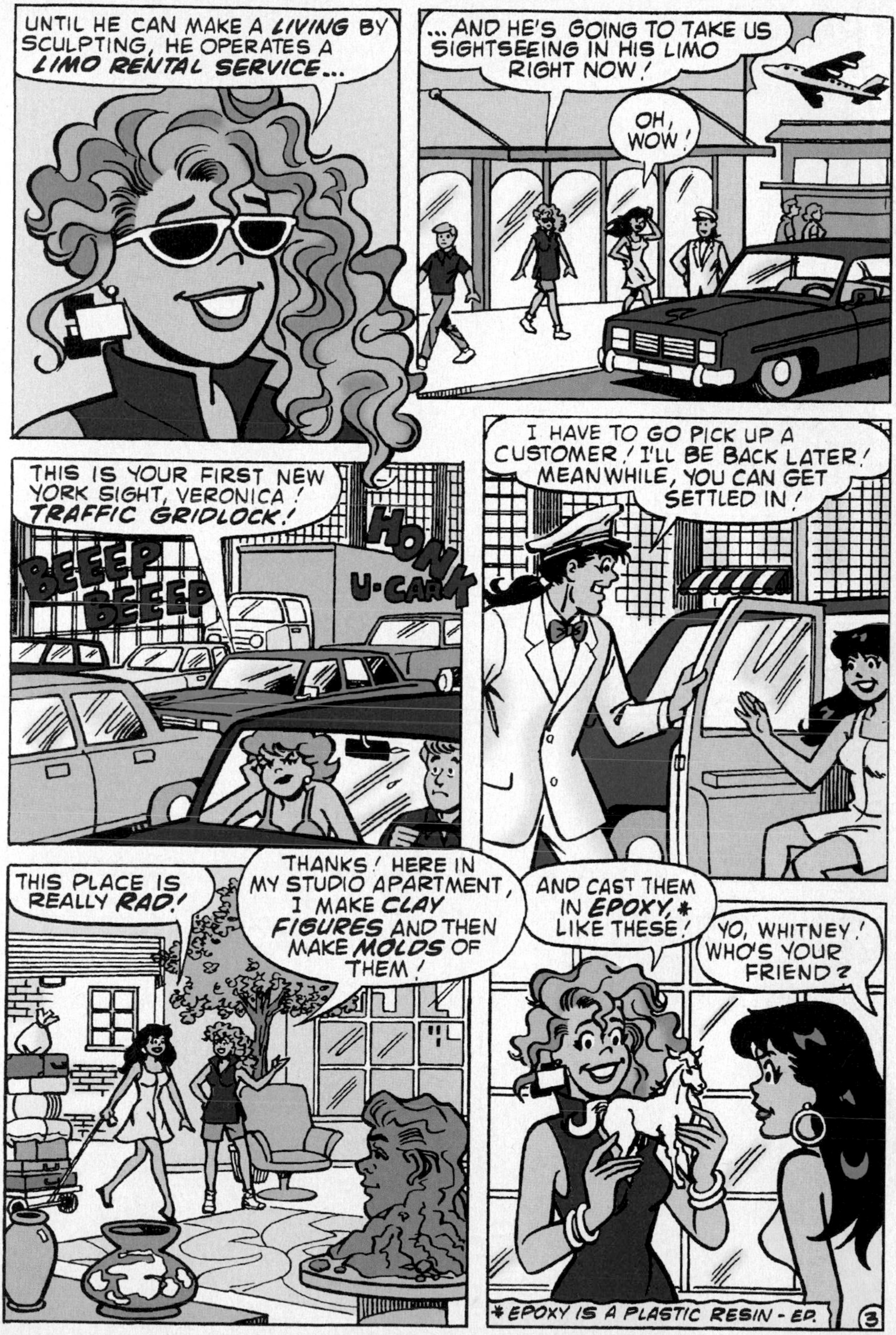

UNTIL HE CAN MAKE A LIVING BY SCULPTING, HE OPERATES A LIMO RENTAL SERVICE...
...AND HE'S GOING TO TAKE US SIGHTSEEING IN HIS LIMO RIGHT NOW!
OH, WOW!
THIS IS YOUR FIRST NEW YORK SIGHT, VERONICA! TRAFFIC GRIDLOCK!
BEEEP BEEEP
HONK
U-CAR
I HAVE TO GO PICK UP A CUSTOMER! I'LL BE BACK LATER! MEANWHILE, YOU CAN GET SETTLED IN!
THIS PLACE IS REALLY RAD!
THANKS! HERE IN MY STUDIO APARTMENT, I MAKE CLAY FIGURES AND THEN MAKE MOLDS OF THEM!
AND CAST THEM IN EPOXY,* LIKE THESE!
YO, WHITNEY! WHO'S YOUR FRIEND?
*EPOXY IS A PLASTIC RESIN - ED.
3

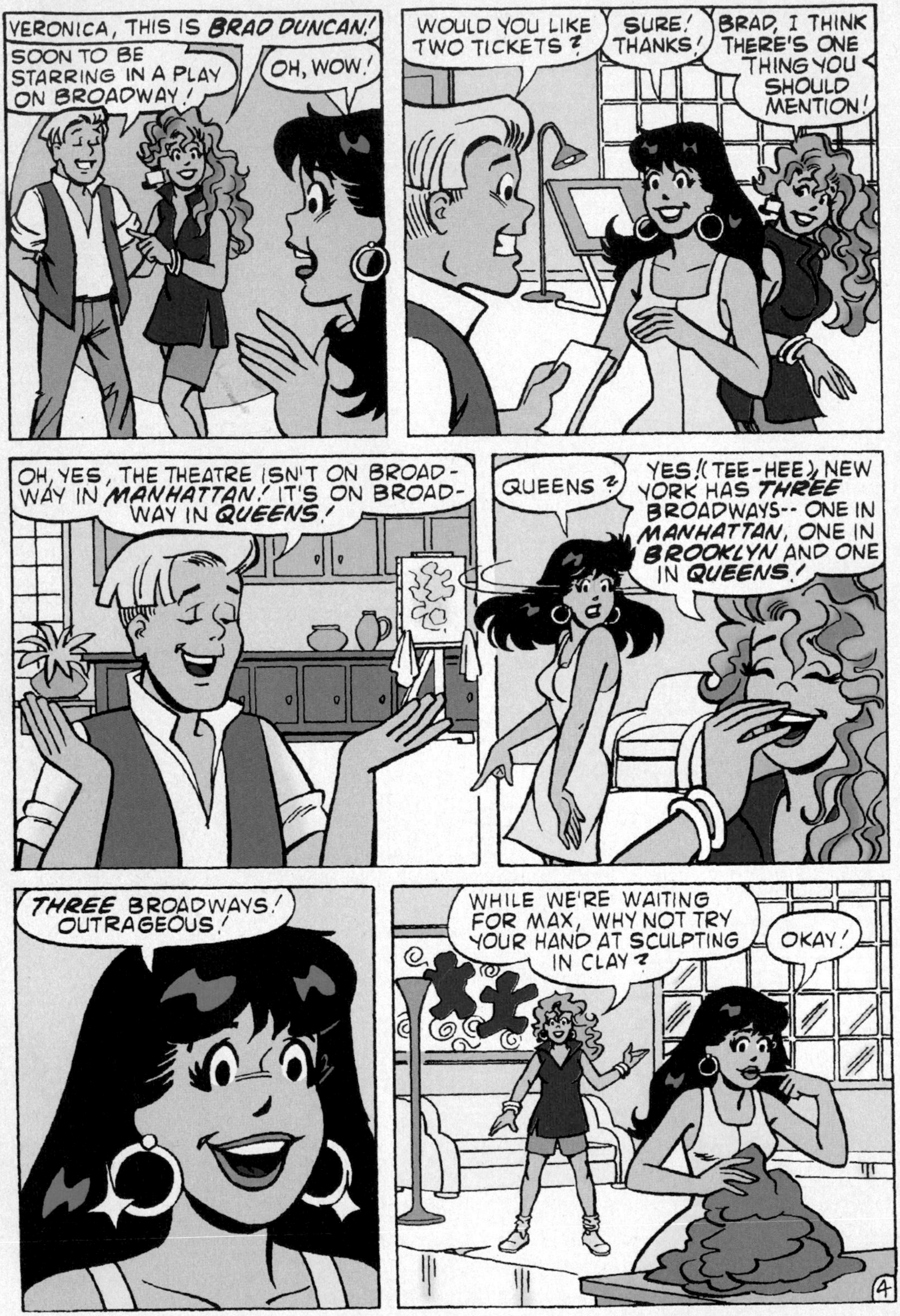
VERONICA, THIS IS BRAD DUNCAN!
SOON TO BE STARRING IN A PLAY ON BROADWAY!
OH, WOW!
WOULD YOU LIKE TWO TICKETS?
SURE! THANKS!
BRAD, I THINK THERE'S ONE THING YOU SHOULD MENTION!
OH, YES, THE THEATRE ISN'T ON BROADWAY IN MANHATTAN! IT'S ON BROADWAY IN QUEENS!
QUEENS?
YES! (TEE-HEE), NEW YORK HAS THREE BROADWAYS-- ONE IN MANHATTAN, ONE IN BROOKLYN AND ONE IN QUEENS!
THREE BROADWAYS! OUTRAGEOUS!
WHILE WE'RE WAITING FOR MAX, WHY NOT TRY YOUR HAND AT SCULPTING IN CLAY?
OKAY!
4

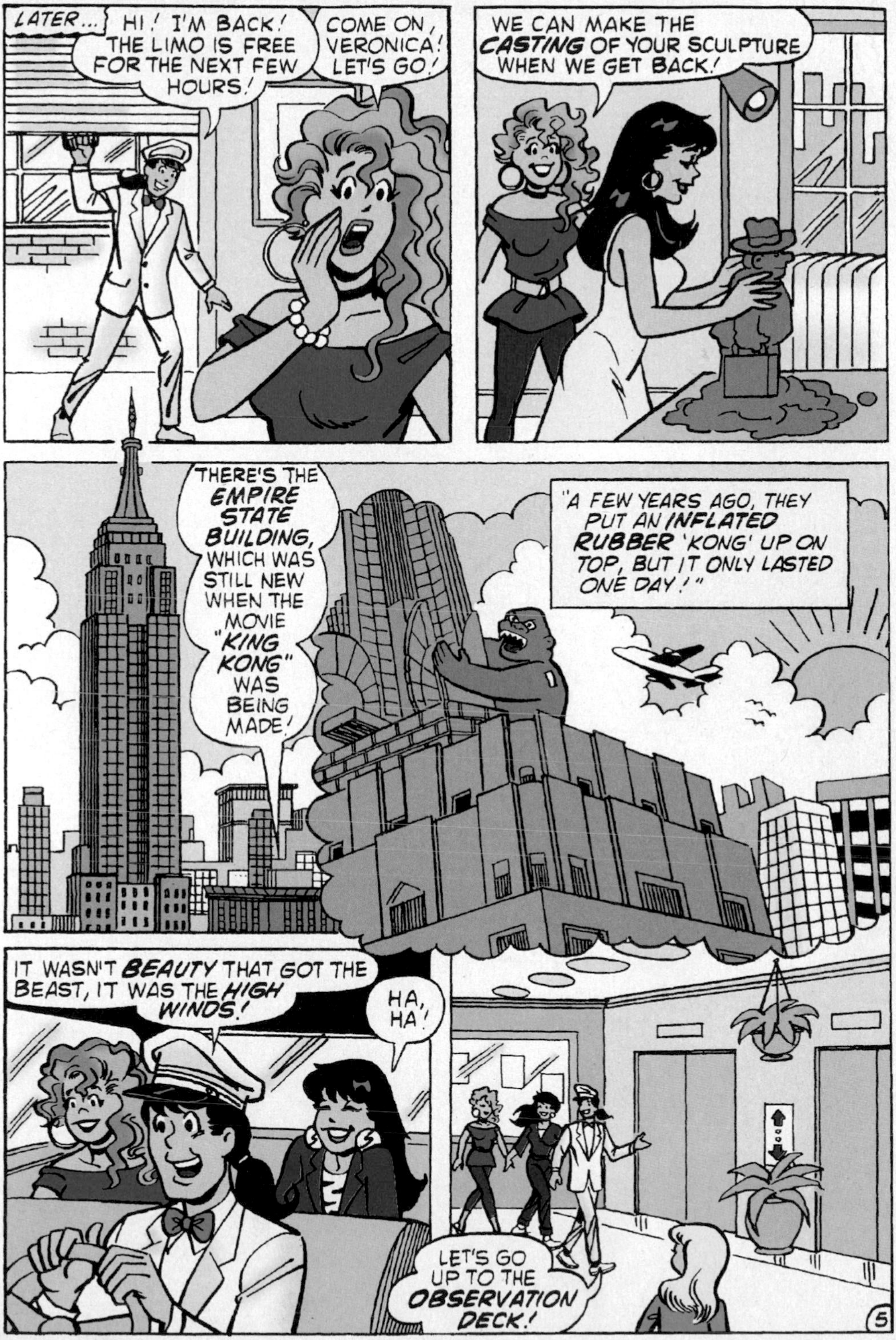
LATER...
HI! I'M BACK! THE LIMO IS FREE FOR THE NEXT FEW HOURS!
COME ON, VERONICA! LET'S GO!
WE CAN MAKE THE CASTING OF YOUR SCULPTURE WHEN WE GET BACK!
THERE'S THE EMPIRE STATE BUILDING, WHICH WAS STILL NEW WHEN THE MOVIE "KING KONG" WAS BEING MADE!
"A FEW YEARS AGO, THEY PUT AN INFLATED RUBBER 'KONG' UP ON TOP, BUT IT ONLY LASTED ONE DAY!"
IT WASN'T BEAUTY THAT GOT THE BEAST, IT WAS THE HIGH WINDS!
HA, HA!
LET'S GO UP TO THE OBSERVATION DECK!
5

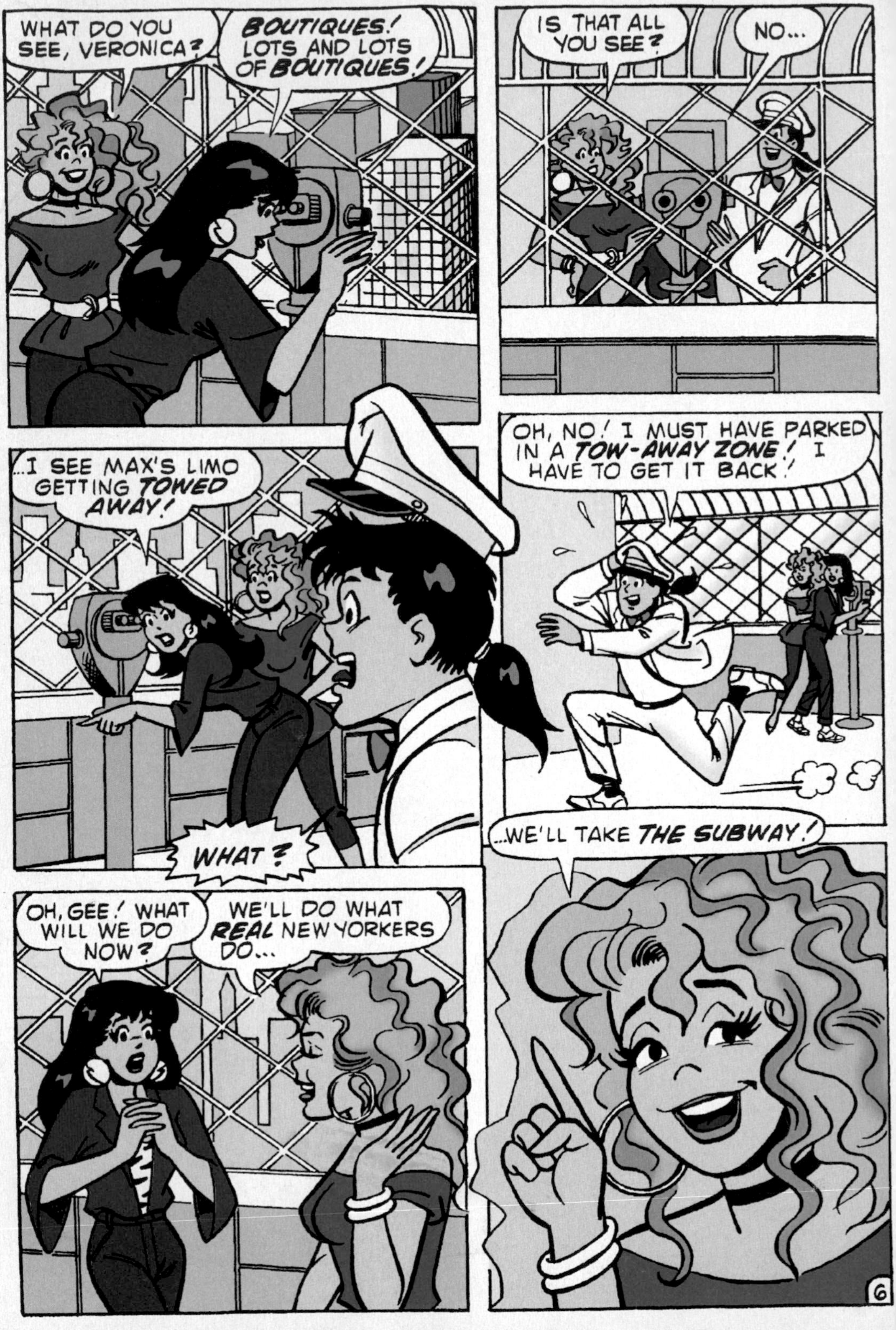
WHAT DO YOU SEE, VERONICA?
BOUTIQUES! LOTS AND LOTS OF BOUTIQUES!
IS THAT ALL YOU SEE?
NO...
...I SEE MAX'S LIMO GETTING TOWED AWAY!
WHAT?
OH, NO! I MUST HAVE PARKED IN A TOW-AWAY ZONE! I HAVE TO GET IT BACK!
OH, GEE! WHAT WILL WE DO NOW?
WE'LL DO WHAT REAL NEW YORKERS DO...
...WE'LL TAKE THE SUBWAY!
6

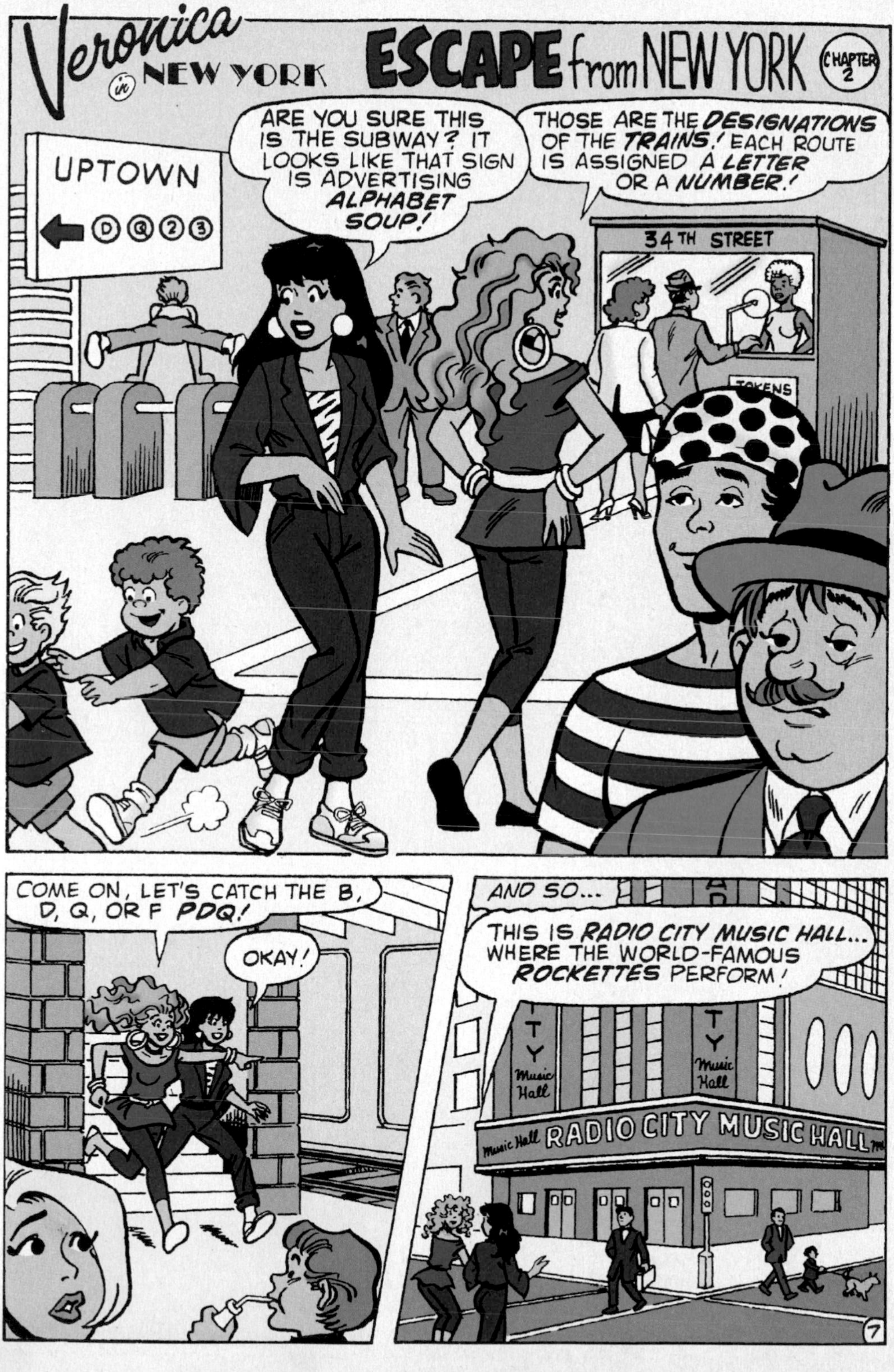
Veronica in NEW YORK
ESCAPE from NEW YORK
CHAPTER 2
UPTOWN
D Q 2 3
ARE YOU SURE THIS IS THE SUBWAY? IT LOOKS LIKE THAT SIGN IS ADVERTISING ALPHABET SOUP!
THOSE ARE THE DESIGNATIONS OF THE TRAINS! EACH ROUTE IS ASSIGNED A LETTER OR A NUMBER!
34TH STREET
TOKENS
COME ON, LET'S CATCH THE B, D, Q, OR F PDQ!
OKAY!
AND SO...
THIS IS RADIO CITY MUSIC HALL... WHERE THE WORLD-FAMOUS ROCKETTES PERFORM!
Music Hall
RADIO CITY MUSIC HALL
7

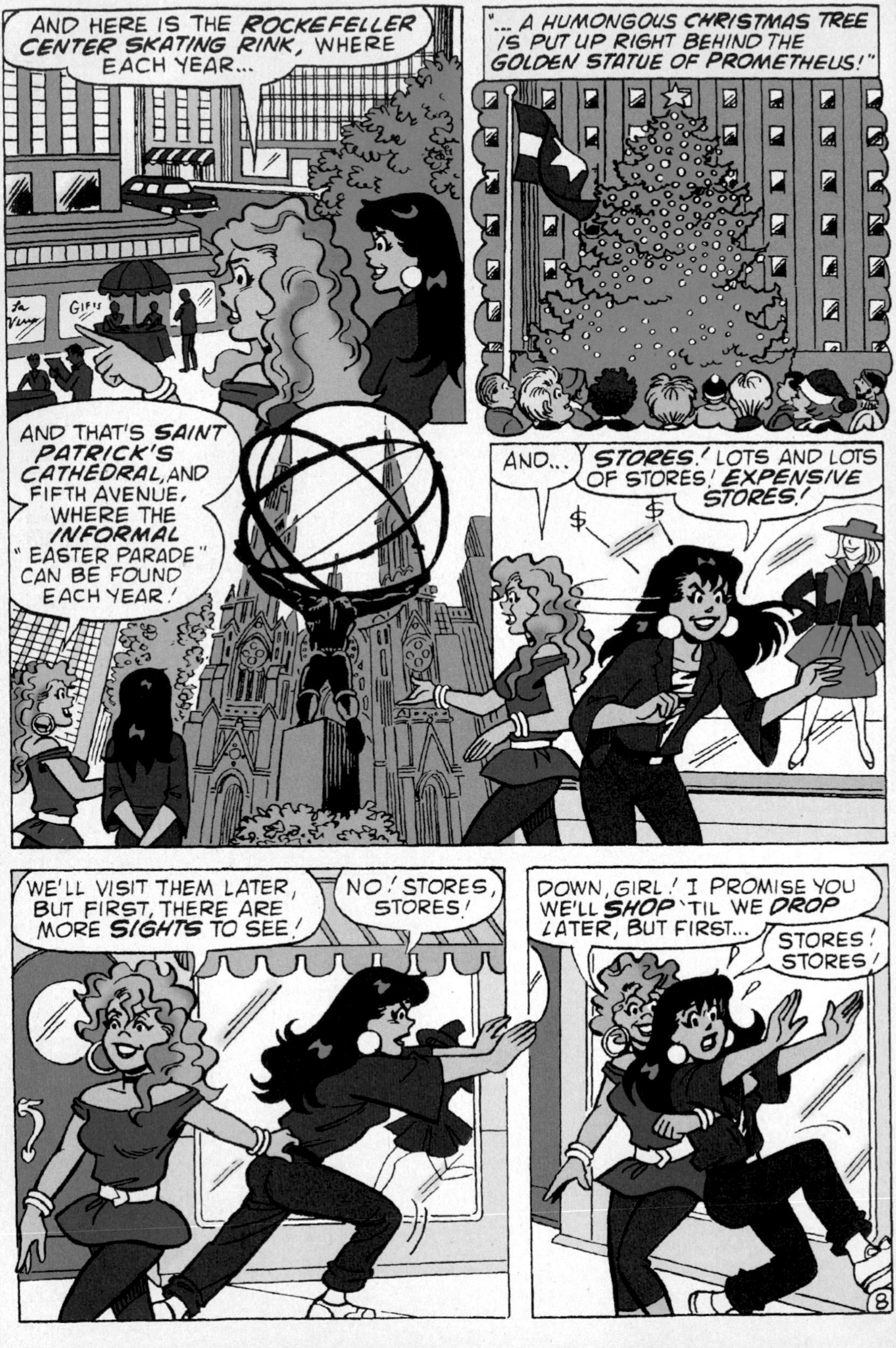
AND HERE IS THE ROCKEFELLER CENTER SKATING RINK, WHERE EACH YEAR...
"... A HUMONGOUS CHRISTMAS TREE IS PUT UP RIGHT BEHIND THE GOLDEN STATUE OF PROMETHEUS!"
GIFTS
AND THAT'S SAINT PATRICK'S CATHEDRAL, AND FIFTH AVENUE, WHERE THE INFORMAL "EASTER PARADE" CAN BE FOUND EACH YEAR!
AND...
STORES! LOTS AND LOTS OF STORES! EXPENSIVE STORES!
WE'LL VISIT THEM LATER, BUT FIRST, THERE ARE MORE SIGHTS TO SEE!
NO! STORES, STORES!
DOWN, GIRL! I PROMISE YOU WE'LL SHOP 'TIL WE DROP LATER, BUT FIRST...
STORES! STORES!
8

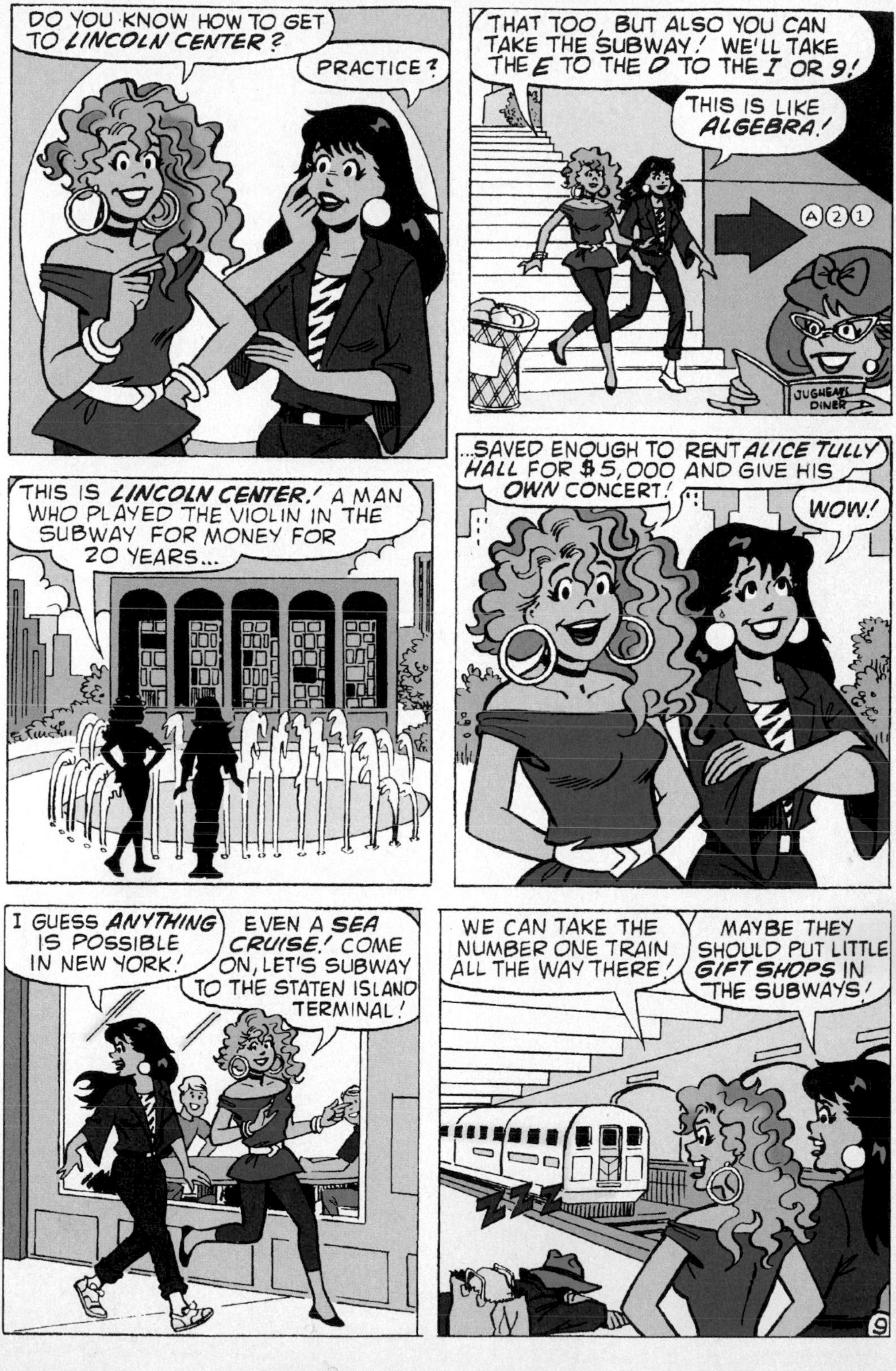
DO YOU KNOW HOW TO GET TO LINCOLN CENTER?
PRACTICE?
THAT TOO, BUT ALSO YOU CAN TAKE THE SUBWAY! WE'LL TAKE THE E TO THE D TO THE 1 OR 9!
THIS IS LIKE ALGEBRA!
A 2 1
JUGHEAD'S DINER
THIS IS LINCOLN CENTER! A MAN WHO PLAYED THE VIOLIN IN THE SUBWAY FOR MONEY FOR 20 YEARS...
...SAVED ENOUGH TO RENT ALICE TULLY HALL FOR $5,000 AND GIVE HIS OWN CONCERT!
WOW!
I GUESS ANYTHING IS POSSIBLE IN NEW YORK!
EVEN A SEA CRUISE! COME ON, LET'S SUBWAY TO THE STATEN ISLAND TERMINAL!
WE CAN TAKE THE NUMBER ONE TRAIN ALL THE WAY THERE!
MAYBE THEY SHOULD PUT LITTLE GIFT SHOPS IN THE SUBWAYS!
ZZZ
9

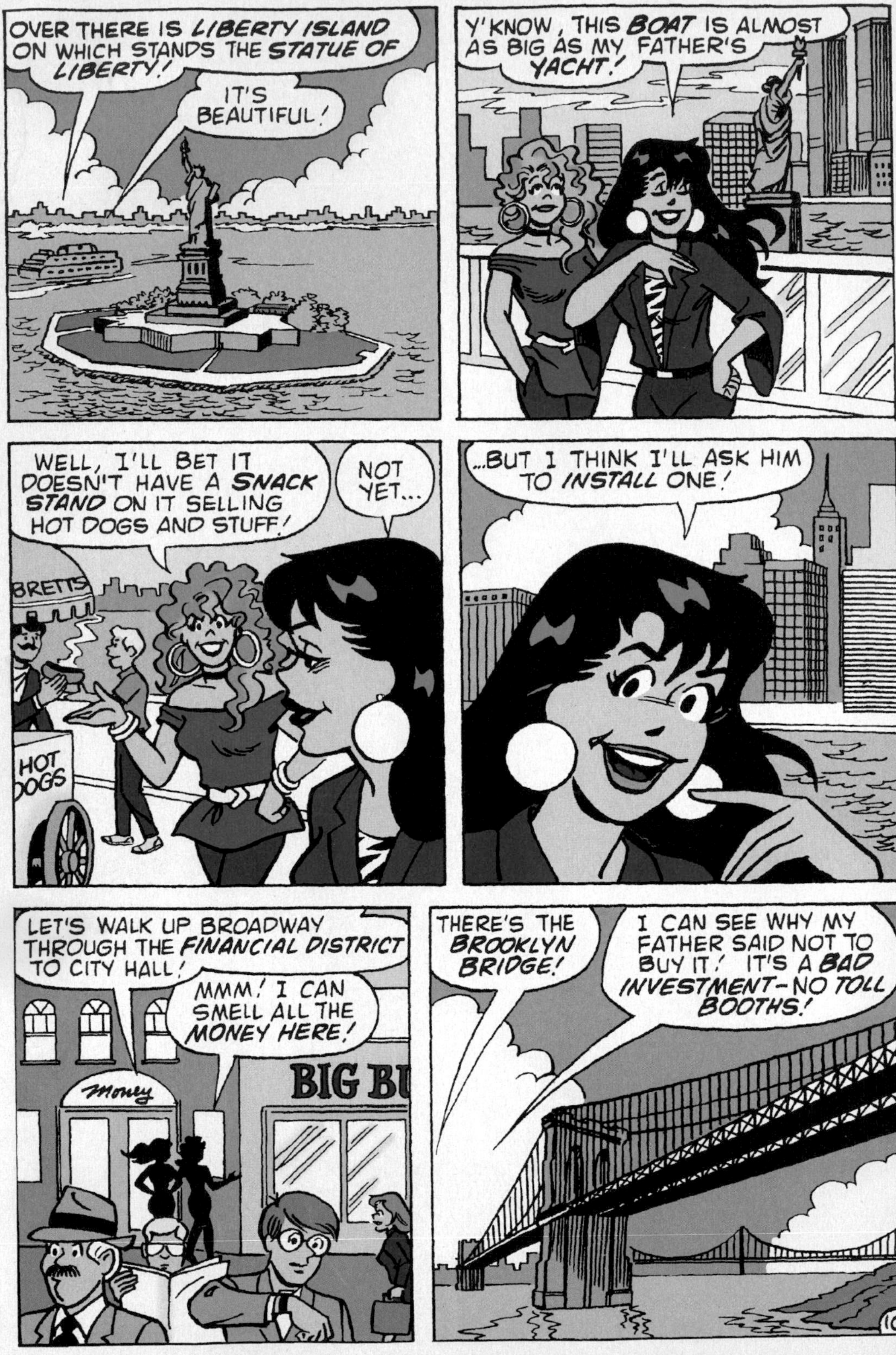
OVER THERE IS LIBERTY ISLAND ON WHICH STANDS THE STATUE OF LIBERTY!
IT'S BEAUTIFUL!
Y'KNOW, THIS BOAT IS ALMOST AS BIG AS MY FATHER'S YACHT!
WELL, I'LL BET IT DOESN'T HAVE A SNACK STAND ON IT SELLING HOT DOGS AND STUFF!
NOT YET...
BRETTS
HOT DOGS
...BUT I THINK I'LL ASK HIM TO INSTALL ONE!
LET'S WALK UP BROADWAY THROUGH THE FINANCIAL DISTRICT TO CITY HALL!
MMM! I CAN SMELL ALL THE MONEY HERE!
Money
BIG BU
THERE'S THE BROOKLYN BRIDGE!
I CAN SEE WHY MY FATHER SAID NOT TO BUY IT! IT'S A BAD INVESTMENT- NO TOLL BOOTHS!
10

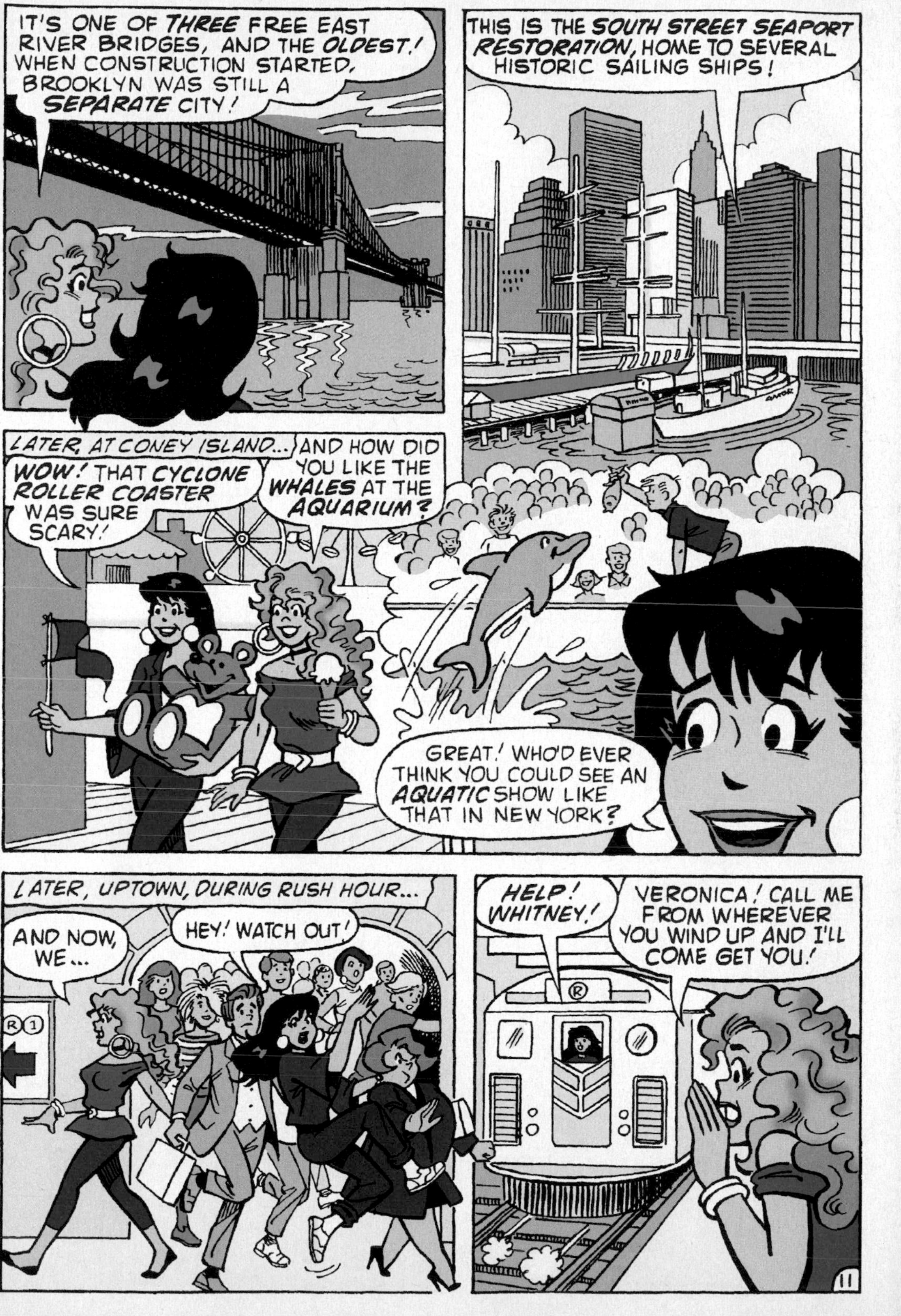
IT'S ONE OF THREE FREE EAST RIVER BRIDGES, AND THE OLDEST! WHEN CONSTRUCTION STARTED, BROOKLYN WAS STILL A SEPARATE CITY!
THIS IS THE SOUTH STREET SEAPORT RESTORATION, HOME TO SEVERAL HISTORIC SAILING SHIPS!
LATER, AT CONEY ISLAND...
WOW! THAT CYCLONE ROLLER COASTER WAS SURE SCARY!
AND HOW DID YOU LIKE THE WHALES AT THE AQUARIUM?
GREAT! WHO'D EVER THINK YOU COULD SEE AN AQUATIC SHOW LIKE THAT IN NEW YORK?
LATER, UPTOWN, DURING RUSH HOUR...
AND NOW, WE...
HEY! WATCH OUT!
HELP! WHITNEY!
VERONICA! CALL ME FROM WHEREVER YOU WIND UP AND I'LL COME GET YOU!
11

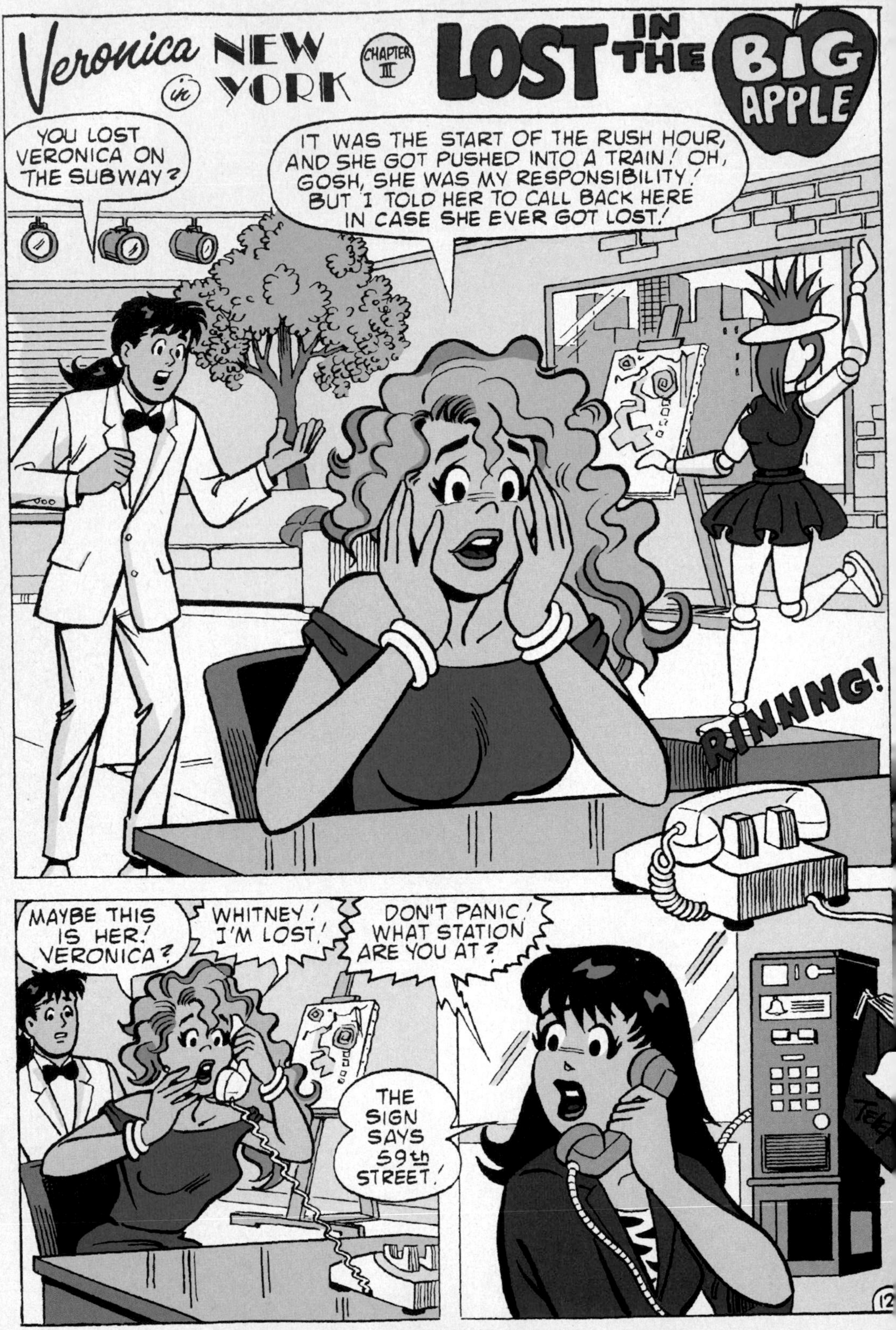
Veronica in NEW YORK
CHAPTER III
LOST IN THE BIG APPLE
YOU LOST VERONICA ON THE SUBWAY?
IT WAS THE START OF THE RUSH HOUR, AND SHE GOT PUSHED INTO A TRAIN! OH, GOSH, SHE WAS MY RESPONSIBILITY! BUT I TOLD HER TO CALL BACK HERE IN CASE SHE EVER GOT LOST!
RINNNG!
MAYBE THIS IS HER! VERONICA?
WHITNEY! I'M LOST!
DON'T PANIC! WHAT STATION ARE YOU AT?
THE SIGN SAYS 59th STREET!
12

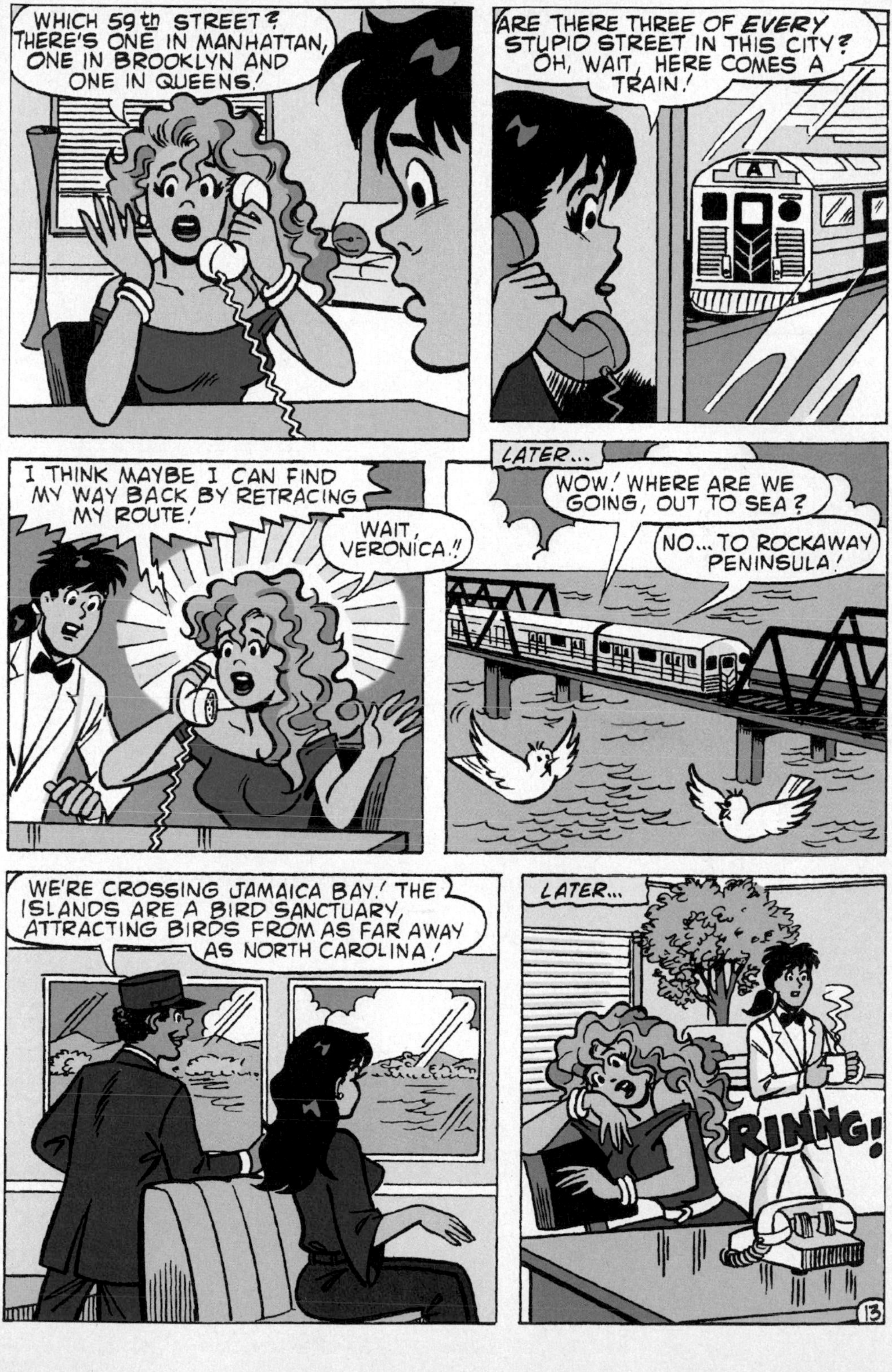
WHICH 59th STREET? THERE'S ONE IN MANHATTAN, ONE IN BROOKLYN AND ONE IN QUEENS!
ARE THERE THREE OF EVERY STUPID STREET IN THIS CITY? OH, WAIT, HERE COMES A TRAIN!
A
I THINK MAYBE I CAN FIND MY WAY BACK BY RETRACING MY ROUTE!
WAIT, VERONICA!!
LATER...
WOW! WHERE ARE WE GOING, OUT TO SEA?
NO... TO ROCKAWAY PENINSULA!
WE'RE CROSSING JAMAICA BAY! THE ISLANDS ARE A BIRD SANCTUARY, ATTRACTING BIRDS FROM AS FAR AWAY AS NORTH CAROLINA!
LATER...
RINNG!
13

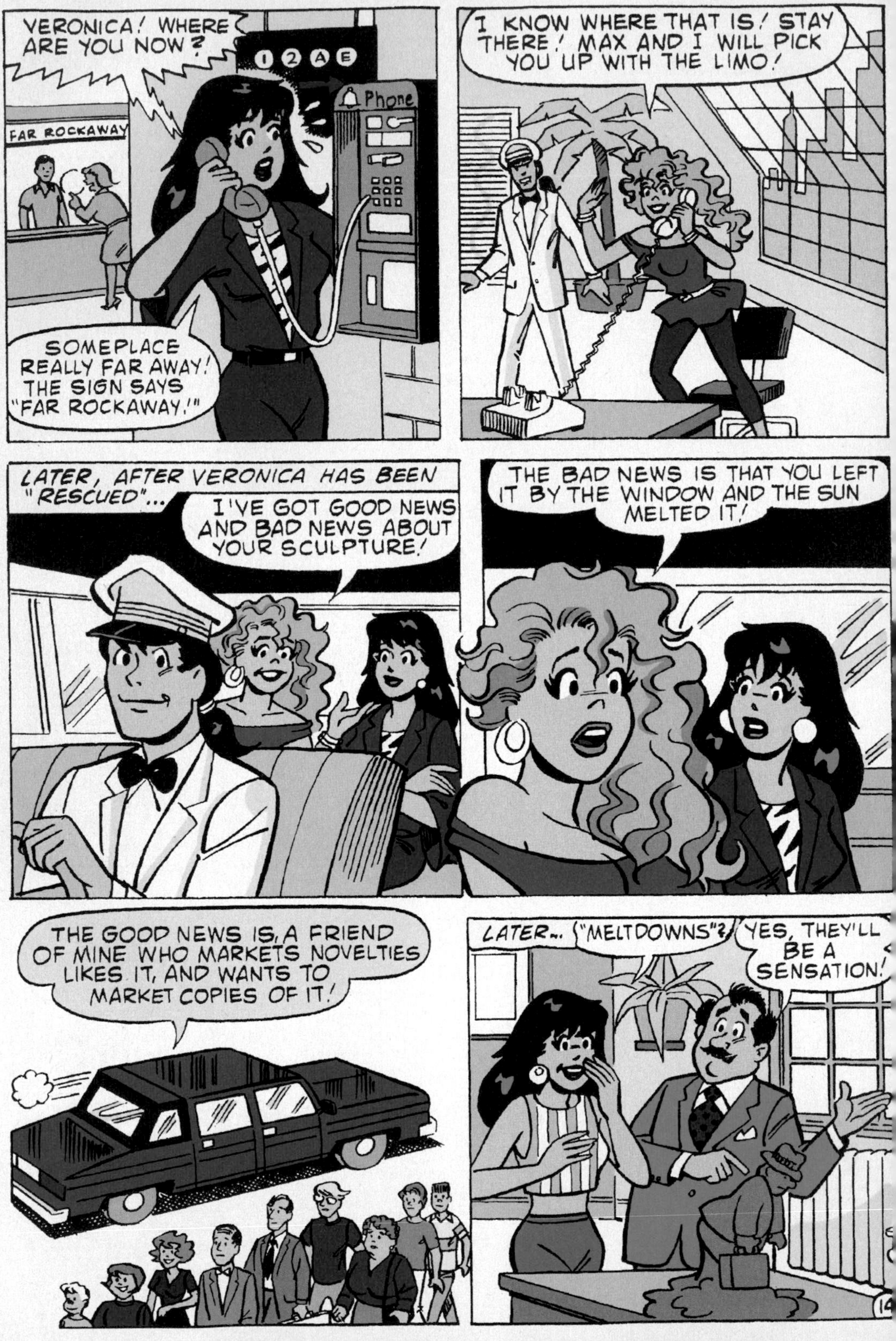
VERONICA! WHERE ARE YOU NOW?
12AE
FAR ROCKAWAY
Phone
SOMEPLACE REALLY FAR AWAY! THE SIGN SAYS "FAR ROCKAWAY!"
I KNOW WHERE THAT IS! STAY THERE! MAX AND I WILL PICK YOU UP WITH THE LIMO!
LATER, AFTER VERONICA HAS BEEN "RESCUED"...
I'VE GOT GOOD NEWS AND BAD NEWS ABOUT YOUR SCULPTURE!
THE BAD NEWS IS THAT YOU LEFT IT BY THE WINDOW AND THE SUN MELTED IT!
THE GOOD NEWS IS, A FRIEND OF MINE WHO MARKETS NOVELTIES LIKES IT, AND WANTS TO MARKET COPIES OF IT!
LATER...
"MELTDOWNS"?
YES, THEY'LL BE A SENSATION!

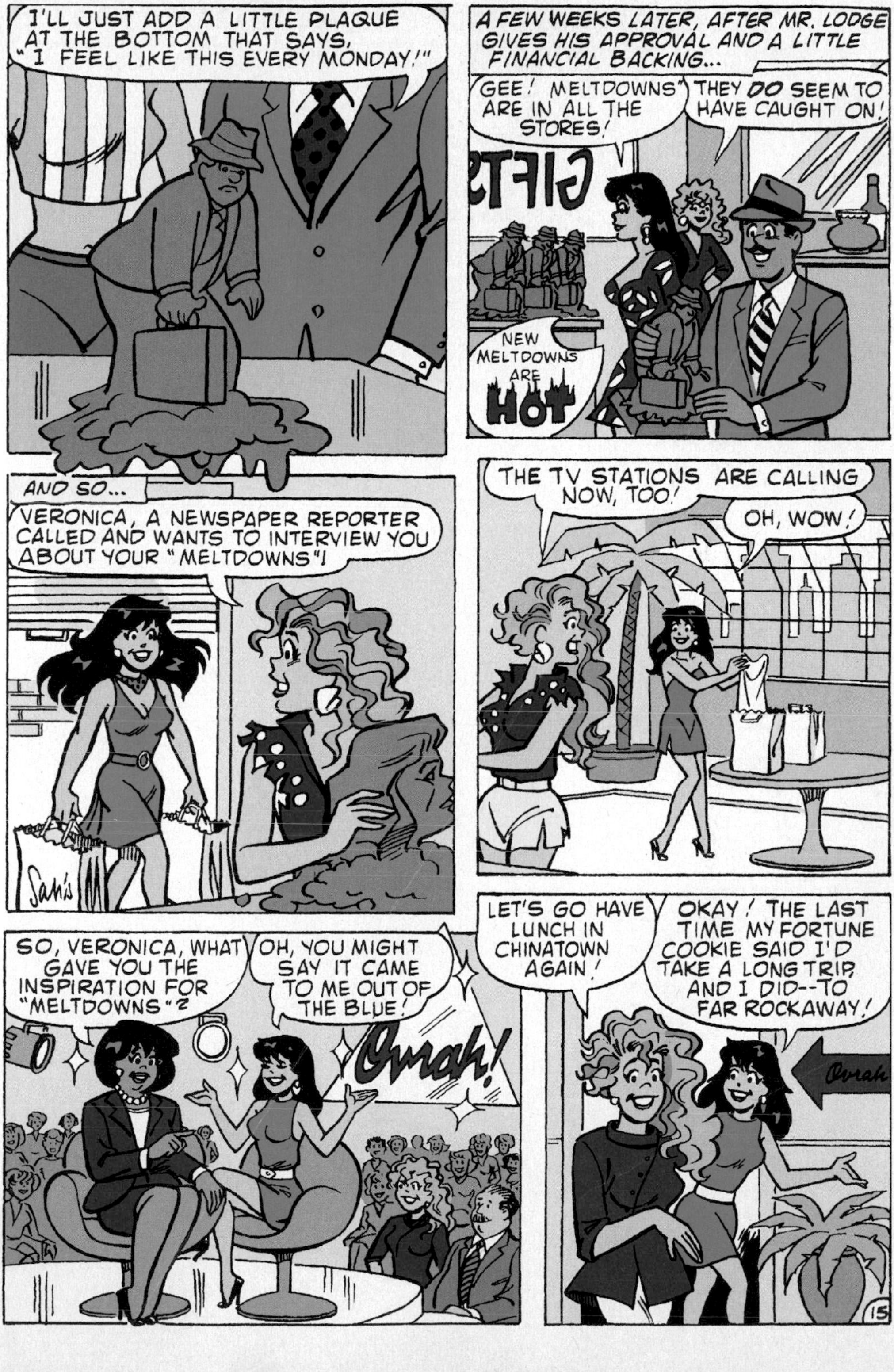
I'LL JUST ADD A LITTLE PLAQUE AT THE BOTTOM THAT SAYS, "I FEEL LIKE THIS EVERY MONDAY!"
A FEW WEEKS LATER, AFTER MR. LODGE GIVES HIS APPROVAL AND A LITTLE FINANCIAL BACKING...
GEE! "MELTDOWNS" ARE IN ALL THE STORES!
THEY DO SEEM TO HAVE CAUGHT ON!
GIFTS
NEW MELTDOWNS ARE HOT
AND SO...
VERONICA, A NEWSPAPER REPORTER CALLED AND WANTS TO INTERVIEW YOU ABOUT YOUR "MELTDOWNS"!
THE TV STATIONS ARE CALLING NOW, TOO!
OH, WOW!
SO, VERONICA, WHAT GAVE YOU THE INSPIRATION FOR "MELTDOWNS"?
OH, YOU MIGHT SAY IT CAME TO ME OUT OF THE BLUE!
Oprah!
LET'S GO HAVE LUNCH IN CHINATOWN AGAIN!
OKAY! THE LAST TIME MY FORTUNE COOKIE SAID I'D TAKE A LONG TRIP, AND I DID--TO FAR ROCKAWAY!
Oprah
15

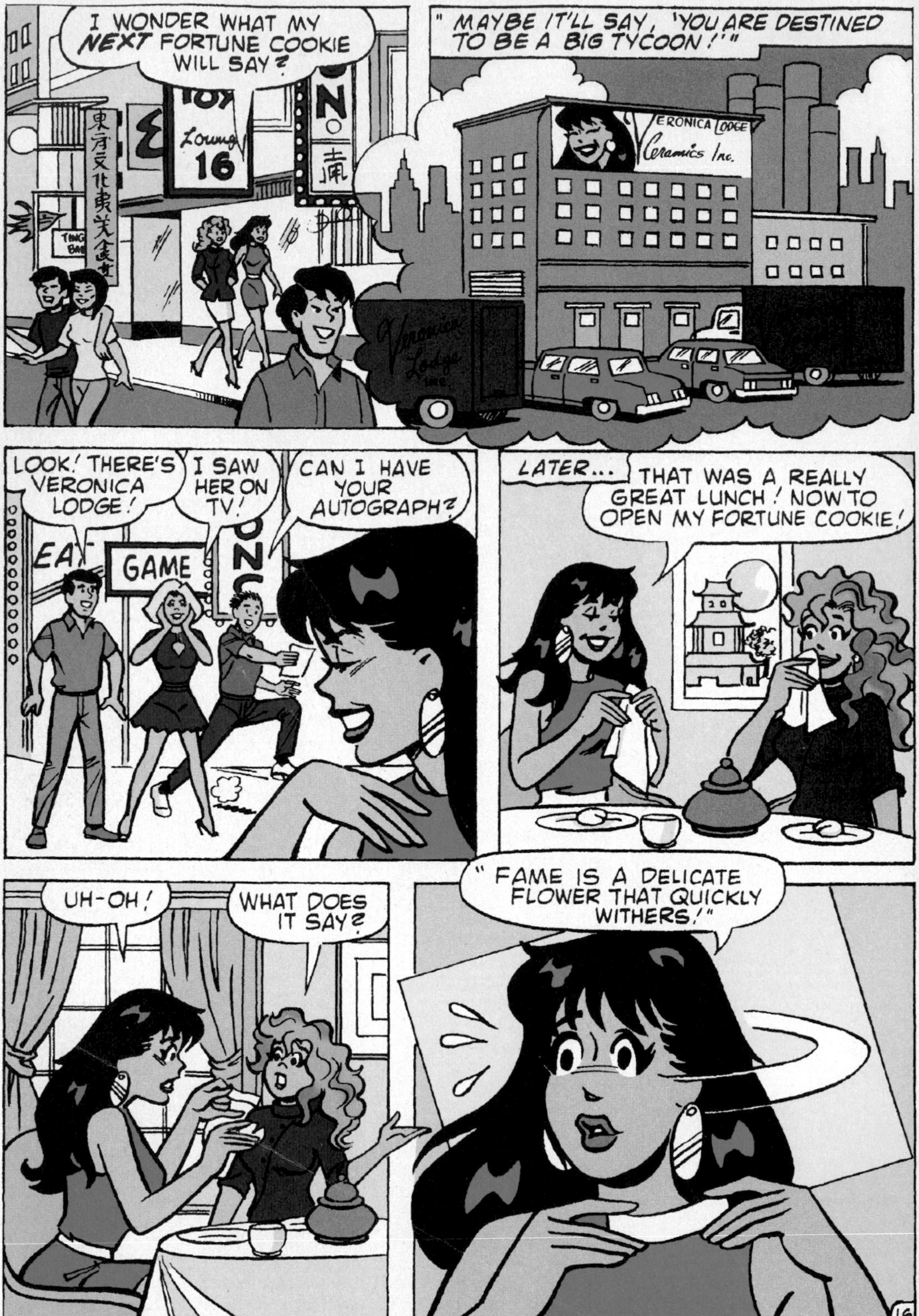
I WONDER WHAT MY NEXT FORTUNE COOKIE WILL SAY?
"MAYBE IT'LL SAY, 'YOU ARE DESTINED TO BE A BIG TYCOON!'"
VERONICA LODGE Ceramics Inc.
Veronica Lodge INC.
LOOK! THERE'S VERONICA LODGE!
I SAW HER ON TV!
CAN I HAVE YOUR AUTOGRAPH?
GAME
LATER...
THAT WAS A REALLY GREAT LUNCH! NOW TO OPEN MY FORTUNE COOKIE!
UH-OH!
WHAT DOES IT SAY?
"FAME IS A DELICATE FLOWER THAT QUICKLY WITHERS!"
16

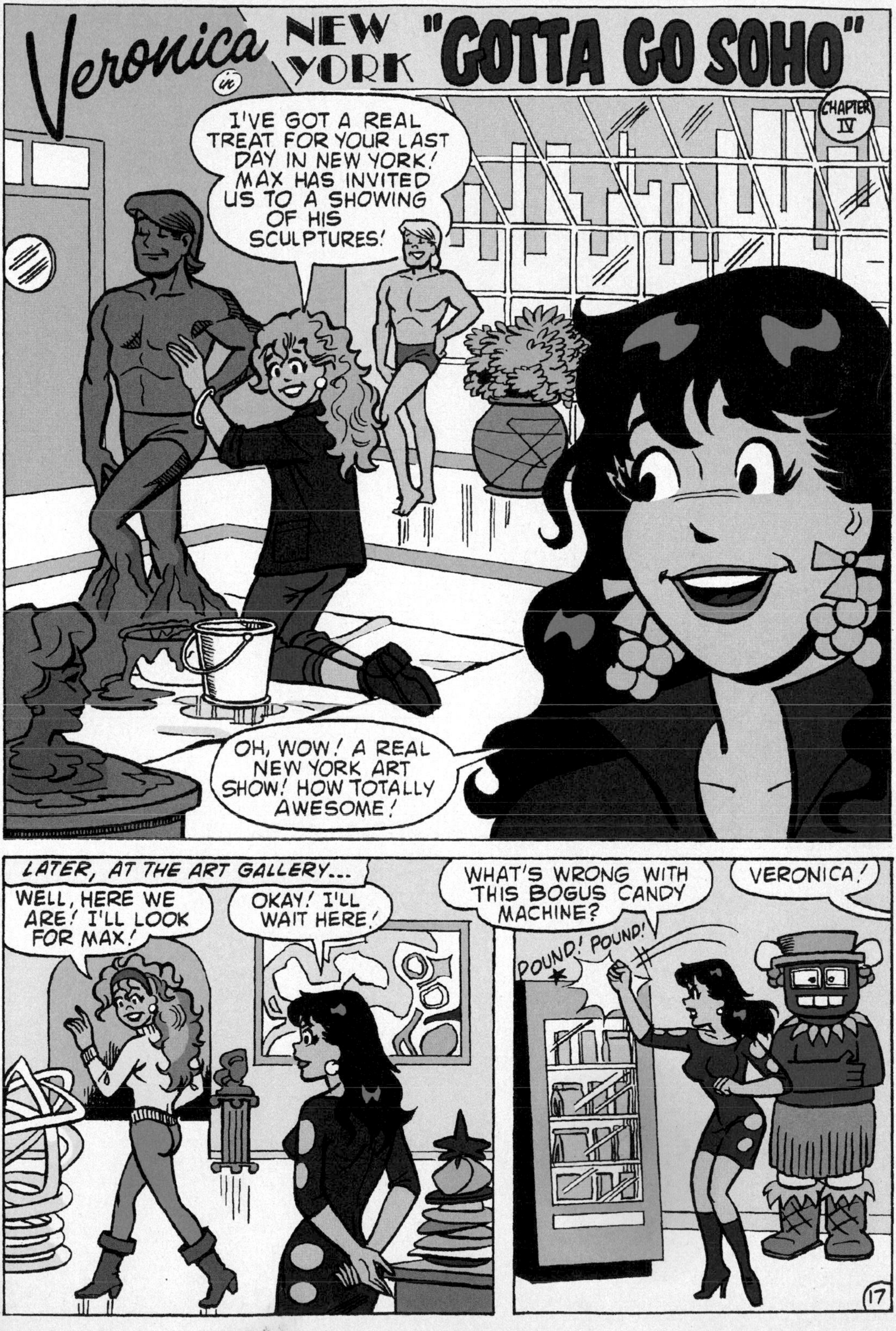
Veronica in NEW YORK
"GOTTA GO SOHO"
CHAPTER IV
I'VE GOT A REAL TREAT FOR YOUR LAST DAY IN NEW YORK! MAX HAS INVITED US TO A SHOWING OF HIS SCULPTURES!
OH, WOW! A REAL NEW YORK ART SHOW! HOW TOTALLY AWESOME!
LATER, AT THE ART GALLERY...
WELL, HERE WE ARE! I'LL LOOK FOR MAX!
OKAY! I'LL WAIT HERE!
WHAT'S WRONG WITH THIS BOGUS CANDY MACHINE?
POUND! POUND!
VERONICA!
17

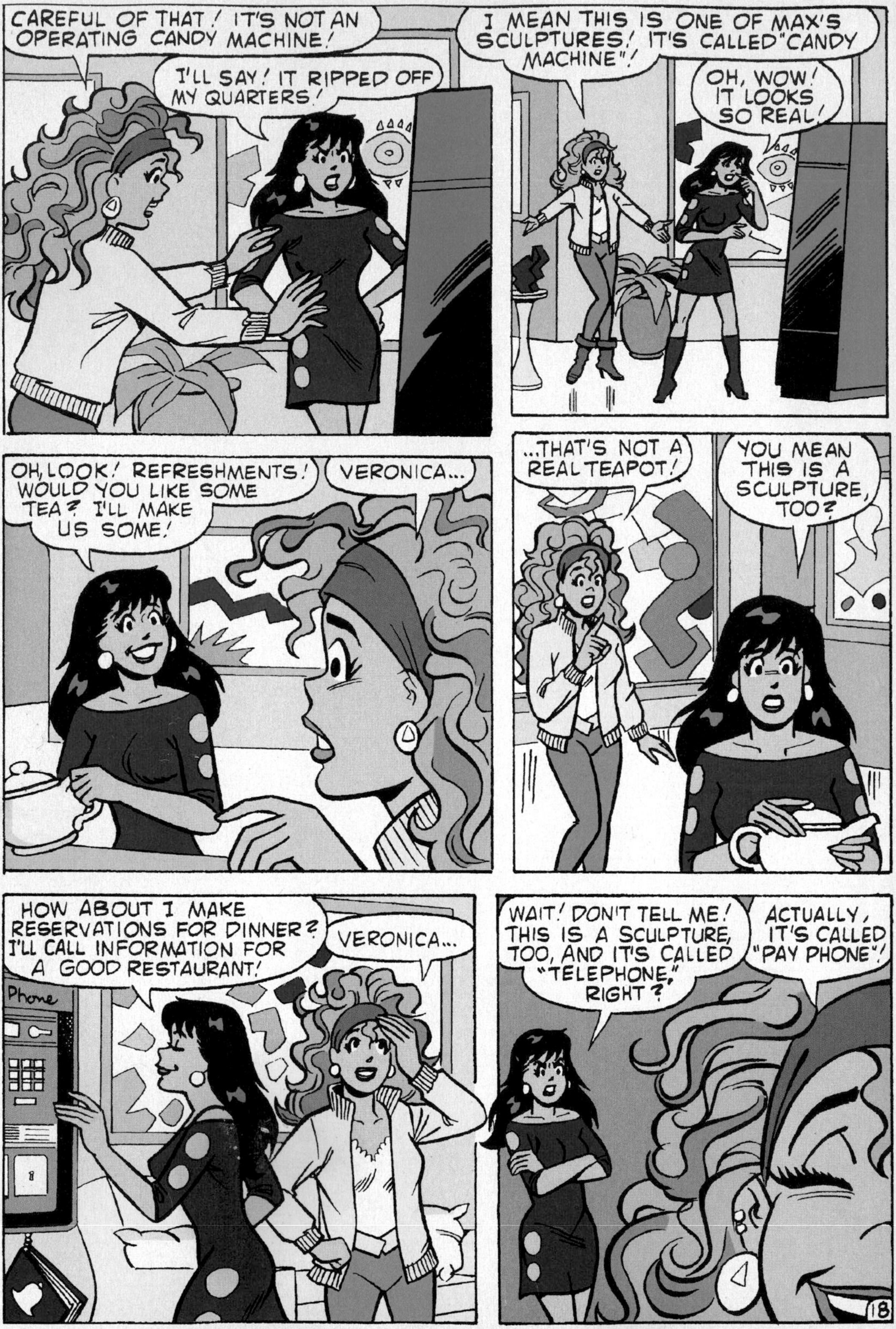
CAREFUL OF THAT! IT'S NOT AN OPERATING CANDY MACHINE!
I'LL SAY! IT RIPPED OFF MY QUARTERS!
I MEAN THIS IS ONE OF MAX'S SCULPTURES! IT'S CALLED "CANDY MACHINE"!
OH, WOW! IT LOOKS SO REAL!
OH, LOOK! REFRESHMENTS! WOULD YOU LIKE SOME TEA? I'LL MAKE US SOME!
VERONICA...
...THAT'S NOT A REAL TEAPOT!
YOU MEAN THIS IS A SCULPTURE, TOO?
HOW ABOUT I MAKE RESERVATIONS FOR DINNER? I'LL CALL INFORMATION FOR A GOOD RESTAURANT!
VERONICA...
Phone
WAIT! DON'T TELL ME! THIS IS A SCULPTURE, TOO, AND IT'S CALLED "TELEPHONE," RIGHT?
ACTUALLY, IT'S CALLED "PAY PHONE"!
18

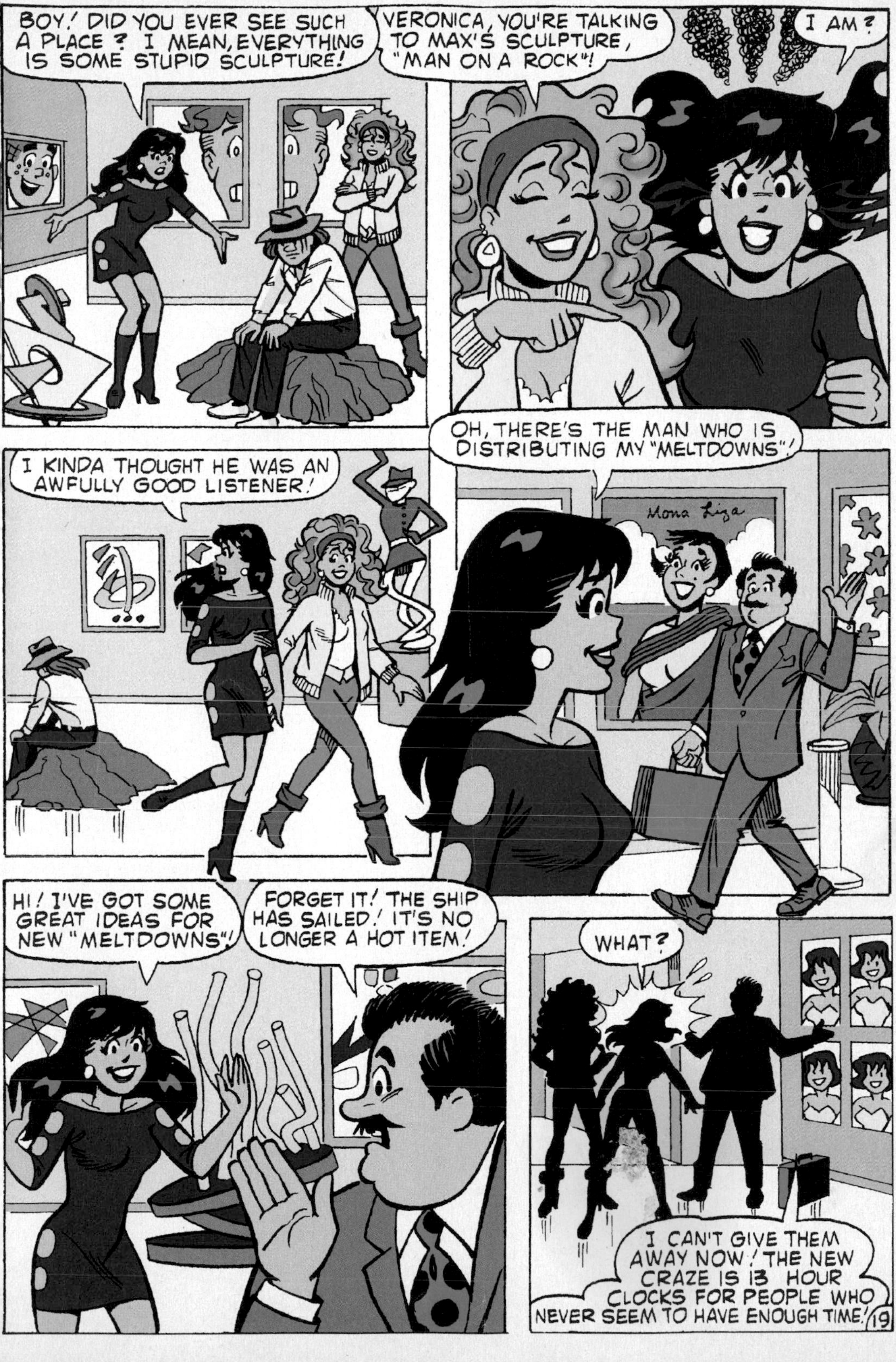
BOY! DID YOU EVER SEE SUCH A PLACE? I MEAN, EVERYTHING IS SOME STUPID SCULPTURE!
VERONICA, YOU'RE TALKING TO MAX'S SCULPTURE, "MAN ON A ROCK"!
I AM?
I KINDA THOUGHT HE WAS AN AWFULLY GOOD LISTENER!
OH, THERE'S THE MAN WHO IS DISTRIBUTING MY "MELTDOWNS"!
Mona Liza
HI! I'VE GOT SOME GREAT IDEAS FOR NEW "MELTDOWNS"!
FORGET IT! THE SHIP HAS SAILED! IT'S NO LONGER A HOT ITEM!
WHAT?
I CAN'T GIVE THEM AWAY NOW! THE NEW CRAZE IS 13 HOUR CLOCKS FOR PEOPLE WHO NEVER SEEM TO HAVE ENOUGH TIME!
19

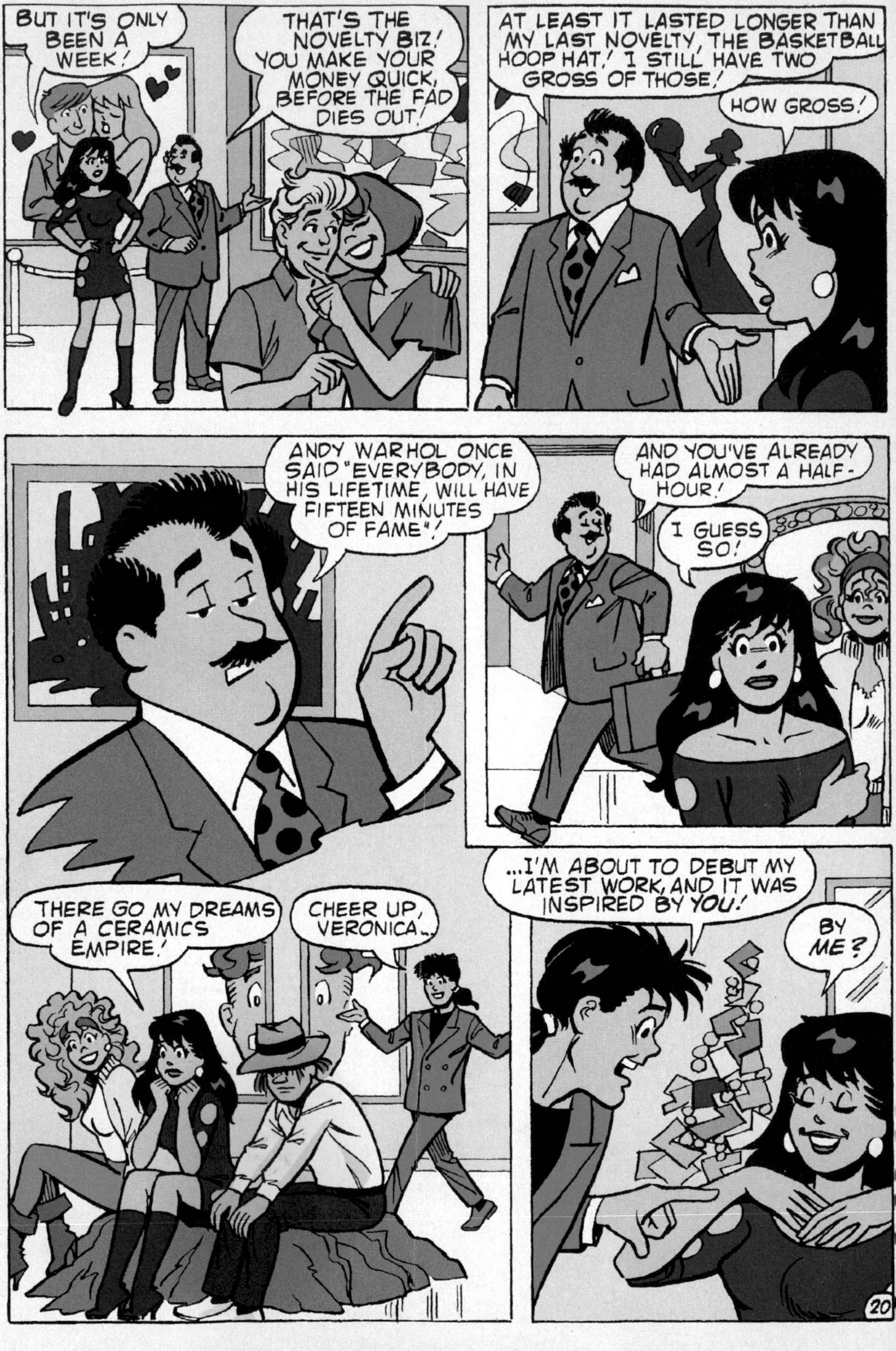
BUT IT'S ONLY BEEN A WEEK!
THAT'S THE NOVELTY BIZ! YOU MAKE YOUR MONEY QUICK, BEFORE THE FAD DIES OUT!
AT LEAST IT LASTED LONGER THAN MY LAST NOVELTY, THE BASKETBALL HOOP HAT! I STILL HAVE TWO GROSS OF THOSE!
HOW GROSS!
ANDY WARHOL ONCE SAID "EVERYBODY, IN HIS LIFETIME, WILL HAVE FIFTEEN MINUTES OF FAME"!
AND YOU'VE ALREADY HAD ALMOST A HALF-HOUR!
I GUESS SO!
THERE GO MY DREAMS OF A CERAMICS EMPIRE!
CHEER UP, VERONICA...
...I'M ABOUT TO DEBUT MY LATEST WORK, AND IT WAS INSPIRED BY YOU!
BY ME?
20

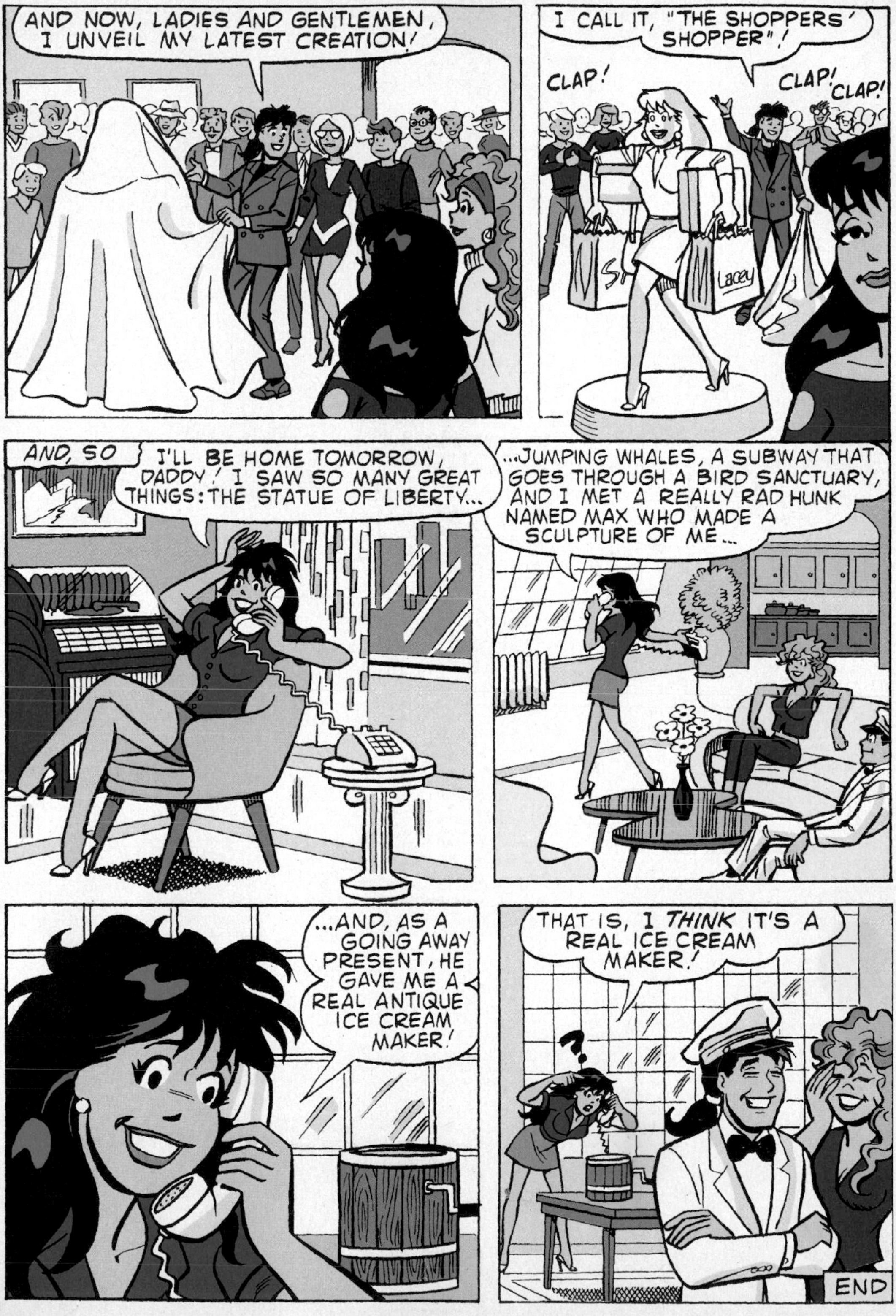
AND NOW, LADIES AND GENTLEMEN, I UNVEIL MY LATEST CREATION!
I CALL IT, "THE SHOPPERS' SHOPPER"!
CLAP!
CLAP! CLAP!
Lacey
AND, SO
I'LL BE HOME TOMORROW, DADDY! I SAW SO MANY GREAT THINGS: THE STATUE OF LIBERTY...
...JUMPING WHALES, A SUBWAY THAT GOES THROUGH A BIRD SANCTUARY, AND I MET A REALLY RAD HUNK NAMED MAX WHO MADE A SCULPTURE OF ME...
...AND, AS A GOING AWAY PRESENT, HE GAVE ME A REAL ANTIQUE ICE CREAM MAKER!
THAT IS, I *THINK* IT'S A REAL ICE CREAM MAKER!
?
END

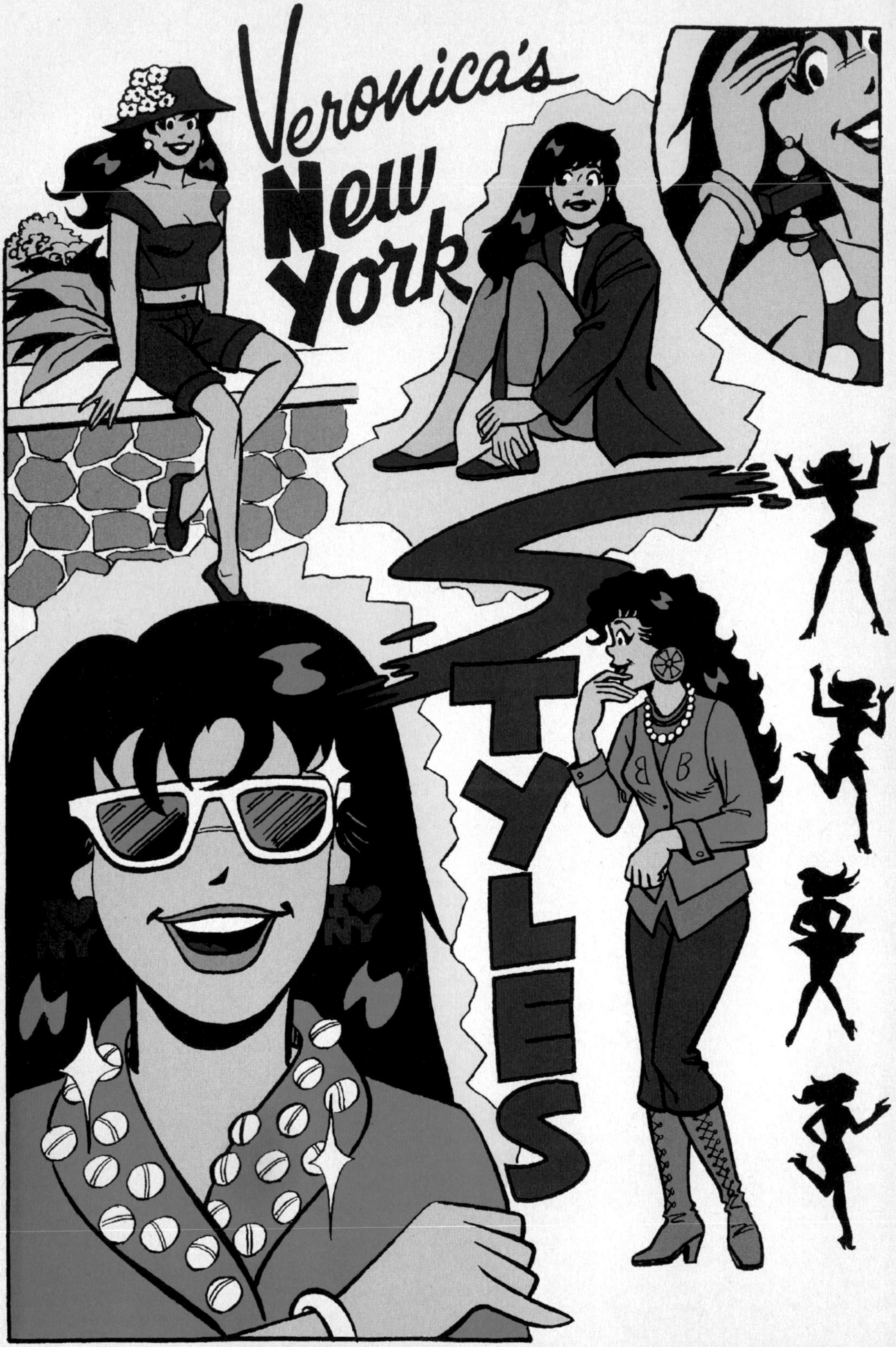
Veronica's
New York
STYLES
I ♥ NY

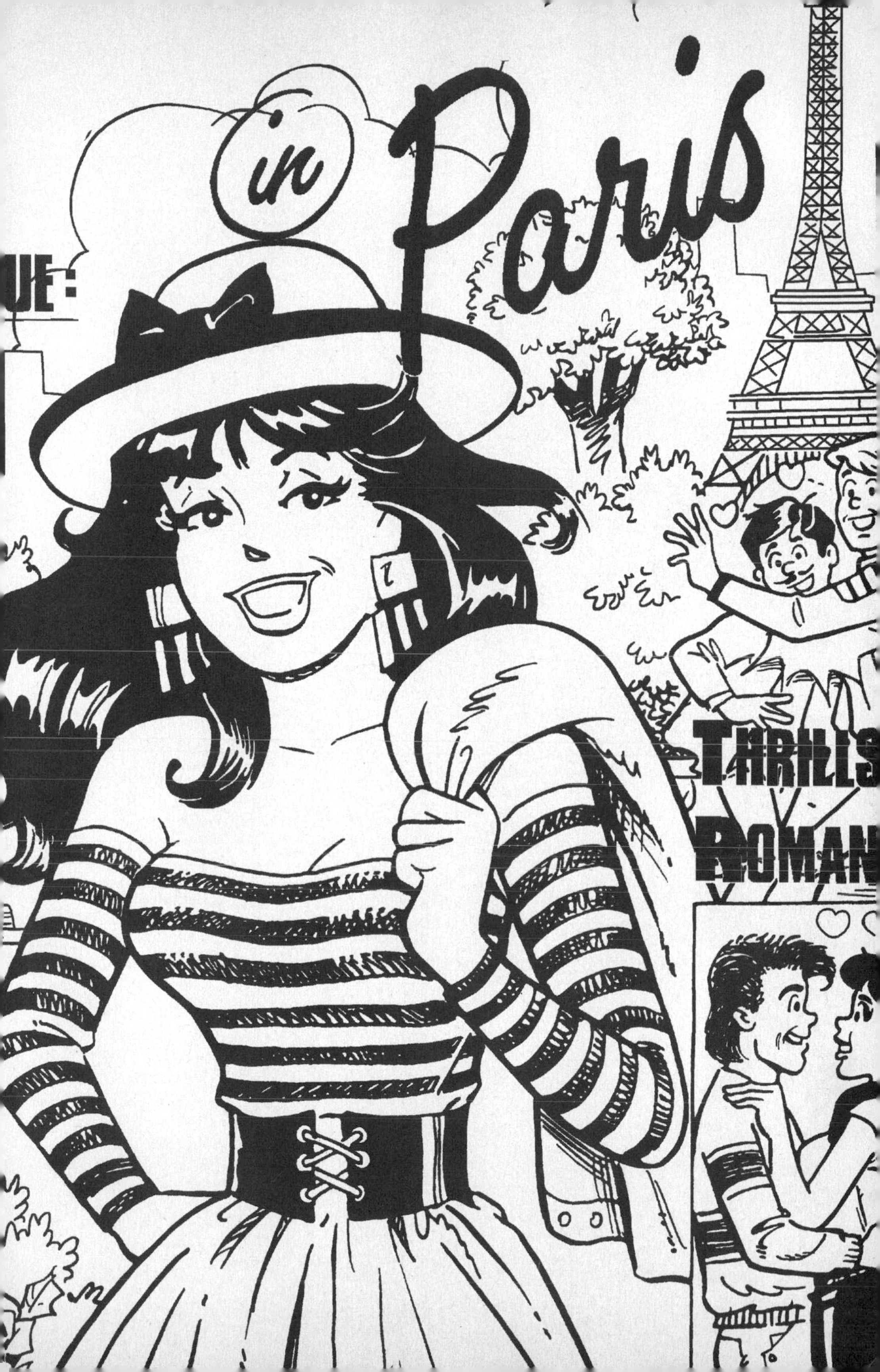

UE:
in Paris
THRILLS
ROMAN

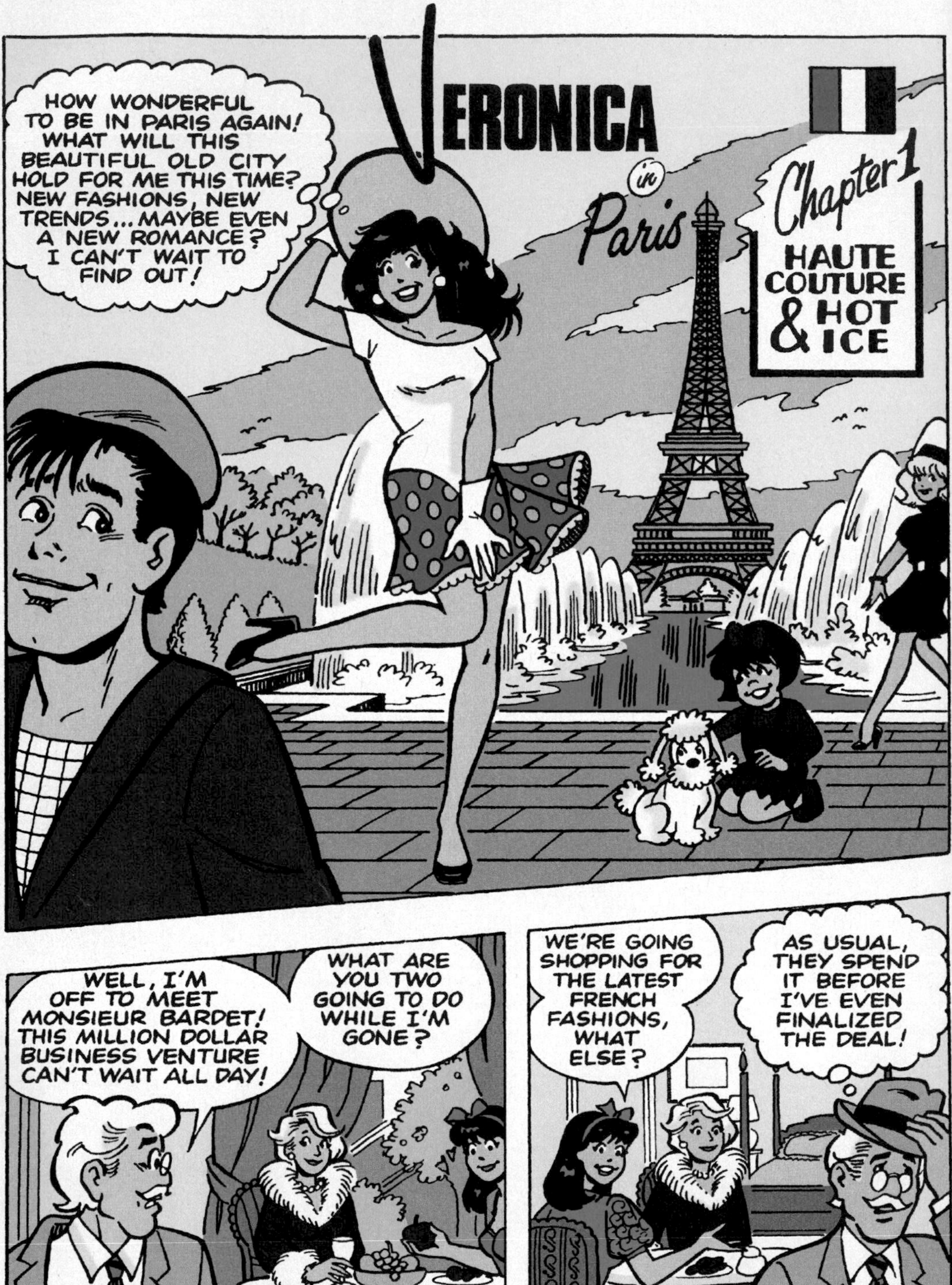
VERONICA in Paris
Chapter 1
HAUTE COUTURE & HOT ICE
HOW WONDERFUL TO BE IN PARIS AGAIN! WHAT WILL THIS BEAUTIFUL OLD CITY HOLD FOR ME THIS TIME? NEW FASHIONS, NEW TRENDS... MAYBE EVEN A NEW ROMANCE? I CAN'T WAIT TO FIND OUT!
WELL, I'M OFF TO MEET MONSIEUR BARDET! THIS MILLION DOLLAR BUSINESS VENTURE CAN'T WAIT ALL DAY!
WHAT ARE YOU TWO GOING TO DO WHILE I'M GONE?
WE'RE GOING SHOPPING FOR THE LATEST FRENCH FASHIONS, WHAT ELSE?
AS USUAL, THEY SPEND IT BEFORE I'VE EVEN FINALIZED THE DEAL!

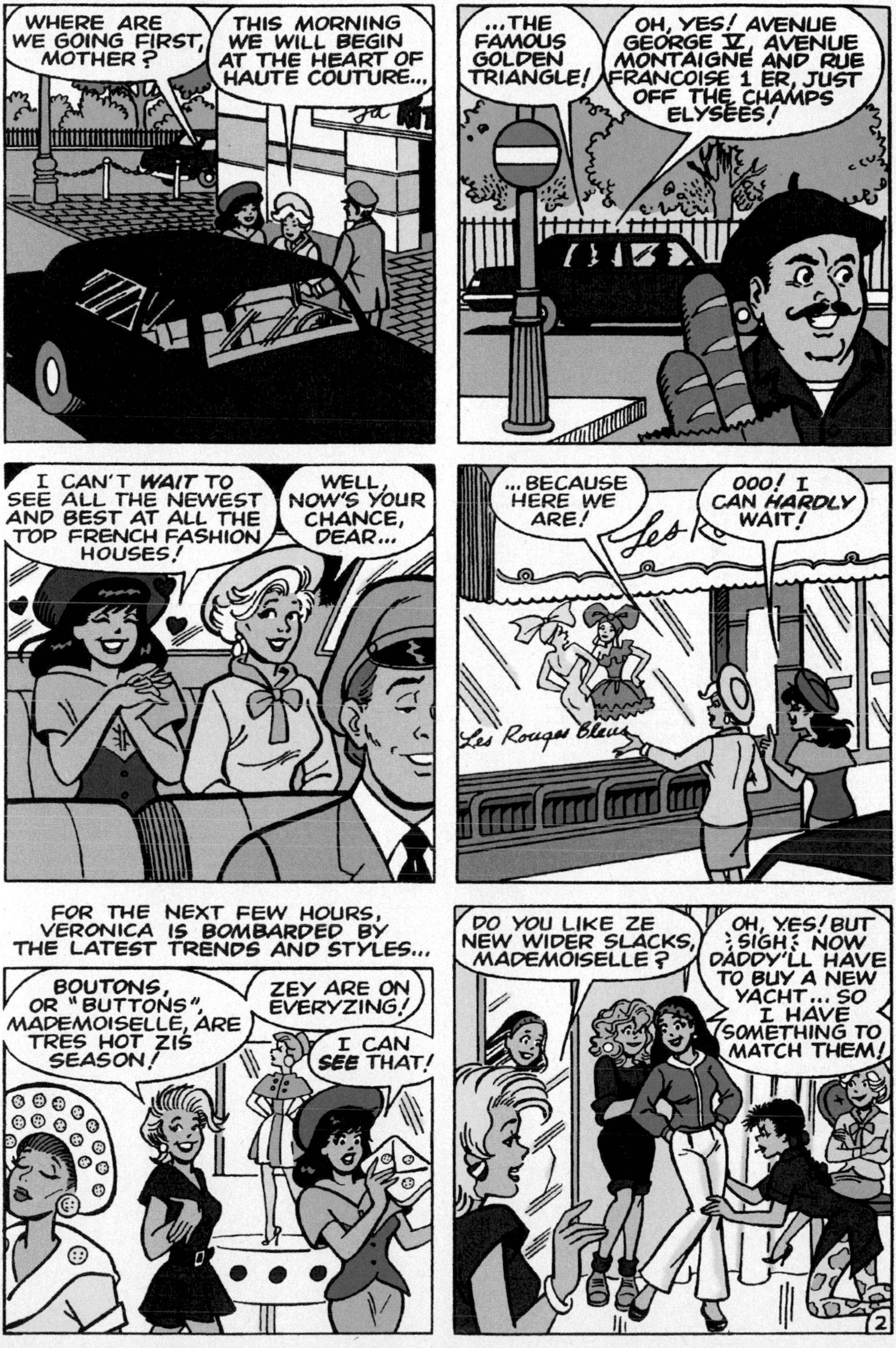
WHERE ARE WE GOING FIRST, MOTHER?
THIS MORNING WE WILL BEGIN AT THE HEART OF HAUTE COUTURE...
...THE FAMOUS GOLDEN TRIANGLE!
OH, YES! AVENUE GEORGE V, AVENUE MONTAIGNÉ AND RUE FRANCOISE 1 ER, JUST OFF THE CHAMPS ELYSÉES!
I CAN'T WAIT TO SEE ALL THE NEWEST AND BEST AT ALL THE TOP FRENCH FASHION HOUSES!
WELL, NOW'S YOUR CHANCE, DEAR...
...BECAUSE HERE WE ARE!
OOO! I CAN HARDLY WAIT!
Les Rouges Bleus
FOR THE NEXT FEW HOURS, VERONICA IS BOMBARDED BY THE LATEST TRENDS AND STYLES...
BOUTONS, OR "BUTTONS", MADEMOISELLE, ARE TRES HOT ZIS SEASON!
ZEY ARE ON EVERYZING!
I CAN SEE THAT!
DO YOU LIKE ZE NEW WIDER SLACKS, MADEMOISELLE?
OH, YES! BUT SIGH NOW DADDY'LL HAVE TO BUY A NEW YACHT... SO I HAVE SOMETHING TO MATCH THEM!

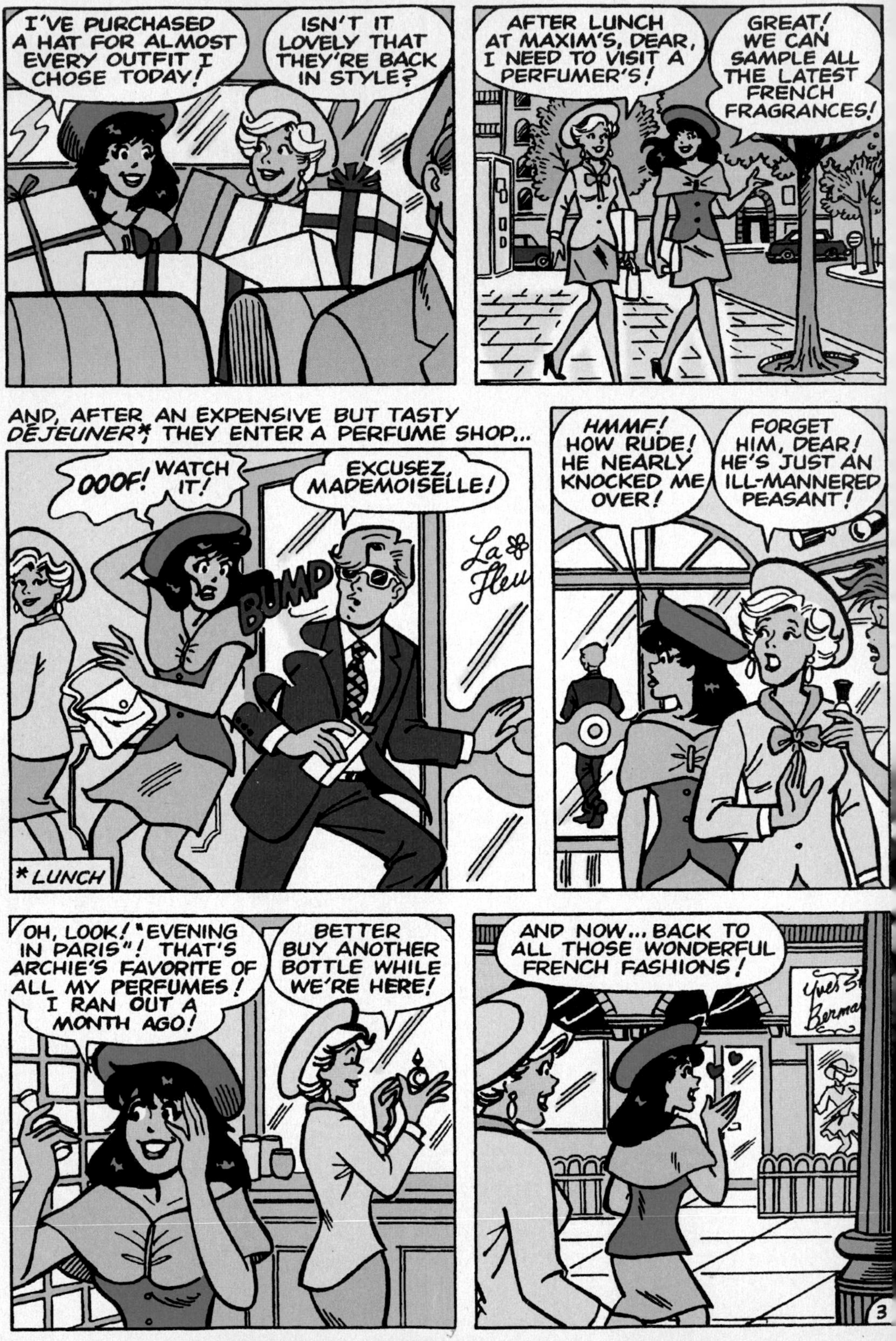
I'VE PURCHASED A HAT FOR ALMOST EVERY OUTFIT I CHOSE TODAY!
ISN'T IT LOVELY THAT THEY'RE BACK IN STYLE?
AFTER LUNCH AT MAXIM'S, DEAR, I NEED TO VISIT A PERFUMER'S!
GREAT! WE CAN SAMPLE ALL THE LATEST FRENCH FRAGRANCES!
AND, AFTER AN EXPENSIVE BUT TASTY DÉJEUNER*, THEY ENTER A PERFUME SHOP...
OOOF! WATCH IT!
EXCUSEZ, MADEMOISELLE!
BUMP
*LUNCH
HMMF! HOW RUDE! HE NEARLY KNOCKED ME OVER!
FORGET HIM, DEAR! HE'S JUST AN ILL-MANNERED PEASANT!
OH, LOOK! "EVENING IN PARIS"! THAT'S ARCHIE'S FAVORITE OF ALL MY PERFUMES! I RAN OUT A MONTH AGO!
BETTER BUY ANOTHER BOTTLE WHILE WE'RE HERE!
AND NOW... BACK TO ALL THOSE WONDERFUL FRENCH FASHIONS!

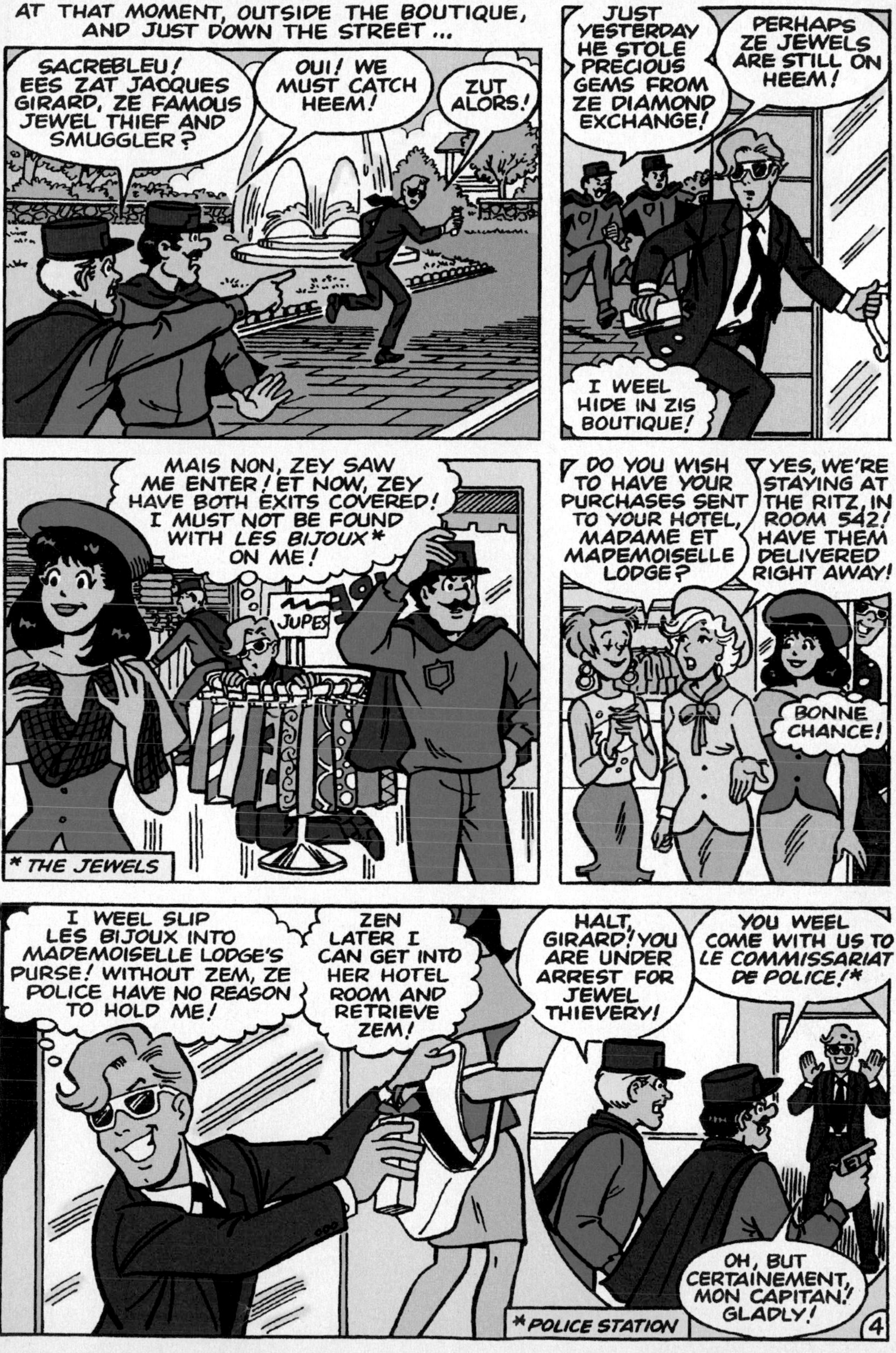
AT THAT MOMENT, OUTSIDE THE BOUTIQUE, AND JUST DOWN THE STREET ...
SACREBLEU! EES ZAT JACQUES GIRARD, ZE FAMOUS JEWEL THIEF AND SMUGGLER?
OUI! WE MUST CATCH HEEM!
ZUT ALORS!
JUST YESTERDAY HE STOLE PRECIOUS GEMS FROM ZE DIAMOND EXCHANGE!
PERHAPS ZE JEWELS ARE STILL ON HEEM!
I WEEL HIDE IN ZIS BOUTIQUE!
MAIS NON, ZEY SAW ME ENTER! ET NOW, ZEY HAVE BOTH EXITS COVERED! I MUST NOT BE FOUND WITH LES BIJOUX* ON ME!
JUPES
* THE JEWELS
DO YOU WISH TO HAVE YOUR PURCHASES SENT TO YOUR HOTEL, MADAME ET MADEMOISELLE LODGE?
YES, WE'RE STAYING AT THE RITZ, IN ROOM 542! HAVE THEM DELIVERED RIGHT AWAY!
BONNE CHANCE!
I WEEL SLIP LES BIJOUX INTO MADEMOISELLE LODGE'S PURSE! WITHOUT ZEM, ZE POLICE HAVE NO REASON TO HOLD ME!
ZEN LATER I CAN GET INTO HER HOTEL ROOM AND RETRIEVE ZEM!
HALT, GIRARD! YOU ARE UNDER ARREST FOR JEWEL THIEVERY!
YOU WEEL COME WITH US TO LE COMMISSARIAT DE POLICE!*
OH, BUT CERTAINEMENT, MON CAPITAN! GLADLY!
* POLICE STATION
4

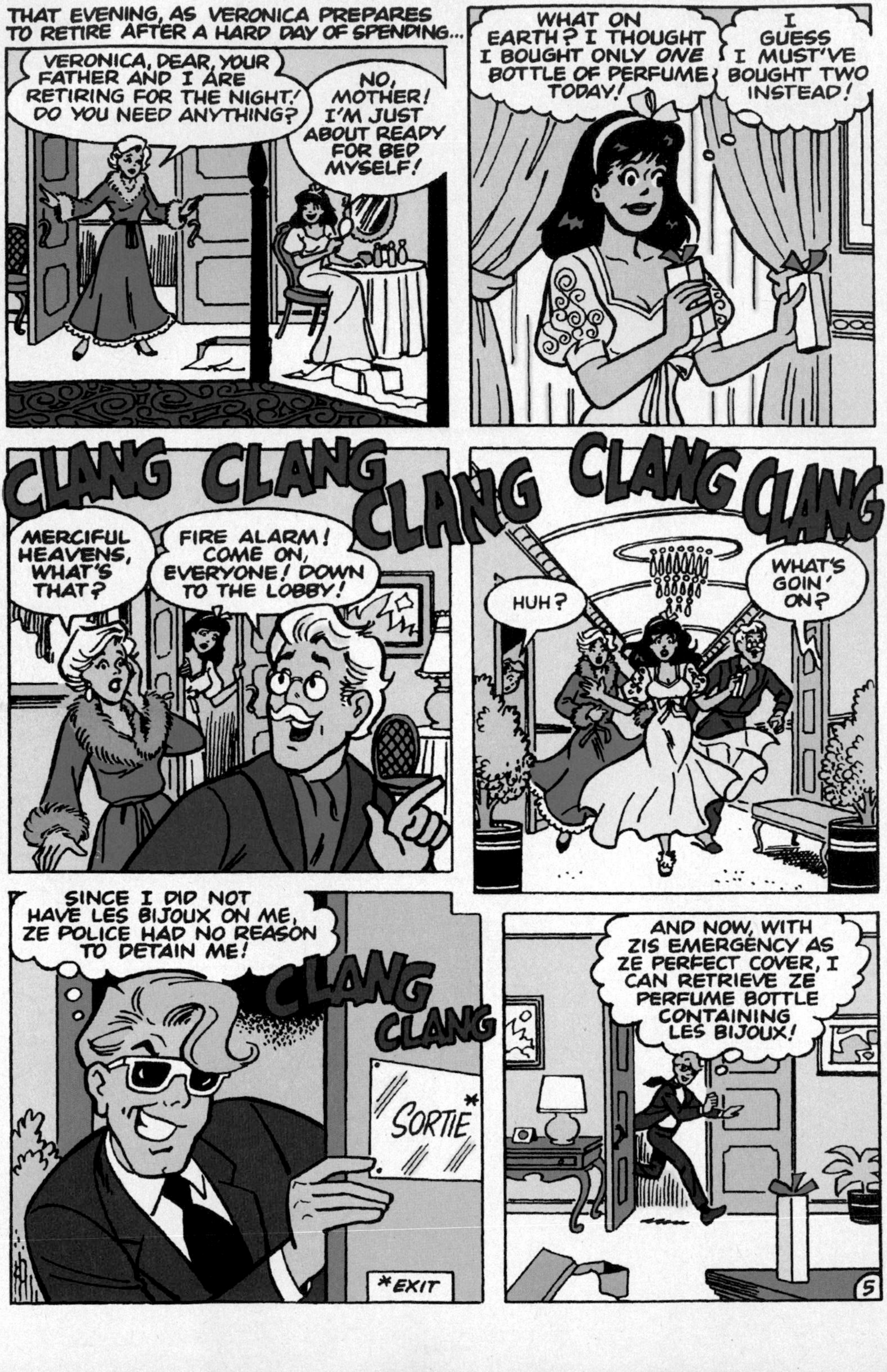
THAT EVENING, AS VERONICA PREPARES TO RETIRE AFTER A HARD DAY OF SPENDING...
VERONICA, DEAR, YOUR FATHER AND I ARE RETIRING FOR THE NIGHT! DO YOU NEED ANYTHING?
NO, MOTHER! I'M JUST ABOUT READY FOR BED MYSELF!
WHAT ON EARTH? I THOUGHT I BOUGHT ONLY ONE BOTTLE OF PERFUME TODAY!
I GUESS I MUST'VE BOUGHT TWO INSTEAD!
CLANG CLANG CLANG CLANG CLANG
MERCIFUL HEAVENS, WHAT'S THAT?
FIRE ALARM! COME ON, EVERYONE! DOWN TO THE LOBBY!
HUH?
WHAT'S GOIN' ON?
SINCE I DID NOT HAVE LES BIJOUX ON ME, ZE POLICE HAD NO REASON TO DETAIN ME!
CLANG CLANG
SORTIE*
*EXIT
AND NOW, WITH ZIS EMERGENCY AS ZE PERFECT COVER, I CAN RETRIEVE ZE PERFUME BOTTLE CONTAINING LES BIJOUX!
5

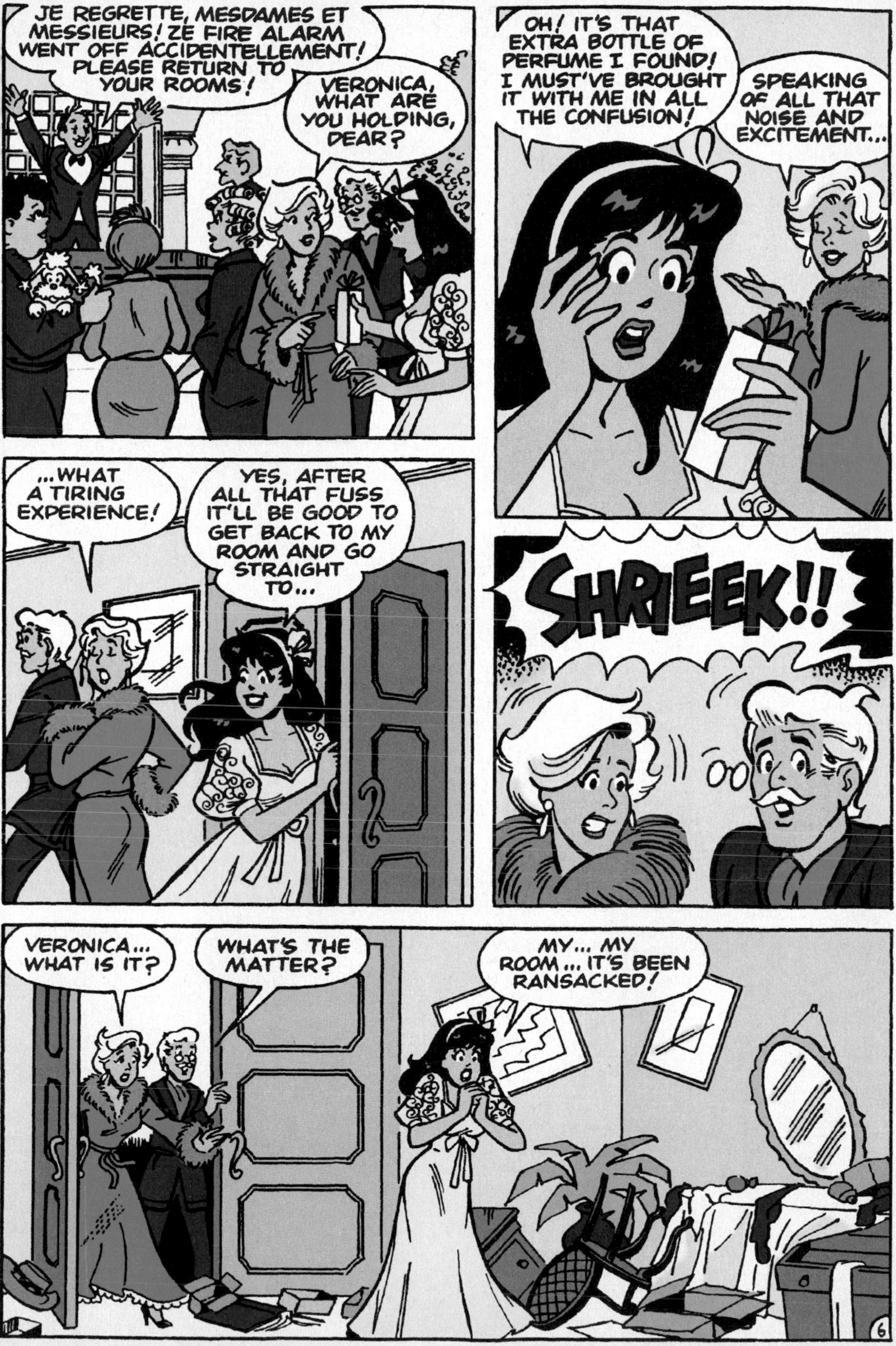
JE REGRETTE, MESDAMES ET MESSIEURS! ZE FIRE ALARM WENT OFF ACCIDENTELLEMENT! PLEASE RETURN TO YOUR ROOMS!
VERONICA, WHAT ARE YOU HOLDING, DEAR?
OH! IT'S THAT EXTRA BOTTLE OF PERFUME I FOUND! I MUST'VE BROUGHT IT WITH ME IN ALL THE CONFUSION!
SPEAKING OF ALL THAT NOISE AND EXCITEMENT...
...WHAT A TIRING EXPERIENCE!
YES, AFTER ALL THAT FUSS IT'LL BE GOOD TO GET BACK TO MY ROOM AND GO STRAIGHT TO...
SHRIEEK!!
VERONICA... WHAT IS IT?
WHAT'S THE MATTER?
MY... MY ROOM... IT'S BEEN RANSACKED!
6

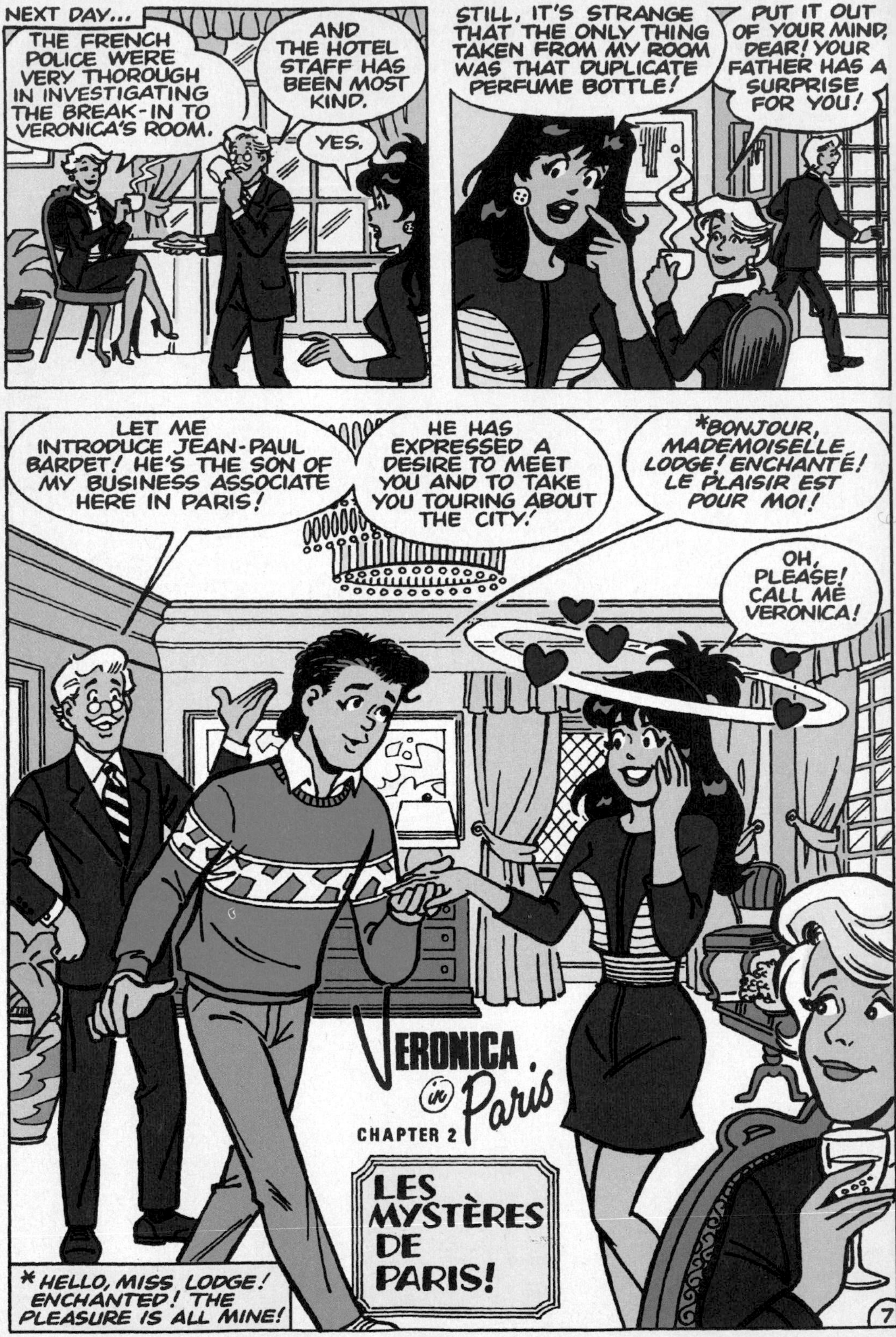
NEXT DAY...
THE FRENCH POLICE WERE VERY THOROUGH IN INVESTIGATING THE BREAK-IN TO VERONICA'S ROOM.
AND THE HOTEL STAFF HAS BEEN MOST KIND.
YES.
STILL, IT'S STRANGE THAT THE ONLY THING TAKEN FROM MY ROOM WAS THAT DUPLICATE PERFUME BOTTLE!
PUT IT OUT OF YOUR MIND, DEAR! YOUR FATHER HAS A SURPRISE FOR YOU!
LET ME INTRODUCE JEAN-PAUL BARDET! HE'S THE SON OF MY BUSINESS ASSOCIATE HERE IN PARIS!
HE HAS EXPRESSED A DESIRE TO MEET YOU AND TO TAKE YOU TOURING ABOUT THE CITY!
*BONJOUR, MADEMOISELLE LODGE! ENCHANTÉ! LE PLAISIR EST POUR MOI!
OH, PLEASE! CALL ME VERONICA!
VERONICA in Paris
CHAPTER 2
LES MYSTÈRES DE PARIS!
* HELLO, MISS LODGE! ENCHANTED! THE PLEASURE IS ALL MINE!
7

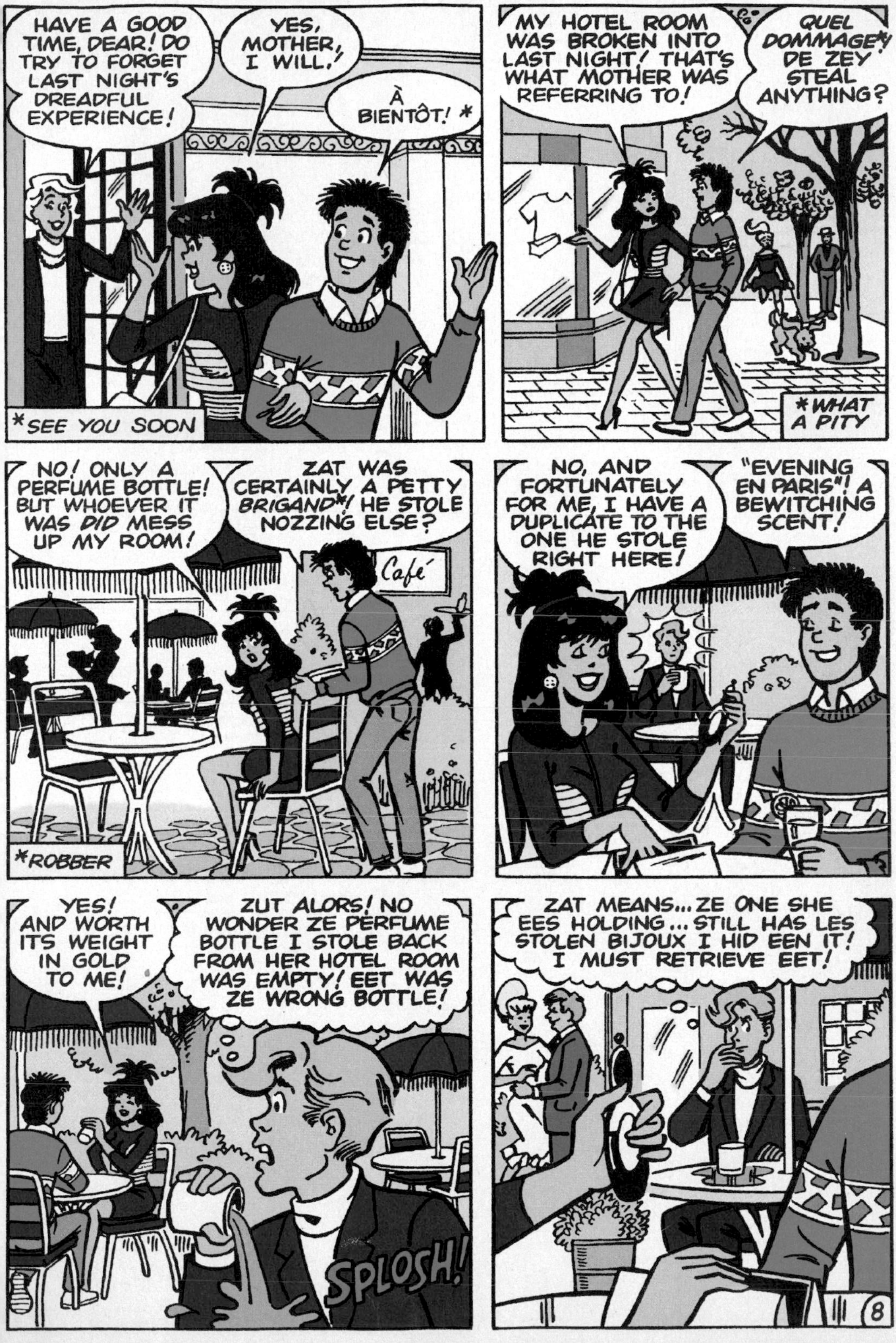
HAVE A GOOD TIME, DEAR! DO TRY TO FORGET LAST NIGHT'S DREADFUL EXPERIENCE!
YES, MOTHER, I WILL.
À BIENTÔT! *
*SEE YOU SOON
MY HOTEL ROOM WAS BROKEN INTO LAST NIGHT! THAT'S WHAT MOTHER WAS REFERRING TO!
QUEL DOMMAGE*! DE ZEY STEAL ANYTHING?
*WHAT A PITY
NO! ONLY A PERFUME BOTTLE! BUT WHOEVER IT WAS DID MESS UP MY ROOM!
ZAT WAS CERTAINLY A PETTY BRIGAND*! HE STOLE NOZZING ELSE?
Café
*ROBBER
NO, AND FORTUNATELY FOR ME, I HAVE A DUPLICATE TO THE ONE HE STOLE RIGHT HERE!
"EVENING EN PARIS"! A BEWITCHING SCENT!
YES! AND WORTH ITS WEIGHT IN GOLD TO ME!
ZUT ALORS! NO WONDER ZE PERFUME BOTTLE I STOLE BACK FROM HER HOTEL ROOM WAS EMPTY! EET WAS ZE WRONG BOTTLE!
SPLOSH!
ZAT MEANS... ZE ONE SHE EES HOLDING... STILL HAS LES STOLEN BIJOUX I HID EEN IT! I MUST RETRIEVE EET!
8

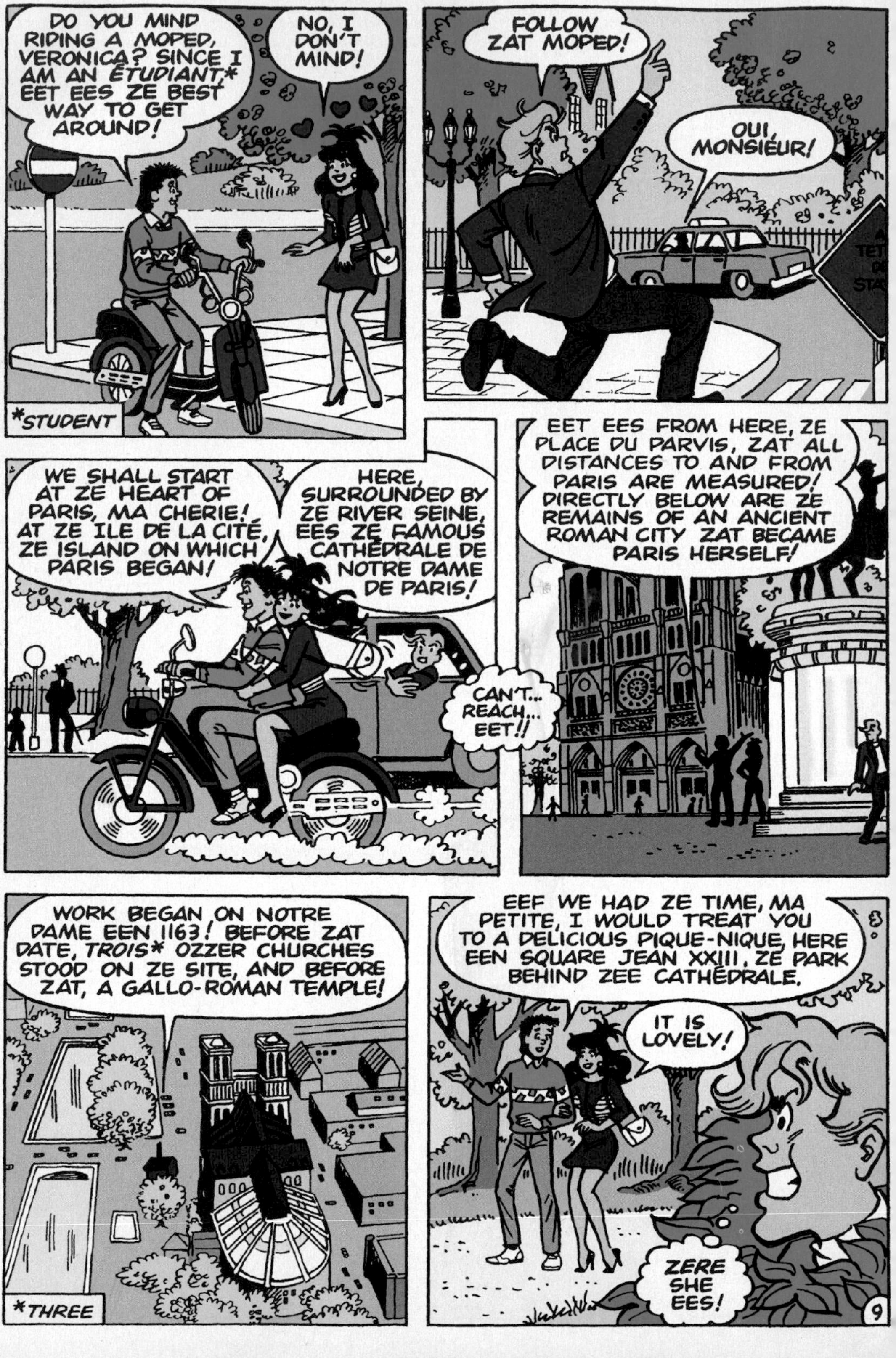
DO YOU MIND RIDING A MOPED, VERONICA? SINCE I AM AN ÉTUDIANT,* EET EES ZE BEST WAY TO GET AROUND!
NO, I DON'T MIND!
*STUDENT
FOLLOW ZAT MOPED!
OUI, MONSIÉUR!
WE SHALL START AT ZE HEART OF PARIS, MA CHERIE! AT ZE ILE DE LA CITÉ, ZE ISLAND ON WHICH PARIS BEGAN!
HERE, SURROUNDED BY ZE RIVER SEINE, EES ZE FAMOUS CATHÉDRALE DE NOTRE DAME DE PARIS!
CAN'T... REACH... EET!!
EET EES FROM HERE, ZE PLACE DU PARVIS, ZAT ALL DISTANCES TO AND FROM PARIS ARE MEASURED! DIRECTLY BELOW ARE ZE REMAINS OF AN ANCIENT ROMAN CITY ZAT BECAME PARIS HERSELF!
WORK BEGAN ON NOTRE DAME EEN 1163! BEFORE ZAT DATE, TROIS* OZZER CHURCHES STOOD ON ZE SITE, AND BEFORE ZAT, A GALLO-ROMAN TEMPLE!
*THREE
EEF WE HAD ZE TIME, MA PETITE, I WOULD TREAT YOU TO A DELICIOUS PIQUE-NIQUE, HERE EEN SQUARE JEAN XXIII, ZE PARK BEHIND ZEE CATHÉDRALE.
IT IS LOVELY!
ZERE SHE EES!
9

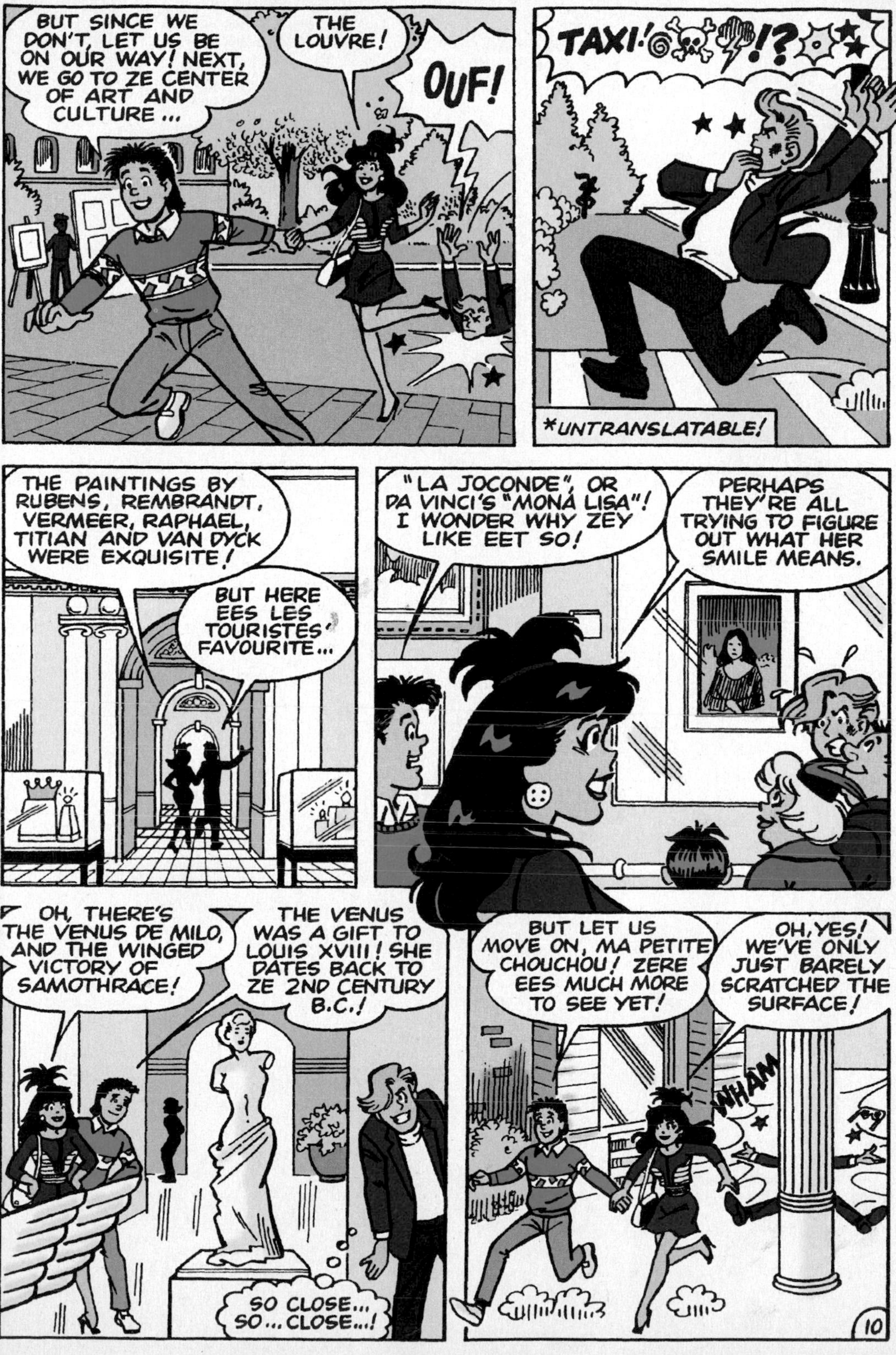

BUT SINCE WE DON'T, LET US BE ON OUR WAY! NEXT, WE GO TO ZE CENTER OF ART AND CULTURE ...
THE LOUVRE!
OUF!
TAXI!*!?
*UNTRANSLATABLE!
THE PAINTINGS BY RUBENS, REMBRANDT, VERMEER, RAPHAEL, TITIAN AND VAN DYCK WERE EXQUISITE!
BUT HERE EES LES TOURISTES' FAVOURITE...
"LA JOCONDE", OR DA VINCI'S "MONA LISA"! I WONDER WHY ZEY LIKE EET SO!
PERHAPS THEY'RE ALL TRYING TO FIGURE OUT WHAT HER SMILE MEANS.
OH, THERE'S THE VENUS DE MILO, AND THE WINGED VICTORY OF SAMOTHRACE!
THE VENUS WAS A GIFT TO LOUIS XVIII! SHE DATES BACK TO ZE 2ND CENTURY B.C.!
SO CLOSE... SO... CLOSE...!
BUT LET US MOVE ON, MA PETITE CHOUCHOU! ZERE EES MUCH MORE TO SEE YET!
OH, YES! WE'VE ONLY JUST BARELY SCRATCHED THE SURFACE!
WHAM
10

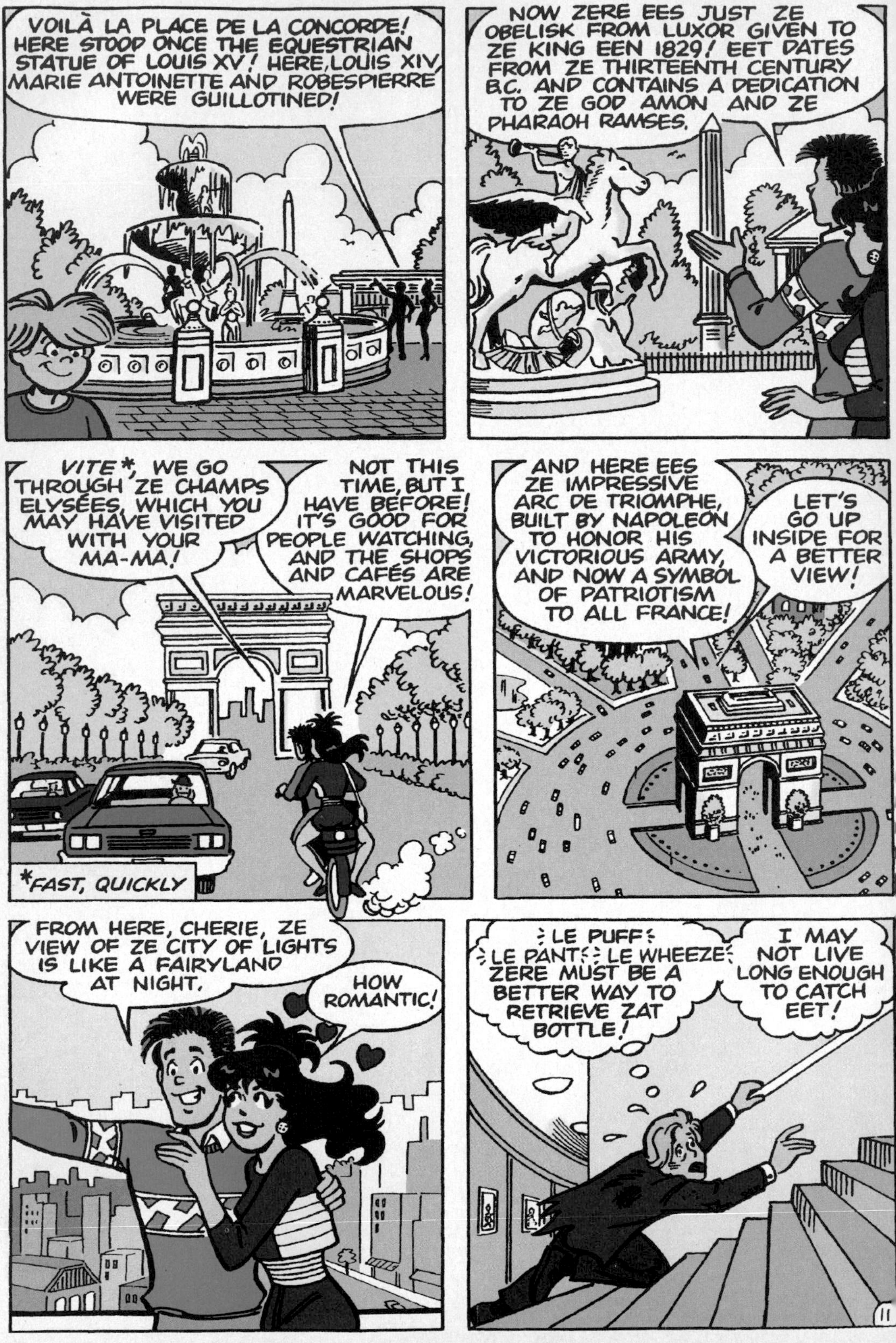
VOILÀ LA PLACE DE LA CONCORDE! HERE STOOD ONCE THE EQUESTRIAN STATUE OF LOUIS XV! HERE, LOUIS XIV, MARIE ANTOINETTE AND ROBESPIERRE WERE GUILLOTINED!
NOW ZERE EES JUST ZE OBELISK FROM LUXOR GIVEN TO ZE KING EEN 1829! EET DATES FROM ZE THIRTEENTH CENTURY B.C. AND CONTAINS A DEDICATION TO ZE GOD AMON AND ZE PHARAOH RAMSES.
VITE*, WE GO THROUGH ZE CHAMPS ELYSÉES, WHICH YOU MAY HAVE VISITED WITH YOUR MA-MA!
NOT THIS TIME, BUT I HAVE BEFORE! IT'S GOOD FOR PEOPLE WATCHING, AND THE SHOPS AND CAFÉS ARE MARVELOUS!
*FAST, QUICKLY
AND HERE EES ZE IMPRESSIVE ARC DE TRIOMPHE, BUILT BY NAPOLEON TO HONOR HIS VICTORIOUS ARMY, AND NOW A SYMBOL OF PATRIOTISM TO ALL FRANCE!
LET'S GO UP INSIDE FOR A BETTER VIEW!
FROM HERE, CHERIE, ZE VIEW OF ZE CITY OF LIGHTS IS LIKE A FAIRYLAND AT NIGHT.
HOW ROMANTIC!
LE PUFF LE PANT LE WHEEZE ZERE MUST BE A BETTER WAY TO RETRIEVE ZAT BOTTLE!
I MAY NOT LIVE LONG ENOUGH TO CATCH EET!
11

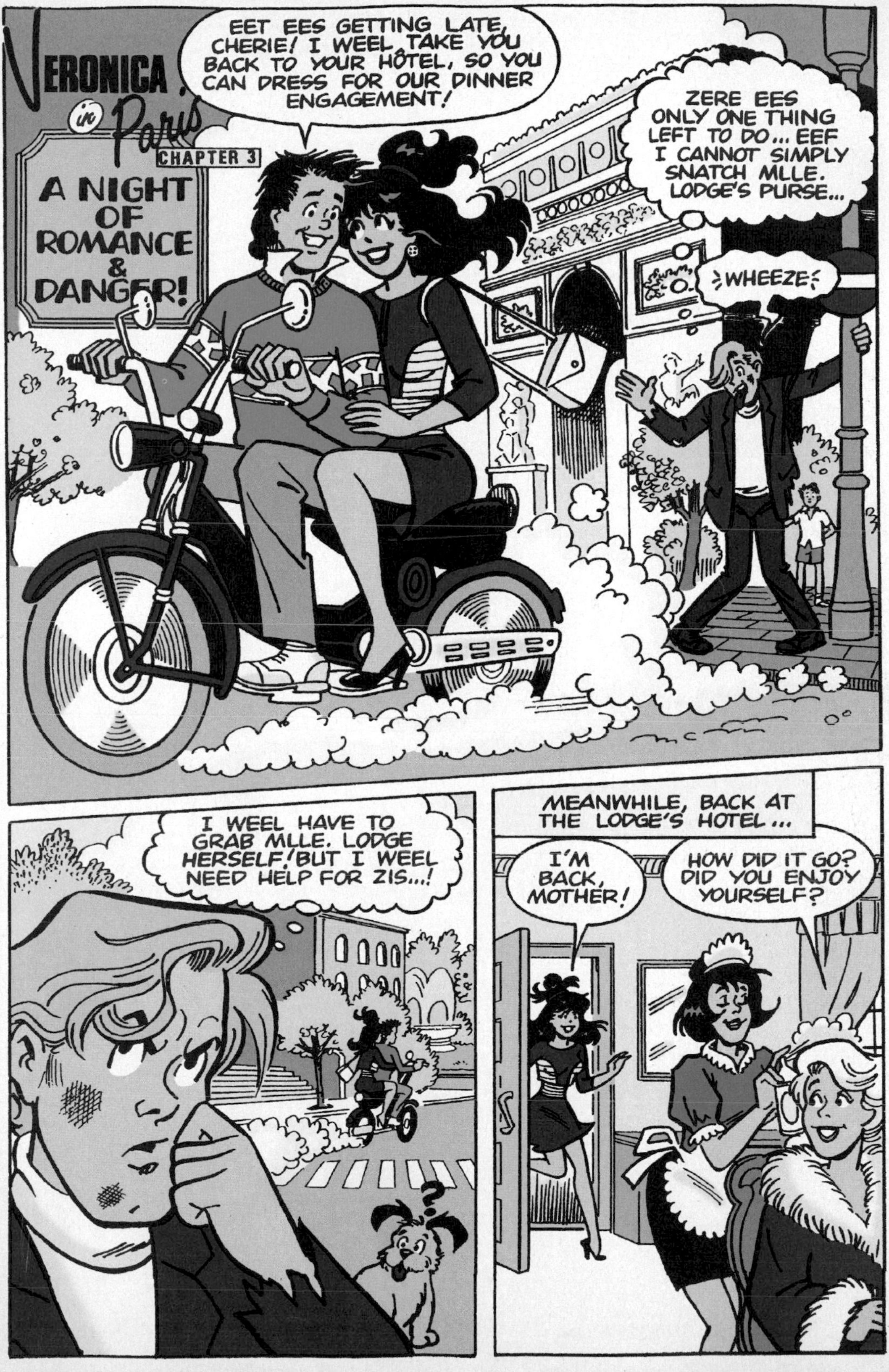
VERONICA in Paris
CHAPTER 3
A NIGHT OF ROMANCE & DANGER!
EET EES GETTING LATE, CHERIE! I WEEL TAKE YOU BACK TO YOUR HÔTEL, SO YOU CAN DRESS FOR OUR DINNER ENGAGEMENT!
ZERE EES ONLY ONE THING LEFT TO DO... EEF I CANNOT SIMPLY SNATCH MLLE. LODGE'S PURSE...
WHEEZE
I WEEL HAVE TO GRAB MLLE. LODGE HERSELF! BUT I WEEL NEED HELP FOR ZIS...!
MEANWHILE, BACK AT THE LODGE'S HOTEL...
I'M BACK, MOTHER!
HOW DID IT GO? DID YOU ENJOY YOURSELF?

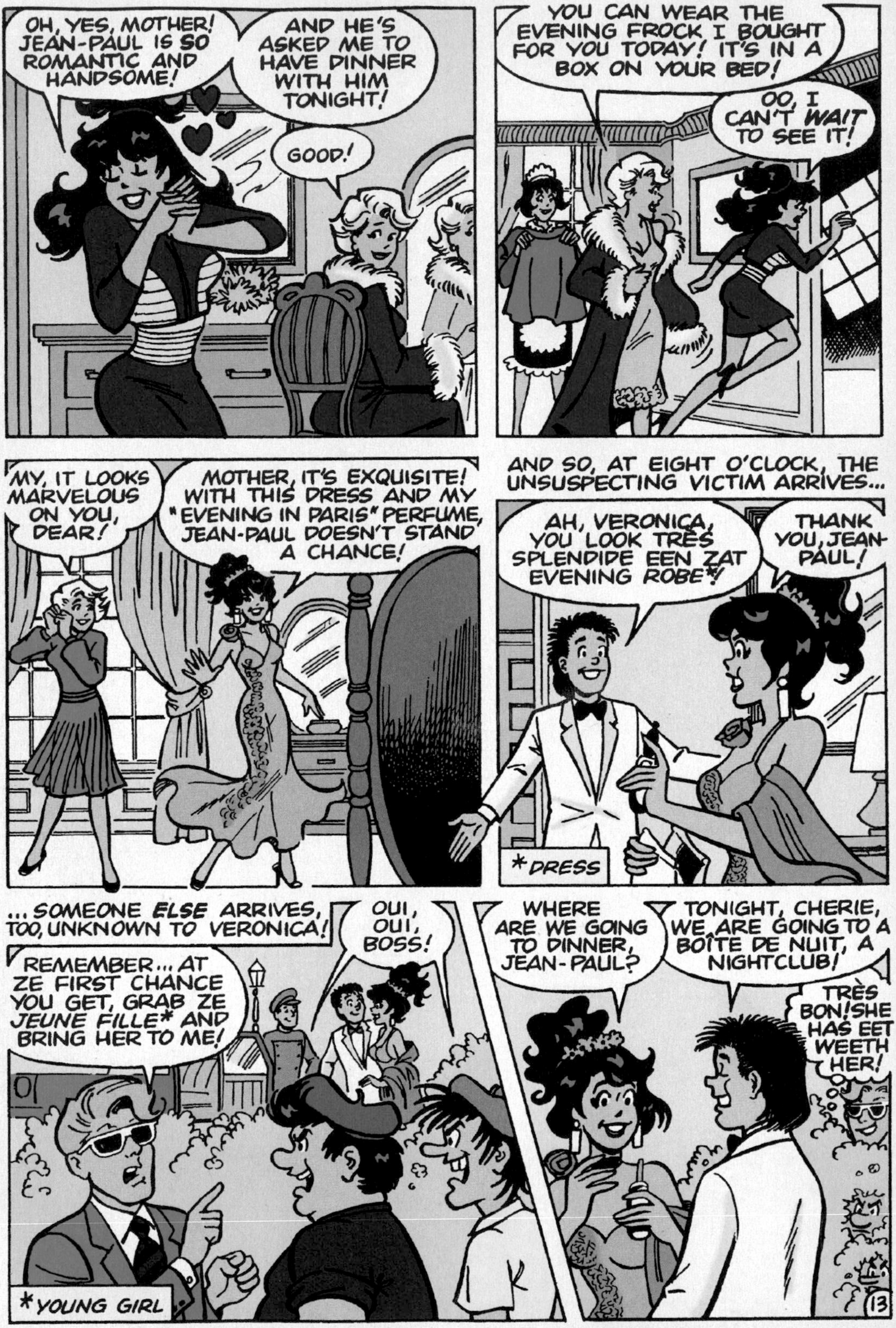
OH, YES, MOTHER! JEAN-PAUL IS SO ROMANTIC AND HANDSOME!
AND HE'S ASKED ME TO HAVE DINNER WITH HIM TONIGHT!
GOOD!
YOU CAN WEAR THE EVENING FROCK I BOUGHT FOR YOU TODAY! IT'S IN A BOX ON YOUR BED!
OO, I CAN'T WAIT TO SEE IT!
MY, IT LOOKS MARVELOUS ON YOU, DEAR!
MOTHER, IT'S EXQUISITE! WITH THIS DRESS AND MY "EVENING IN PARIS" PERFUME, JEAN-PAUL DOESN'T STAND A CHANCE!
AND SO, AT EIGHT O'CLOCK, THE UNSUSPECTING VICTIM ARRIVES...
AH, VERONICA, YOU LOOK TRÈS SPLENDIDE EEN ZAT EVENING ROBE*!
THANK YOU, JEAN-PAUL!
*DRESS
...SOMEONE ELSE ARRIVES, TOO, UNKNOWN TO VERONICA!
OUI, OUI, BOSS!
REMEMBER... AT ZE FIRST CHANCE YOU GET, GRAB ZE JEUNE FILLE* AND BRING HER TO ME!
*YOUNG GIRL
WHERE ARE WE GOING TO DINNER, JEAN-PAUL?
TONIGHT, CHERIE, WE ARE GOING TO A BOÎTE DE NUIT, A NIGHTCLUB!
TRÈS BON! SHE HAS EET WEETH HER!
13

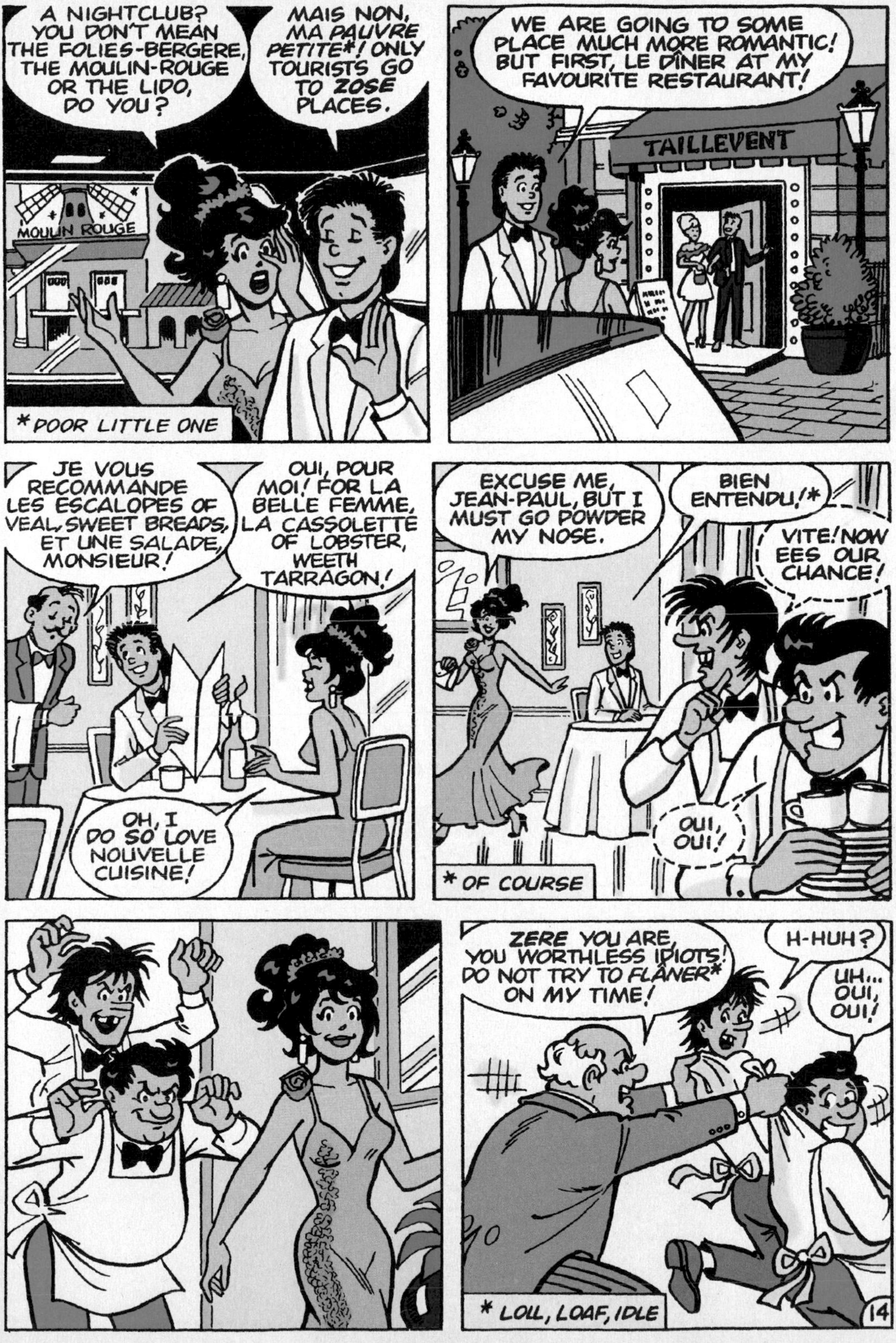
A NIGHTCLUB? YOU DON'T MEAN THE FOLIES-BERGERE, THE MOULIN-ROUGE OR THE LIDO, DO YOU?
MAIS NON, MA PAUVRE PETITE*! ONLY TOURISTS GO TO ZOSE PLACES.
MOULIN ROUGE
*POOR LITTLE ONE
WE ARE GOING TO SOME PLACE MUCH MORE ROMANTIC! BUT FIRST, LE DÎNER AT MY FAVOURITE RESTAURANT!
TAILLEVENT
JE VOUS RECOMMANDE LES ESCALOPES OF VEAL, SWEET BREADS, ET UNE SALADE, MONSIEUR!
OUI, POUR MOI! FOR LA BELLE FEMME, LA CASSOLETTE OF LOBSTER, WEETH TARRAGON!
OH, I DO SO LOVE NOUVELLE CUISINE!
EXCUSE ME, JEAN-PAUL, BUT I MUST GO POWDER MY NOSE.
BIEN ENTENDU!*
VITE! NOW EES OUR CHANCE!
OUI, OUI!
*OF COURSE
ZERE YOU ARE, YOU WORTHLESS IDIOTS! DO NOT TRY TO FLÂNER* ON MY TIME!
H-HUH?
UH... OUI, OUI!
*LOLL, LOAF, IDLE
14

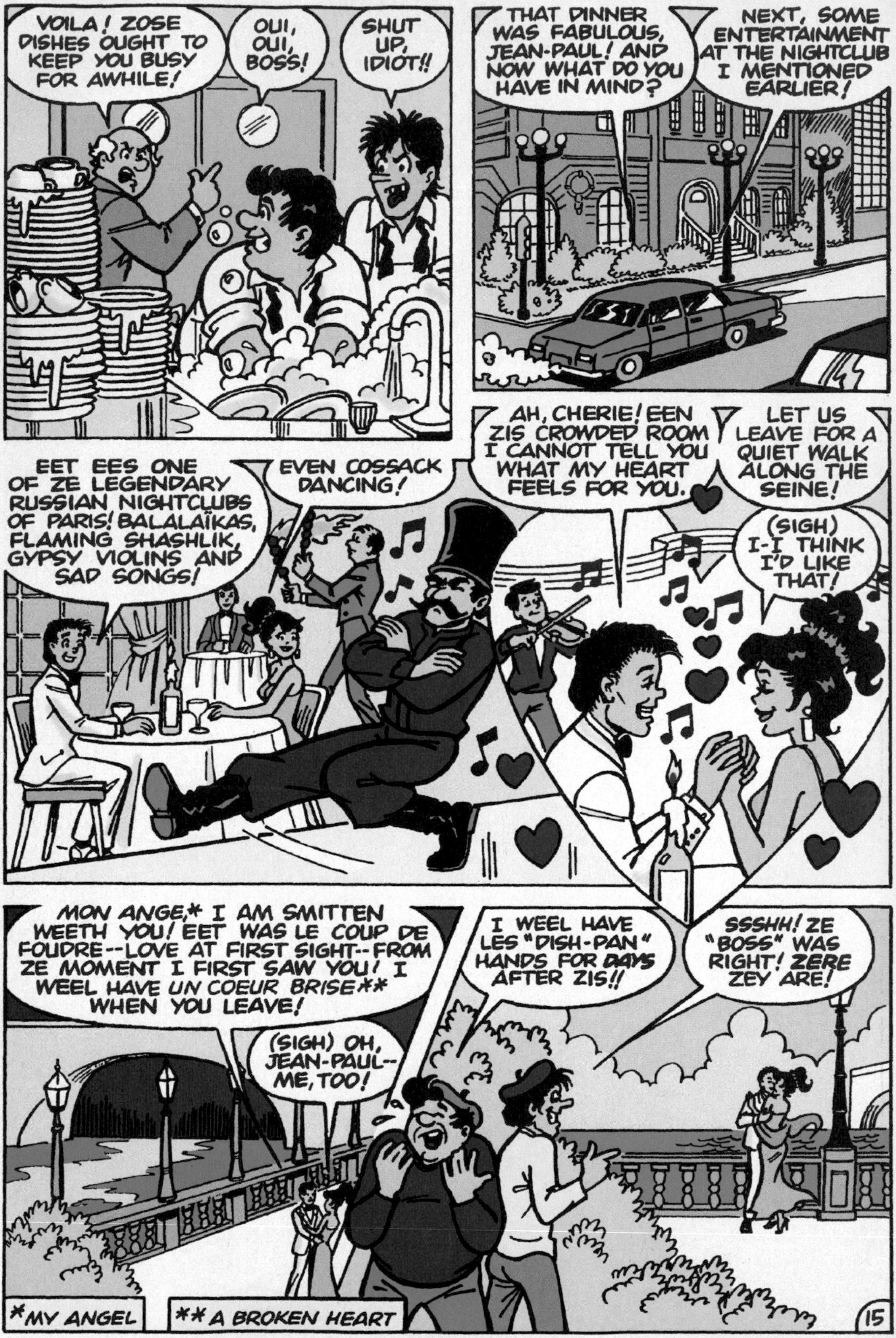
VOILA! ZOSE DISHES OUGHT TO KEEP YOU BUSY FOR AWHILE!
OUI, OUI, BOSS!
SHUT UP, IDIOT!!
THAT DINNER WAS FABULOUS, JEAN-PAUL! AND NOW WHAT DO YOU HAVE IN MIND?
NEXT, SOME ENTERTAINMENT AT THE NIGHTCLUB I MENTIONED EARLIER!
EET EES ONE OF ZE LEGENDARY RUSSIAN NIGHTCLUBS OF PARIS! BALALAÏKAS, FLAMING SHASHLIK, GYPSY VIOLINS AND SAD SONGS!
EVEN COSSACK DANCING!
AH, CHERIE! EEN ZIS CROWDED ROOM I CANNOT TELL YOU WHAT MY HEART FEELS FOR YOU.
LET US LEAVE FOR A QUIET WALK ALONG THE SEINE!
(SIGH) I-I THINK I'D LIKE THAT!
MON ANGE,* I AM SMITTEN WEETH YOU! EET WAS LE COUP DE FOUDRE--LOVE AT FIRST SIGHT--FROM ZE MOMENT I FIRST SAW YOU! I WEEL HAVE UN COEUR BRISE** WHEN YOU LEAVE!
(SIGH) OH, JEAN-PAUL--ME, TOO!
I WEEL HAVE LES "DISH-PAN" HANDS FOR DAYS AFTER ZIS!!
SSSHH! ZE "BOSS" WAS RIGHT! ZERE ZEY ARE!
*MY ANGEL
**A BROKEN HEART
15

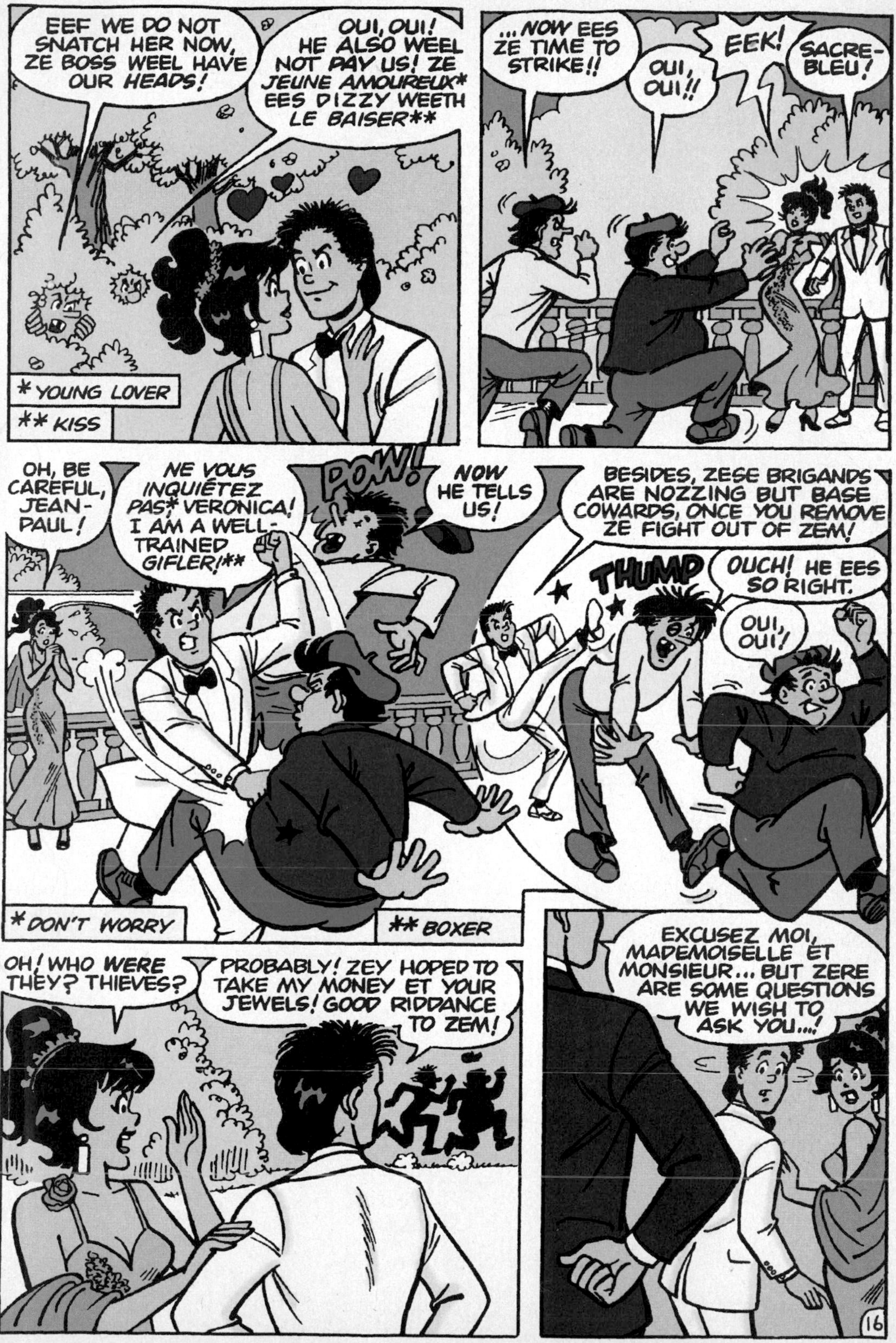
EEF WE DO NOT SNATCH HER NOW, ZE BOSS WEEL HAVE OUR HEADS!
OUI, OUI! HE ALSO WEEL NOT PAY US! ZE JEUNE AMOUREUX* EES DIZZY WEETH LE BAISER**
* YOUNG LOVER
** KISS
...NOW EES ZE TIME TO STRIKE!!
OUI, OUI!!
EEK!
SACRE-BLEU!
OH, BE CAREFUL, JEAN-PAUL!
NE VOUS INQUIÉTEZ PAS* VERONICA! I AM A WELL-TRAINED GIFLER!**
POW!
NOW HE TELLS US!
BESIDES, ZESE BRIGANDS ARE NOZZING BUT BASE COWARDS, ONCE YOU REMOVE ZE FIGHT OUT OF ZEM!
THUMP
OUCH! HE EES SO RIGHT.
OUI, OUI!
* DON'T WORRY
** BOXER
OH! WHO WERE THEY? THIEVES?
PROBABLY! ZEY HOPED TO TAKE MY MONEY ET YOUR JEWELS! GOOD RIDDANCE TO ZEM!
EXCUSEZ MOI, MADEMOISELLE ET MONSIEUR... BUT ZERE ARE SOME QUESTIONS WE WISH TO ASK YOU...!
16

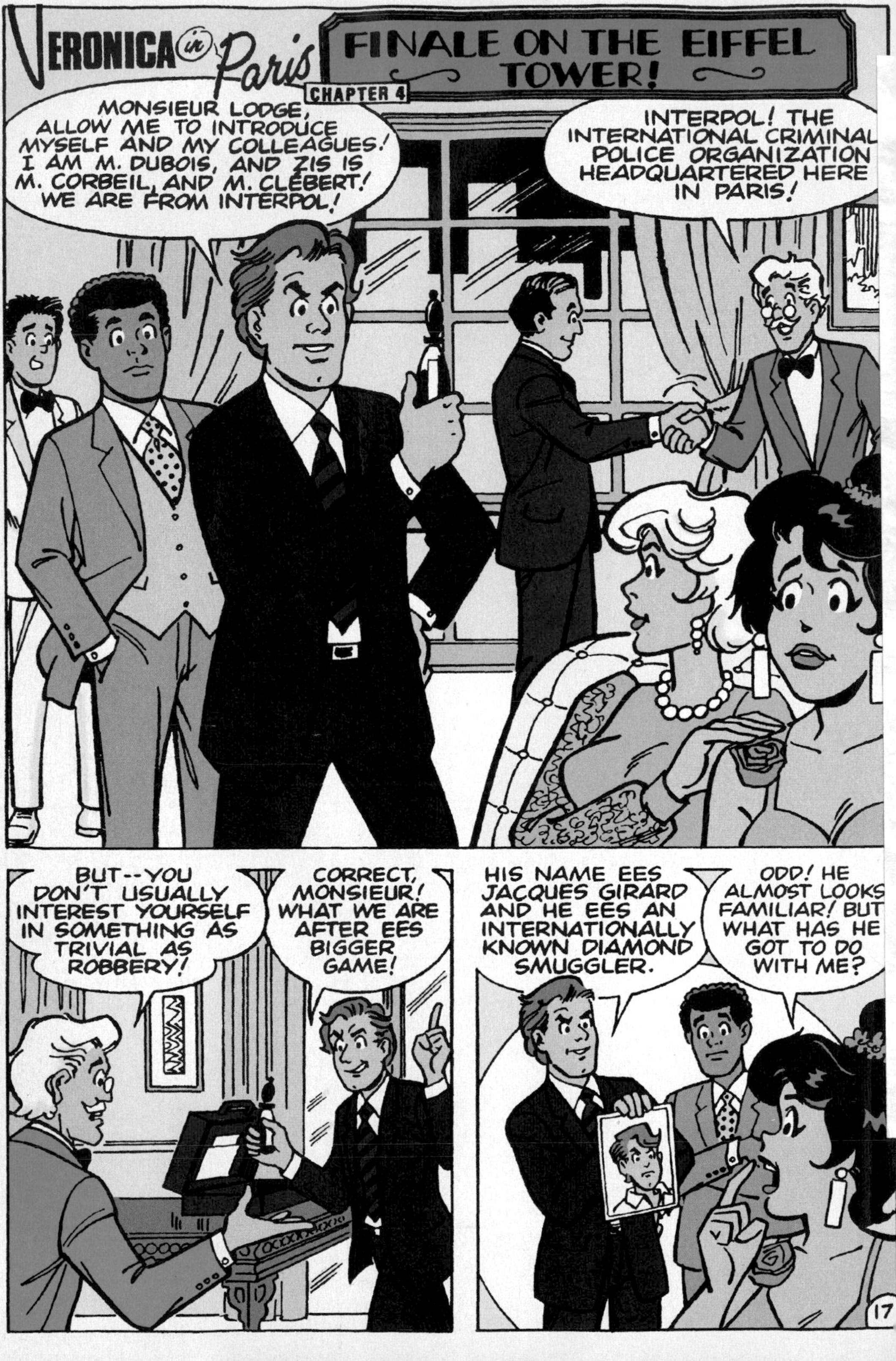
VERONICA in Paris
CHAPTER 4
FINALE ON THE EIFFEL TOWER!
MONSIEUR LODGE, ALLOW ME TO INTRODUCE MYSELF AND MY COLLEAGUES! I AM M. DUBOIS, AND ZIS IS M. CORBEIL, AND M. CLÉBERT! WE ARE FROM INTERPOL!
INTERPOL! THE INTERNATIONAL CRIMINAL POLICE ORGANIZATION HEADQUARTERED HERE IN PARIS!
BUT--YOU DON'T USUALLY INTEREST YOURSELF IN SOMETHING AS TRIVIAL AS ROBBERY!
CORRECT, MONSIEUR! WHAT WE ARE AFTER EES BIGGER GAME!
HIS NAME EES JACQUES GIRARD AND HE EES AN INTERNATIONALLY KNOWN DIAMOND SMUGGLER.
ODD! HE ALMOST LOOKS FAMILIAR! BUT WHAT HAS HE GOT TO DO WITH ME?
17

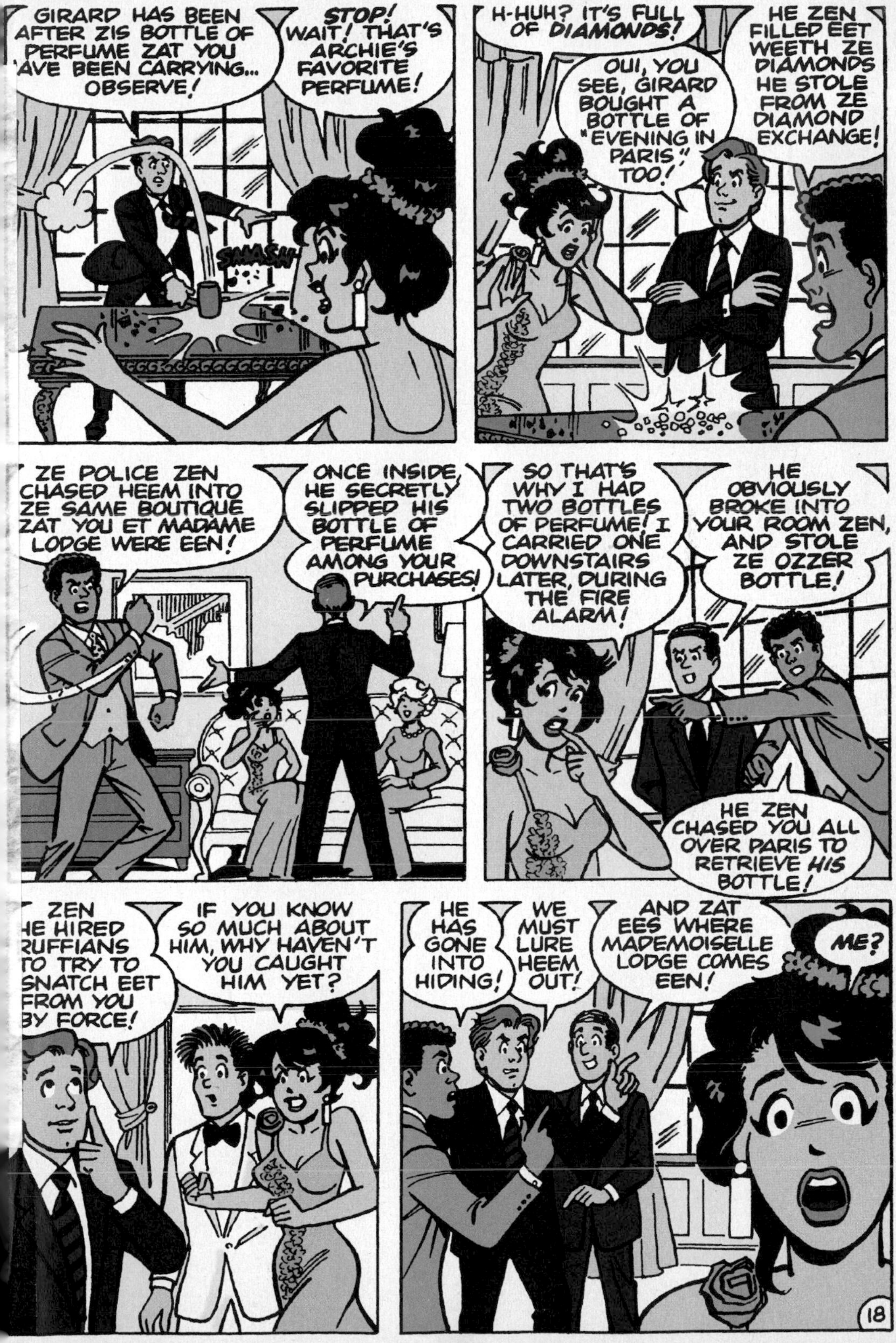
GIRARD HAS BEEN AFTER ZIS BOTTLE OF PERFUME ZAT YOU 'AVE BEEN CARRYING... OBSERVE!
STOP! WAIT! THAT'S ARCHIE'S FAVORITE PERFUME!
SMASH!
H-HUH? IT'S FULL OF DIAMONDS!
OUI, YOU SEE, GIRARD BOUGHT A BOTTLE OF "EVENING IN PARIS," TOO!
HE ZEN FILLED EET WEETH ZE DIAMONDS HE STOLE FROM ZE DIAMOND EXCHANGE!
ZE POLICE ZEN CHASED HEEM INTO ZE SAME BOUTIQUE ZAT YOU ET MADAME LODGE WERE EEN!
ONCE INSIDE, HE SECRETLY SLIPPED HIS BOTTLE OF PERFUME AMONG YOUR PURCHASES!
SO THAT'S WHY I HAD TWO BOTTLES OF PERFUME! I CARRIED ONE DOWNSTAIRS LATER, DURING THE FIRE ALARM!
HE OBVIOUSLY BROKE INTO YOUR ROOM ZEN, AND STOLE ZE OZZER BOTTLE!
HE ZEN CHASED YOU ALL OVER PARIS TO RETRIEVE HIS BOTTLE!
ZEN HE HIRED RUFFIANS TO TRY TO SNATCH EET FROM YOU BY FORCE!
IF YOU KNOW SO MUCH ABOUT HIM, WHY HAVEN'T YOU CAUGHT HIM YET?
HE HAS GONE INTO HIDING!
WE MUST LURE HEEM OUT!
AND ZAT EES WHERE MADEMOISELLE LODGE COMES EEN!
ME?
18

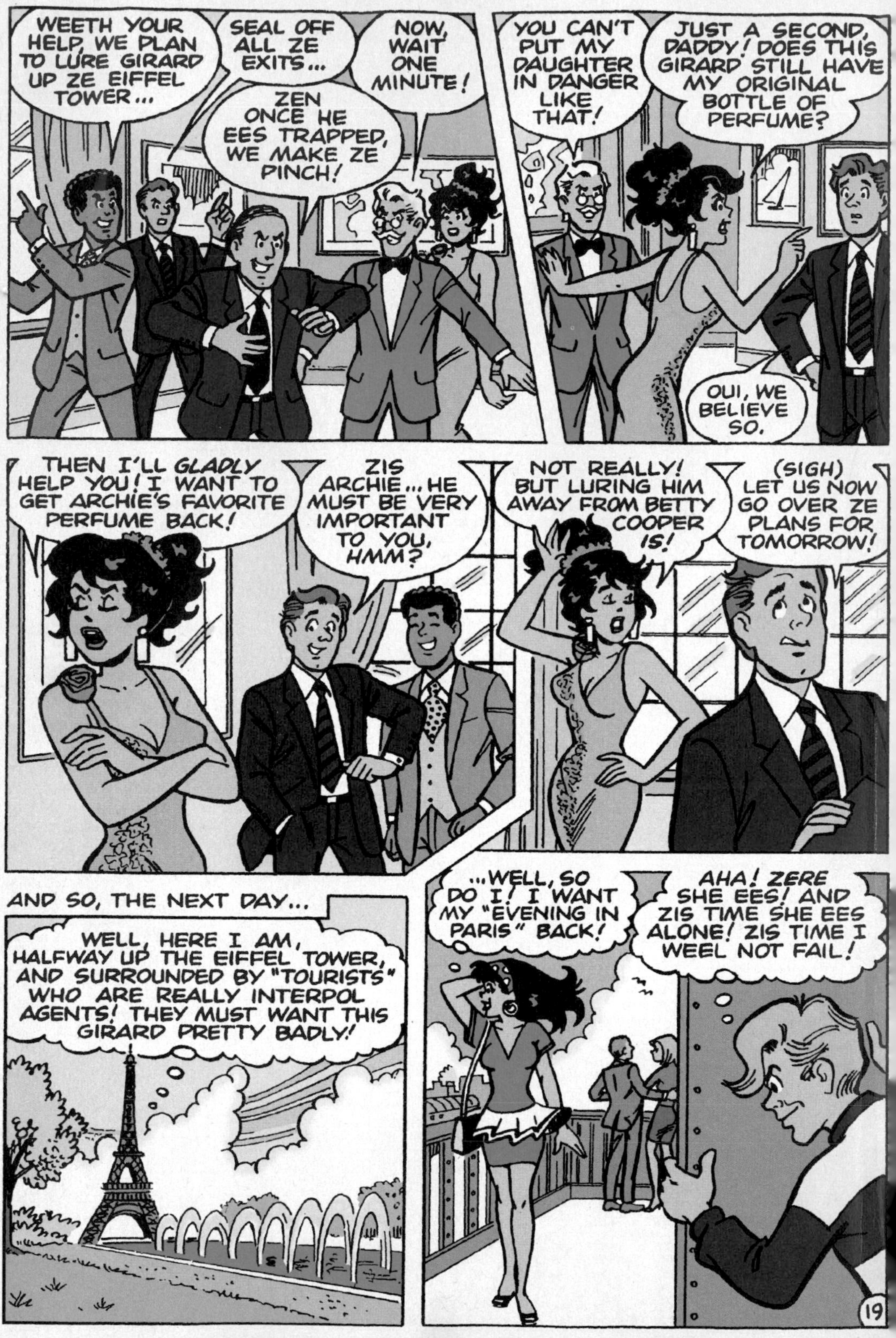
WEETH YOUR HELP, WE PLAN TO LURE GIRARD UP ZE EIFFEL TOWER...
SEAL OFF ALL ZE EXITS...
ZEN ONCE HE EES TRAPPED, WE MAKE ZE PINCH!
NOW, WAIT ONE MINUTE!
YOU CAN'T PUT MY DAUGHTER IN DANGER LIKE THAT!
JUST A SECOND, DADDY! DOES THIS GIRARD STILL HAVE MY ORIGINAL BOTTLE OF PERFUME?
OUI, WE BELIEVE SO.
THEN I'LL GLADLY HELP YOU! I WANT TO GET ARCHIE'S FAVORITE PERFUME BACK!
ZIS ARCHIE... HE MUST BE VERY IMPORTANT TO YOU, HMM?
NOT REALLY! BUT LURING HIM AWAY FROM BETTY COOPER IS!
(SIGH) LET US NOW GO OVER ZE PLANS FOR TOMORROW!
AND SO, THE NEXT DAY...
WELL, HERE I AM, HALFWAY UP THE EIFFEL TOWER, AND SURROUNDED BY "TOURISTS" WHO ARE REALLY INTERPOL AGENTS! THEY MUST WANT THIS GIRARD PRETTY BADLY!
...WELL, SO DO I! I WANT MY "EVENING IN PARIS" BACK!
AHA! ZERE SHE EES! AND ZIS TIME SHE EES ALONE! ZIS TIME I WEEL NOT FAIL!
19

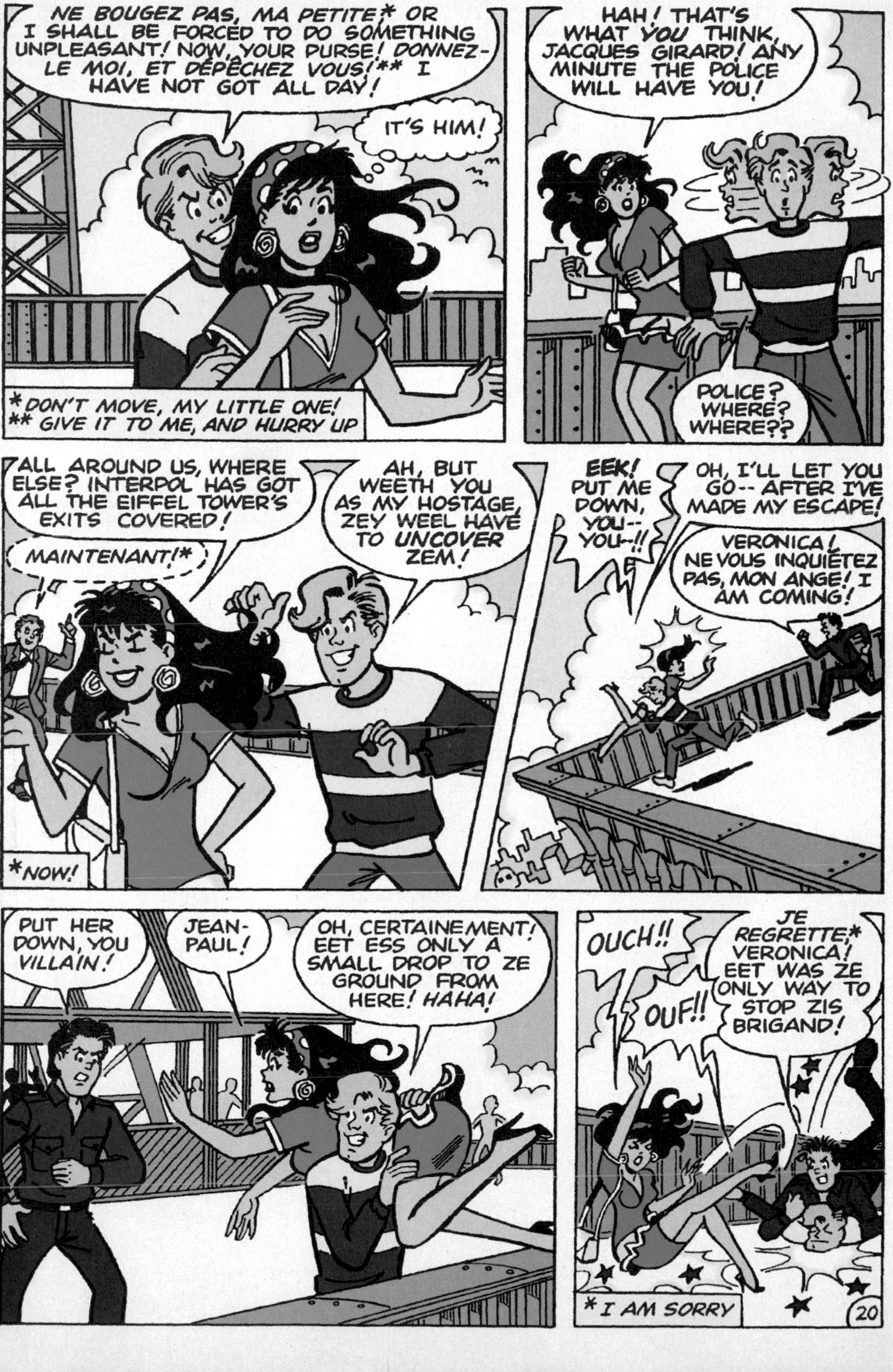

NE BOUGEZ PAS, MA PETITE* OR I SHALL BE FORCED TO DO SOMETHING UNPLEASANT! NOW, YOUR PURSE! DONNEZ-LE MOI, ET DÉPÊCHEZ VOUS!** I HAVE NOT GOT ALL DAY!
IT'S HIM!
*DON'T MOVE, MY LITTLE ONE!
** GIVE IT TO ME, AND HURRY UP
HAH! THAT'S WHAT YOU THINK, JACQUES GIRARD! ANY MINUTE THE POLICE WILL HAVE YOU!
POLICE? WHERE? WHERE??
ALL AROUND US, WHERE ELSE? INTERPOL HAS GOT ALL THE EIFFEL TOWER'S EXITS COVERED!
MAINTENANT!*
AH, BUT WEETH YOU AS MY HOSTAGE, ZEY WEEL HAVE TO UNCOVER ZEM!
*NOW!
EEK! PUT ME DOWN, YOU-- YOU--!!
OH, I'LL LET YOU GO-- AFTER I'VE MADE MY ESCAPE!
VERONICA! NE VOUS INQUIÉTEZ PAS, MON ANGE! I AM COMING!
PUT HER DOWN, YOU VILLAIN!
JEAN-PAUL!
OH, CERTAINEMENT! EET ESS ONLY A SMALL DROP TO ZE GROUND FROM HERE! HAHA!
OUCH!!
OUF!!
JE REGRETTE,* VERONICA! EET WAS ZE ONLY WAY TO STOP ZIS BRIGAND!
*I AM SORRY
20

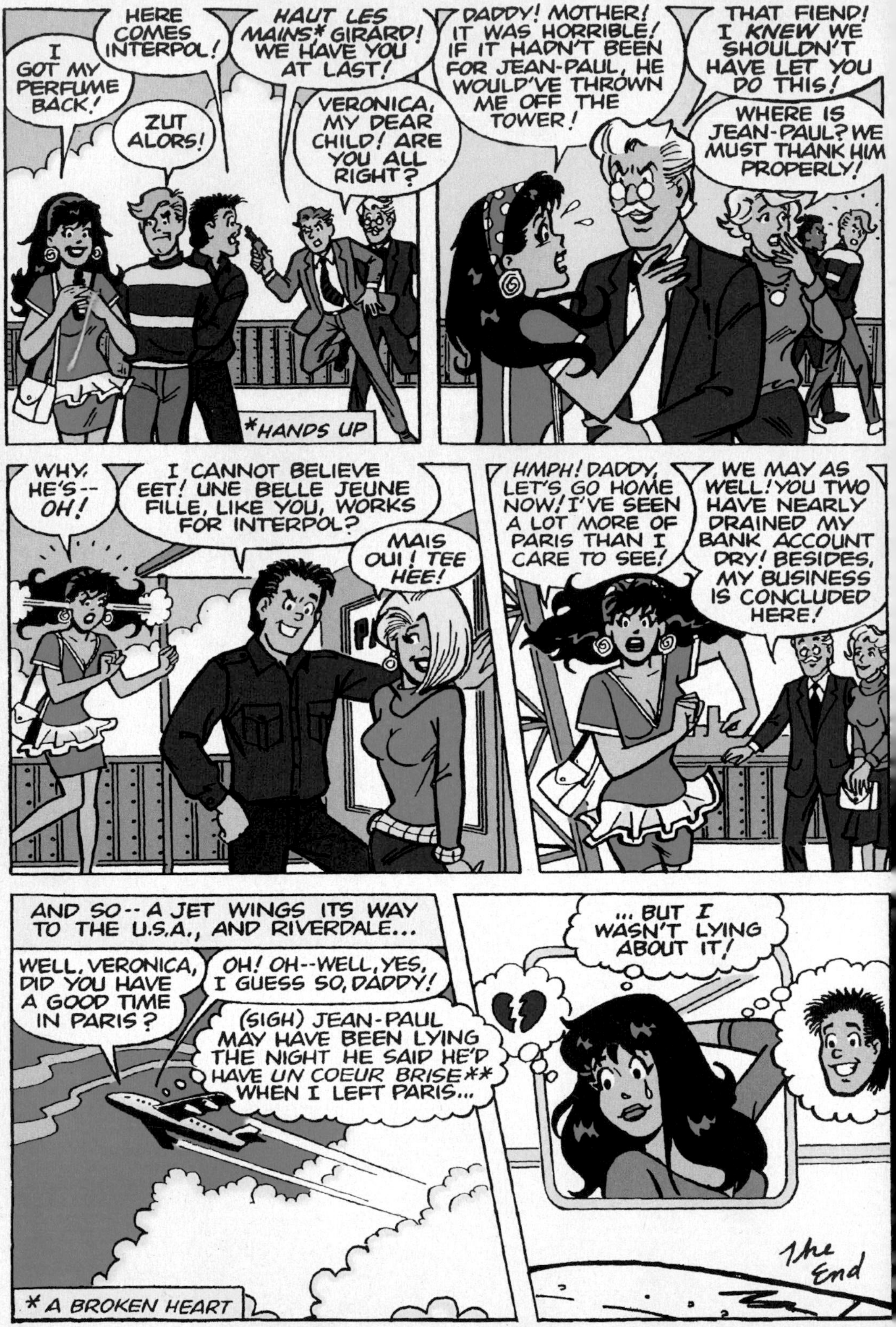

I GOT MY PERFUME BACK!
HERE COMES INTERPOL!
ZUT ALORS!
HAUT LES MAINS* GIRARD! WE HAVE YOU AT LAST!
VERONICA, MY DEAR CHILD! ARE YOU ALL RIGHT?
*HANDS UP
DADDY! MOTHER! IT WAS HORRIBLE! IF IT HADN'T BEEN FOR JEAN-PAUL, HE WOULD'VE THROWN ME OFF THE TOWER!
THAT FIEND! I KNEW WE SHOULDN'T HAVE LET YOU DO THIS!
WHERE IS JEAN-PAUL? WE MUST THANK HIM PROPERLY!
WHY, HE'S-- OH!
I CANNOT BELIEVE EET! UNE BELLE JEUNE FILLE, LIKE YOU, WORKS FOR INTERPOL?
MAIS OUI! TEE HEE!
HMPH! DADDY, LET'S GO HOME NOW! I'VE SEEN A LOT MORE OF PARIS THAN I CARE TO SEE!
WE MAY AS WELL! YOU TWO HAVE NEARLY DRAINED MY BANK ACCOUNT DRY! BESIDES, MY BUSINESS IS CONCLUDED HERE!
AND SO-- A JET WINGS ITS WAY TO THE U.S.A., AND RIVERDALE...
WELL, VERONICA, DID YOU HAVE A GOOD TIME IN PARIS?
OH! OH--WELL, YES, I GUESS SO, DADDY!
(SIGH) JEAN-PAUL MAY HAVE BEEN LYING THE NIGHT HE SAID HE'D HAVE UN COEUR BRISE** WHEN I LEFT PARIS...
...BUT I WASN'T LYING ABOUT IT!
The End
*A BROKEN HEART

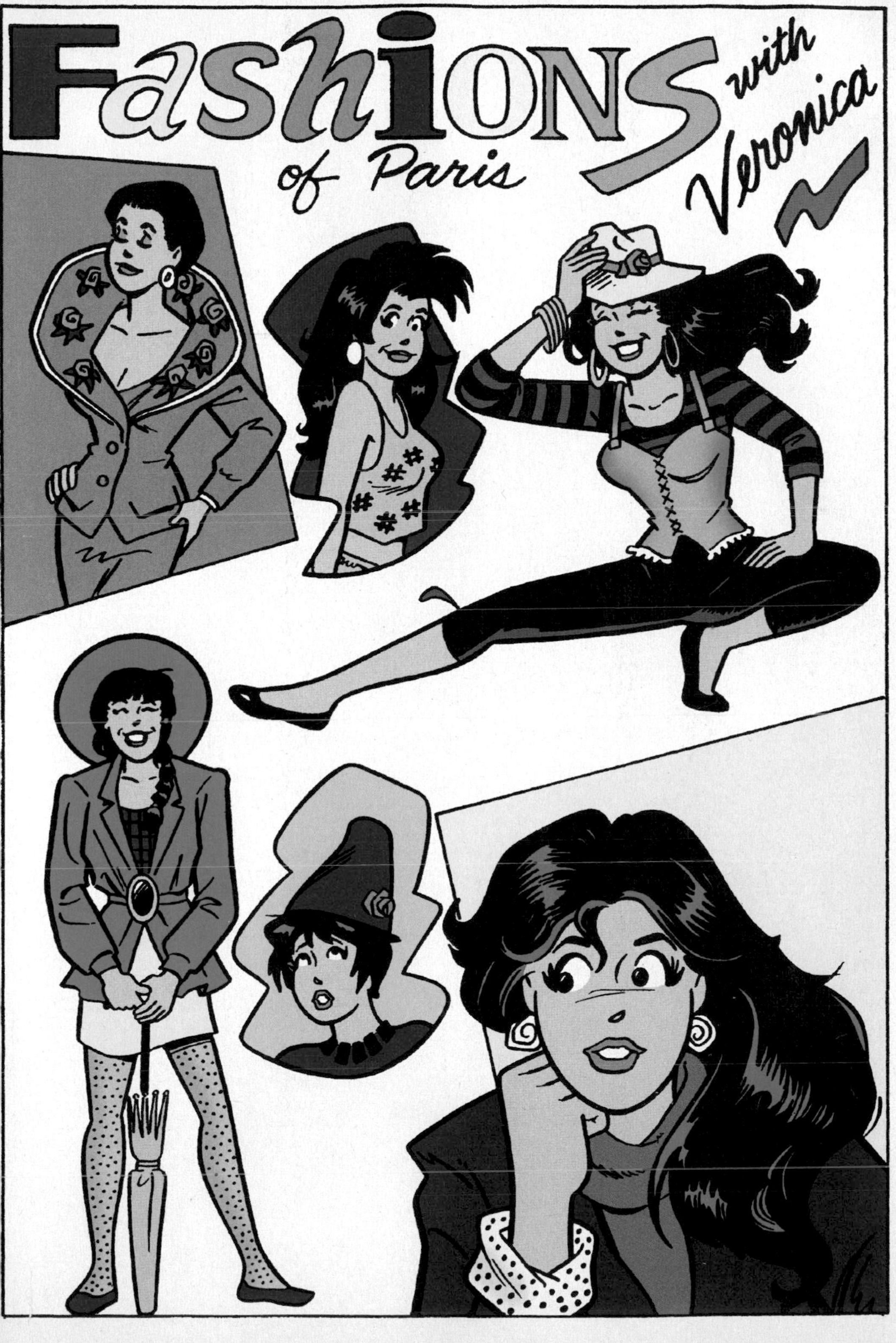
Fashions of Paris
with Veronica

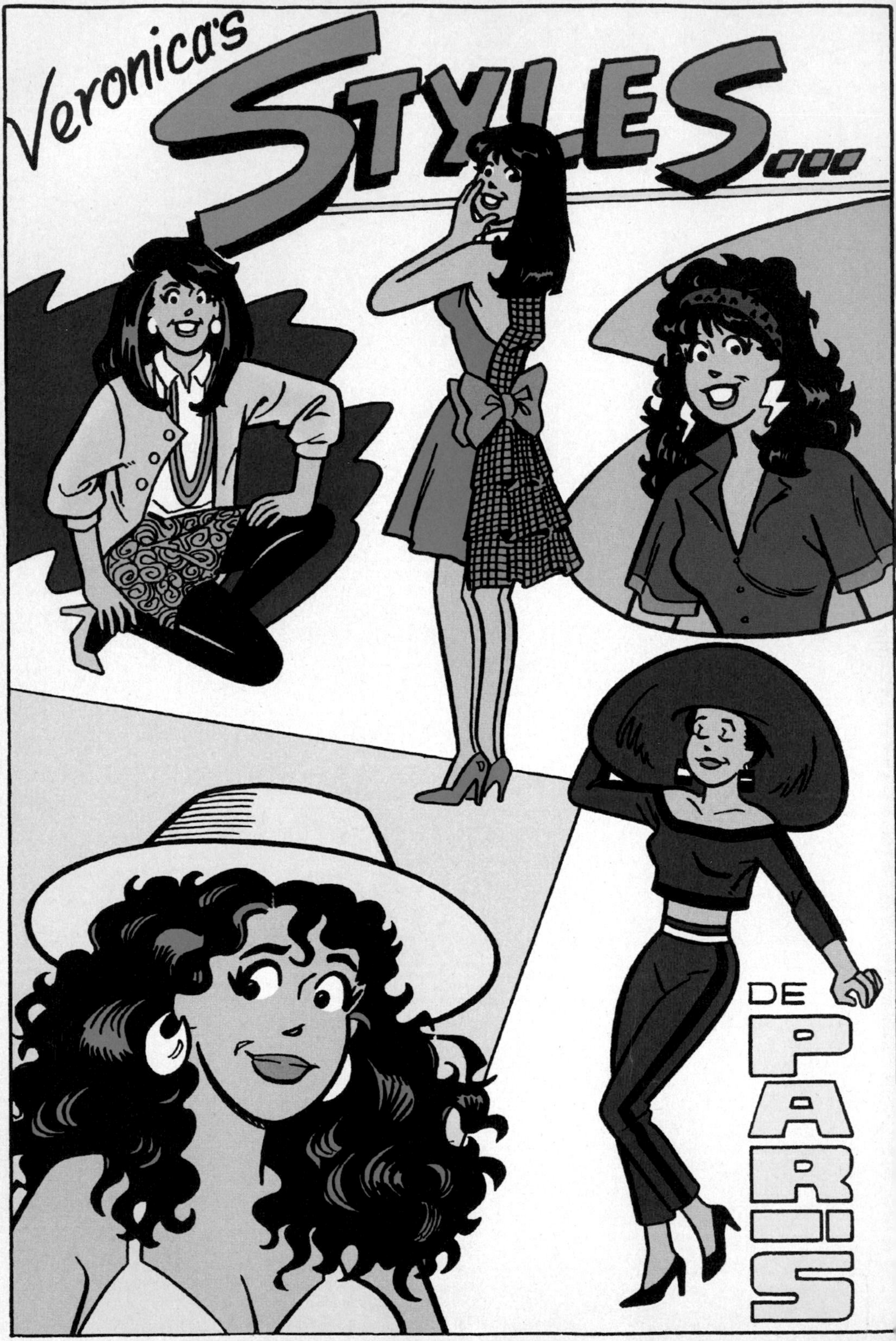
Veronica's STYLES...
DE PARIS

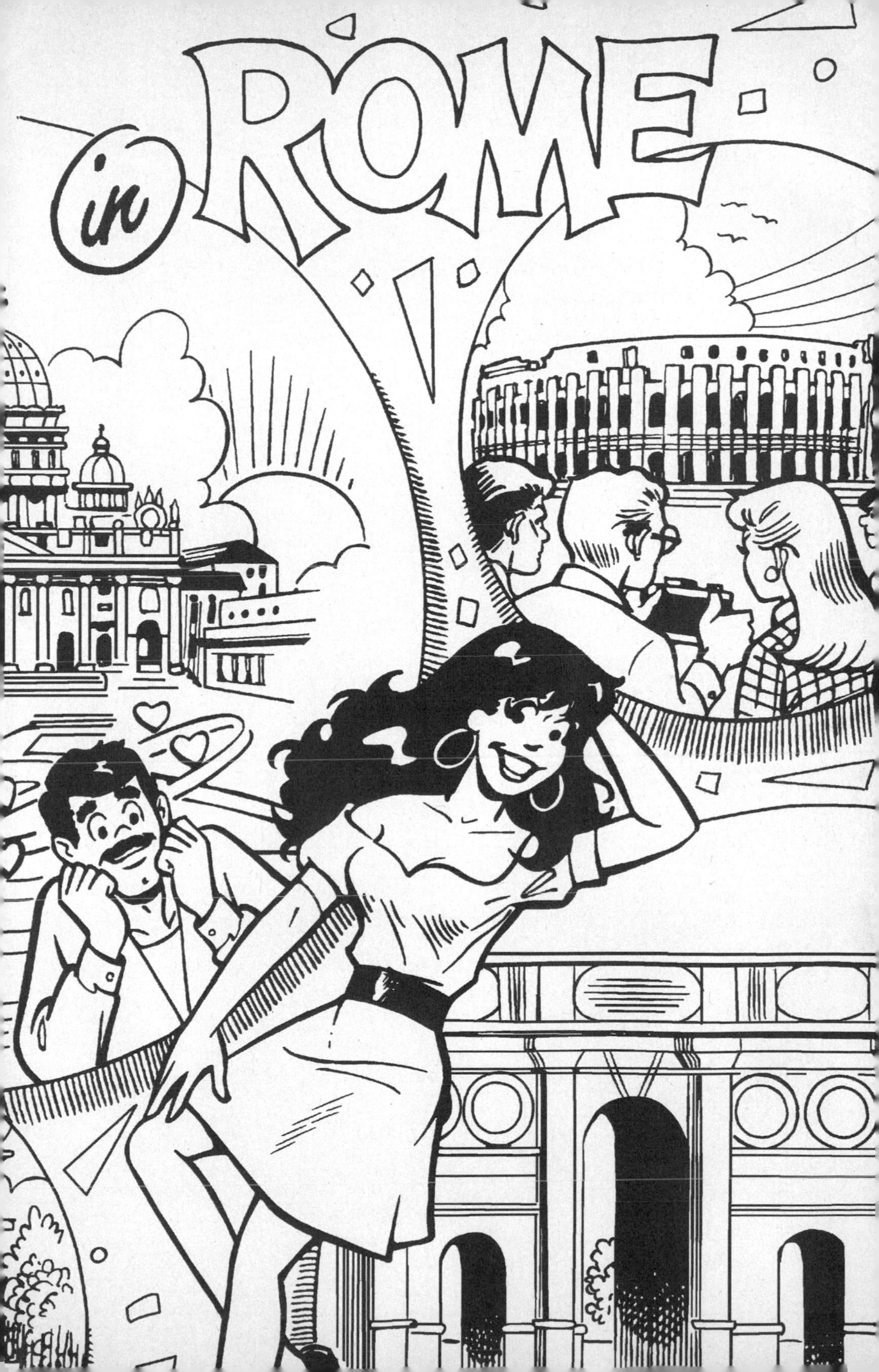

in ROME

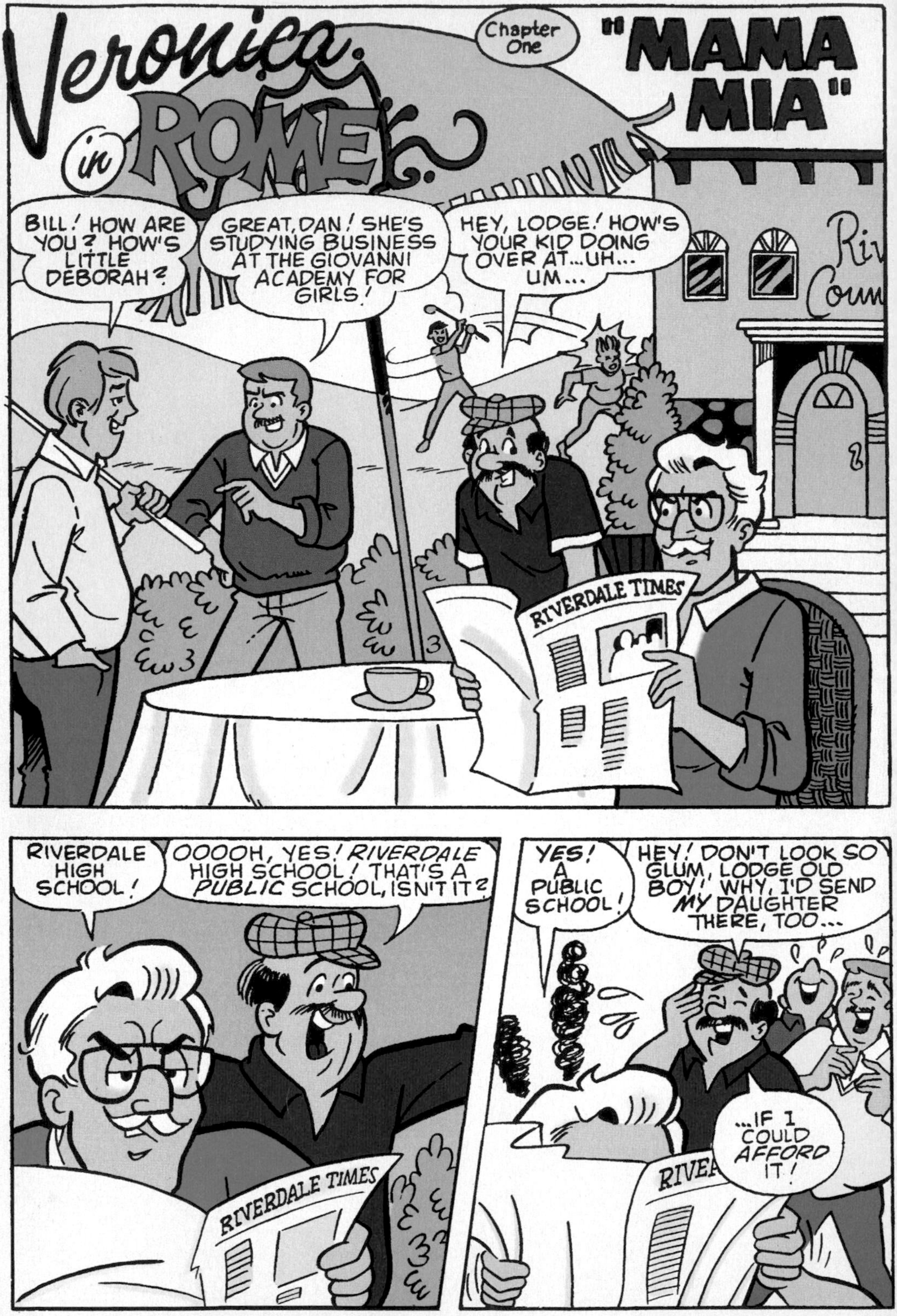
Veronica in ROME
Chapter One
"MAMA MIA"
BILL! HOW ARE YOU? HOW'S LITTLE DEBORAH?
GREAT, DAN! SHE'S STUDYING BUSINESS AT THE GIOVANNI ACADEMY FOR GIRLS!
HEY, LODGE! HOW'S YOUR KID DOING OVER AT...UH... UM...
RIVERDALE TIMES
RIVERDALE HIGH SCHOOL!
OOOOH, YES! RIVERDALE HIGH SCHOOL! THAT'S A PUBLIC SCHOOL, ISN'T IT?
RIVERDALE TIMES
YES! A PUBLIC SCHOOL!
HEY! DON'T LOOK SO GLUM, LODGE OLD BOY! WHY, I'D SEND MY DAUGHTER THERE, TOO...
...IF I COULD AFFORD IT!

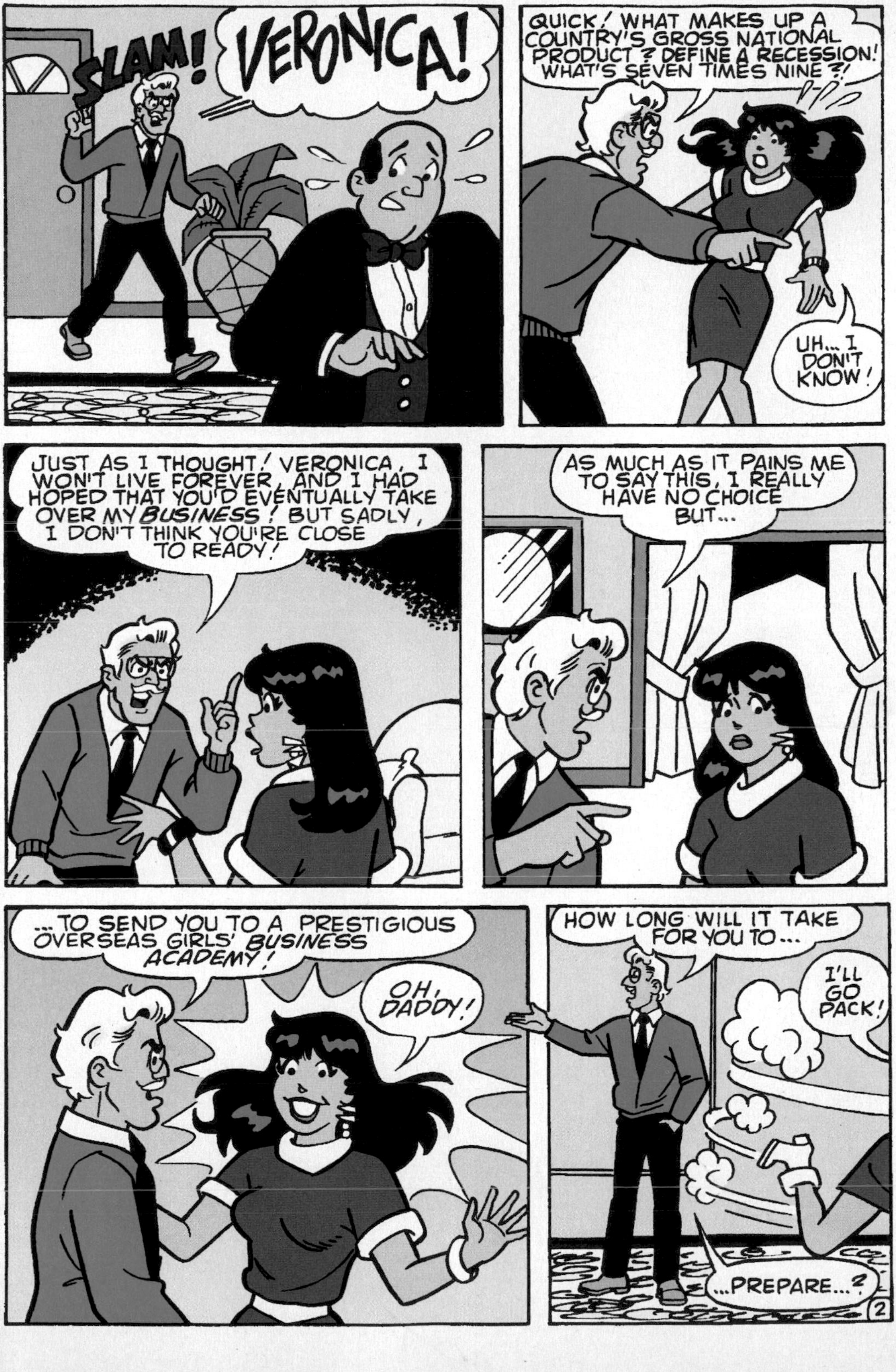
SLAM!
VERONICA!
QUICK! WHAT MAKES UP A COUNTRY'S GROSS NATIONAL PRODUCT? DEFINE A RECESSION! WHAT'S SEVEN TIMES NINE?!
UH... I DON'T KNOW!
JUST AS I THOUGHT! VERONICA, I WON'T LIVE FOREVER, AND I HAD HOPED THAT YOU'D EVENTUALLY TAKE OVER MY BUSINESS! BUT SADLY, I DON'T THINK YOU'RE CLOSE TO READY!
AS MUCH AS IT PAINS ME TO SAY THIS, I REALLY HAVE NO CHOICE BUT...
...TO SEND YOU TO A PRESTIGIOUS OVERSEAS GIRLS' BUSINESS ACADEMY!
OH, DADDY!
HOW LONG WILL IT TAKE FOR YOU TO...
I'LL GO PACK!
...PREPARE...?
2

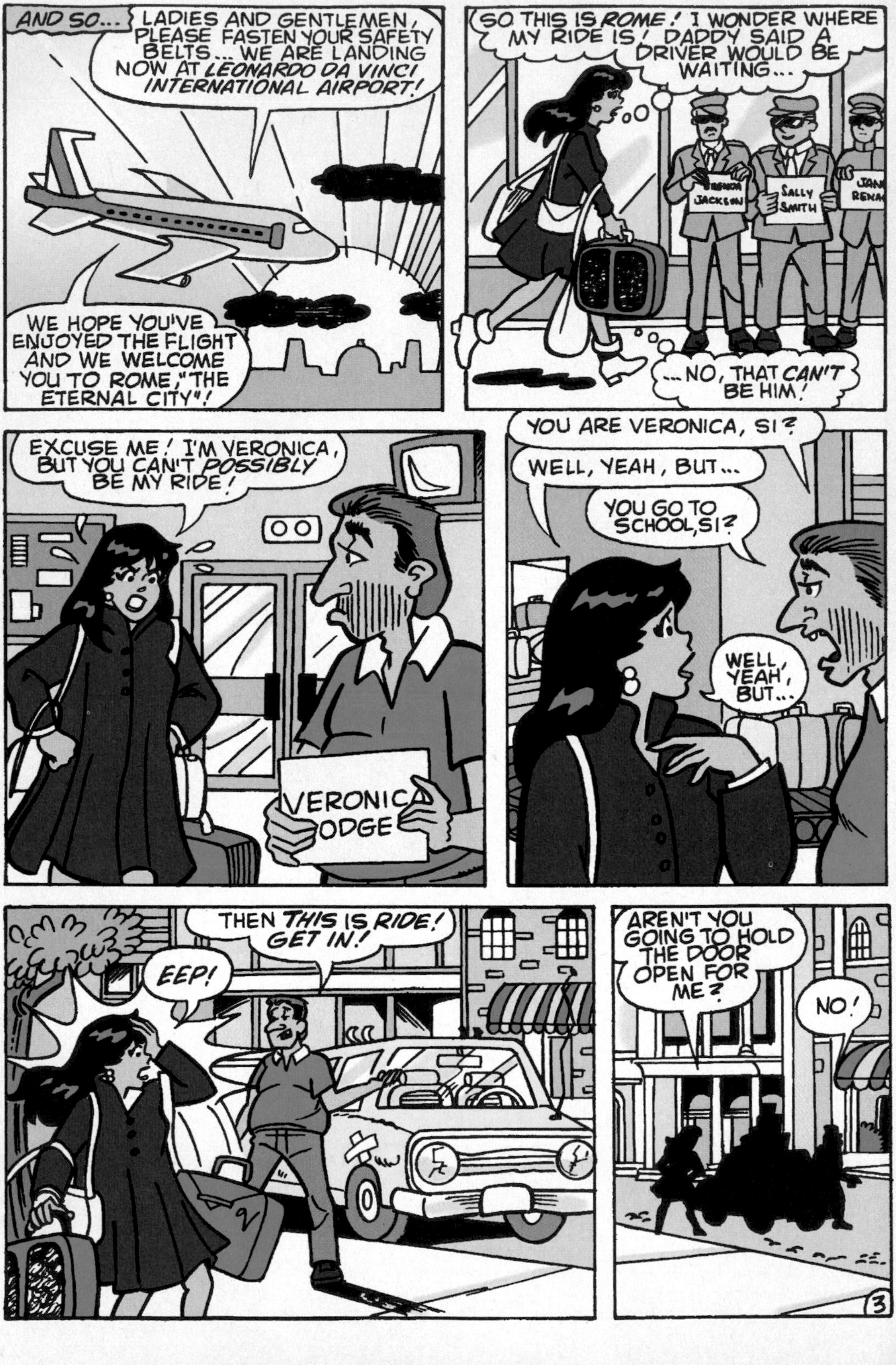
AND SO...
LADIES AND GENTLEMEN, PLEASE FASTEN YOUR SAFETY BELTS... WE ARE LANDING NOW AT LEONARDO DA VINCI INTERNATIONAL AIRPORT!
WE HOPE YOU'VE ENJOYED THE FLIGHT AND WE WELCOME YOU TO ROME, "THE ETERNAL CITY"!
SO THIS IS ROME! I WONDER WHERE MY RIDE IS! DADDY SAID A DRIVER WOULD BE WAITING...
JACKSON
SALLY SMITH
...NO, THAT CAN'T BE HIM!
EXCUSE ME! I'M VERONICA, BUT YOU CAN'T POSSIBLY BE MY RIDE!
VERONICA
ODGE
YOU ARE VERONICA, SI?
WELL, YEAH, BUT...
YOU GO TO SCHOOL, SI?
WELL, YEAH, BUT...
THEN THIS IS RIDE! GET IN!
EEP!
AREN'T YOU GOING TO HOLD THE DOOR OPEN FOR ME?
NO!
3

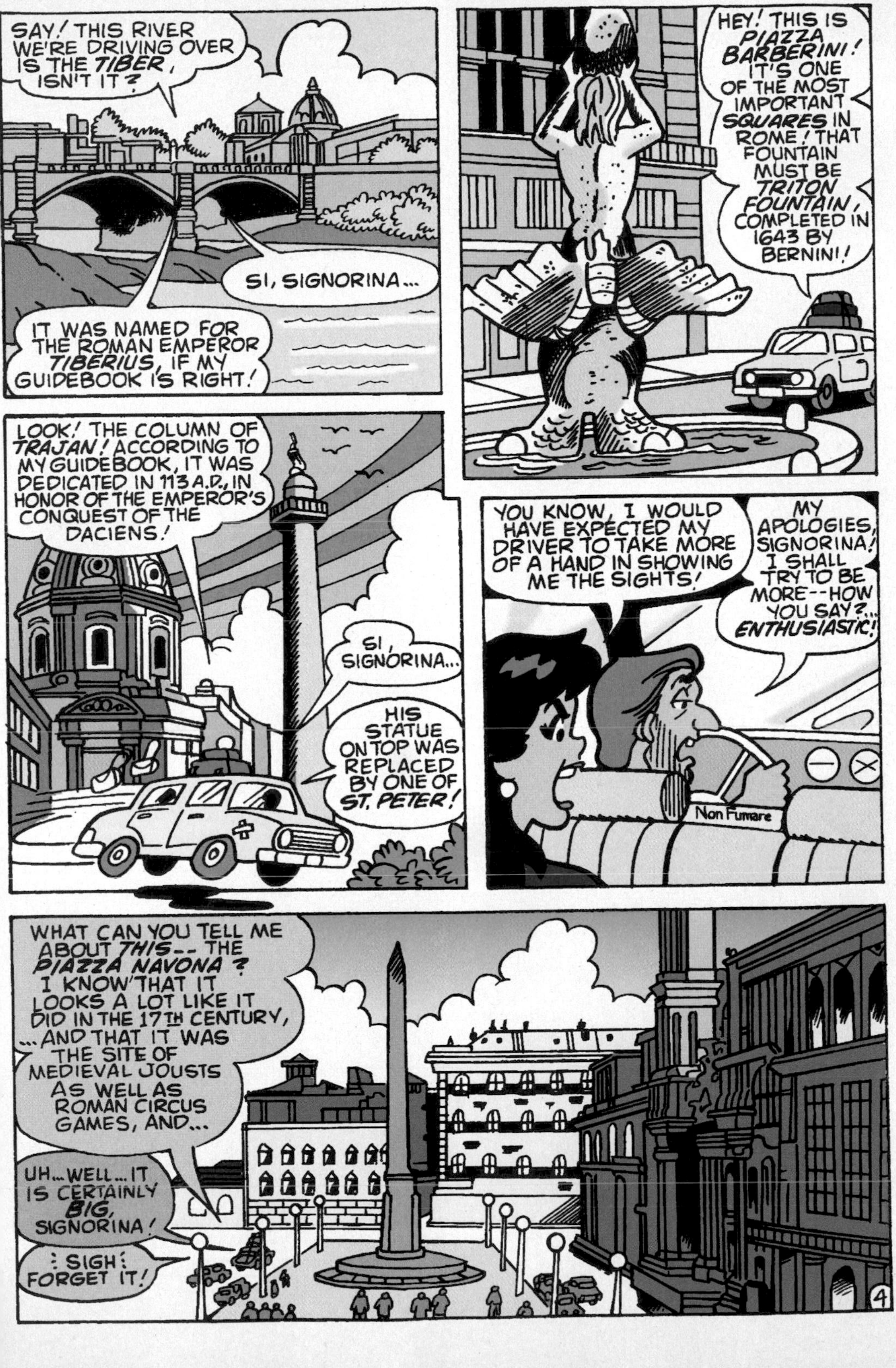
SAY! THIS RIVER WE'RE DRIVING OVER IS THE TIBER, ISN'T IT?
SI, SIGNORINA...
IT WAS NAMED FOR THE ROMAN EMPEROR TIBERIUS, IF MY GUIDEBOOK IS RIGHT!
HEY! THIS IS PIAZZA BARBERINI! IT'S ONE OF THE MOST IMPORTANT SQUARES IN ROME! THAT FOUNTAIN MUST BE TRITON FOUNTAIN, COMPLETED IN 1643 BY BERNINI!
LOOK! THE COLUMN OF TRAJAN! ACCORDING TO MY GUIDEBOOK, IT WAS DEDICATED IN 113 A.D., IN HONOR OF THE EMPEROR'S CONQUEST OF THE DACIENS!
SI, SIGNORINA...
HIS STATUE ON TOP WAS REPLACED BY ONE OF ST. PETER!
YOU KNOW, I WOULD HAVE EXPECTED MY DRIVER TO TAKE MORE OF A HAND IN SHOWING ME THE SIGHTS!
MY APOLOGIES, SIGNORINA! I SHALL TRY TO BE MORE--HOW YOU SAY?... ENTHUSIASTIC!
Non Fumare
WHAT CAN YOU TELL ME ABOUT THIS-- THE PIAZZA NAVONA? I KNOW THAT IT LOOKS A LOT LIKE IT DID IN THE 17TH CENTURY, ...AND THAT IT WAS THE SITE OF MEDIEVAL JOUSTS AS WELL AS ROMAN CIRCUS GAMES, AND...
UH...WELL...IT IS CERTAINLY BIG, SIGNORINA!
SIGH FORGET IT!
4

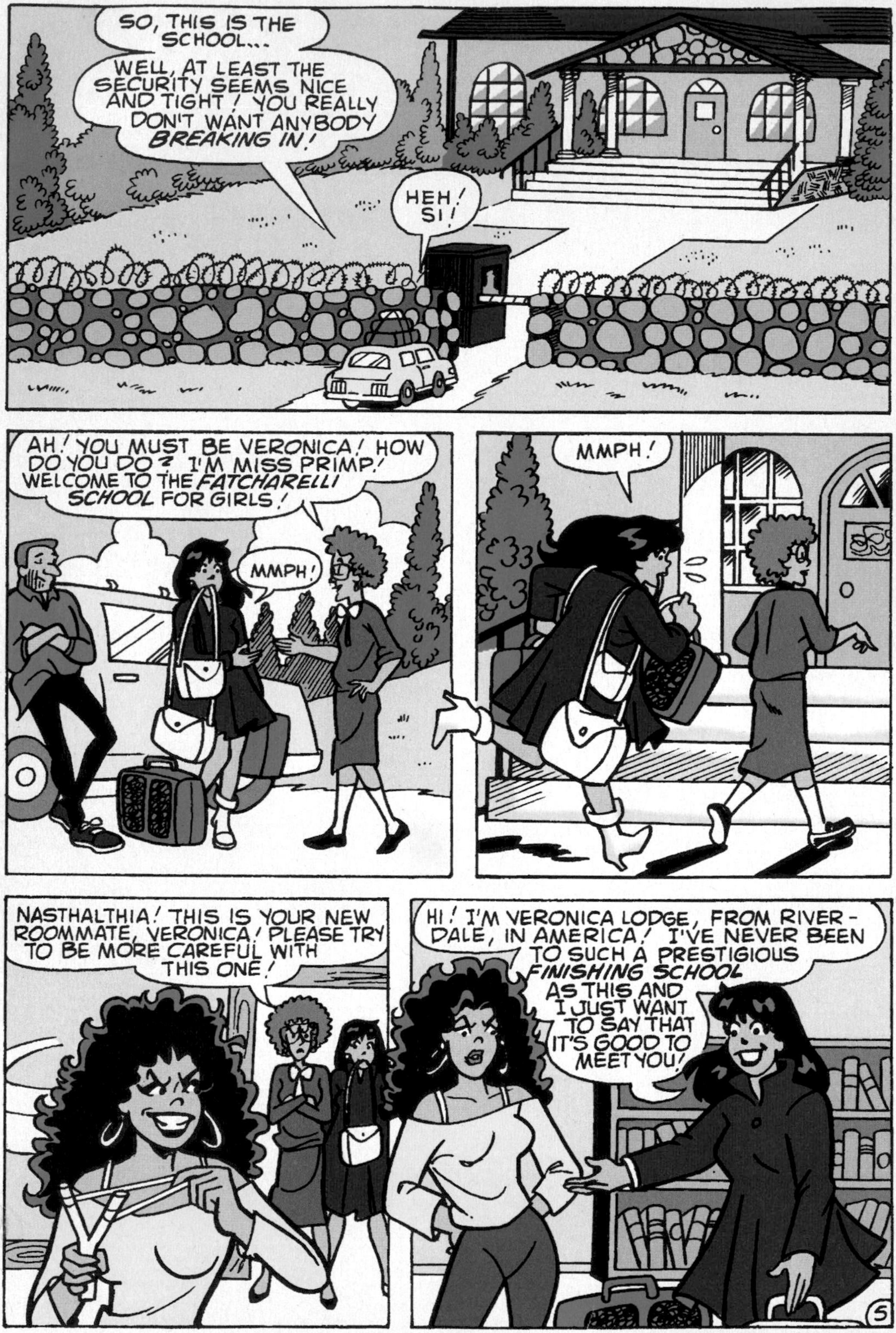
SO, THIS IS THE SCHOOL...
WELL, AT LEAST THE SECURITY SEEMS NICE AND TIGHT! YOU REALLY DON'T WANT ANYBODY BREAKING IN!
HEH! SI!
AH! YOU MUST BE VERONICA! HOW DO YOU DO? I'M MISS PRIMP! WELCOME TO THE FATCHARELLI SCHOOL FOR GIRLS!
MMPH!
MMPH!
NASTHALTHIA! THIS IS YOUR NEW ROOMMATE, VERONICA! PLEASE TRY TO BE MORE CAREFUL WITH THIS ONE!
HI! I'M VERONICA LODGE, FROM RIVER-DALE, IN AMERICA! I'VE NEVER BEEN TO SUCH A PRESTIGIOUS FINISHING SCHOOL AS THIS AND I JUST WANT TO SAY THAT IT'S GOOD TO MEET YOU!
5

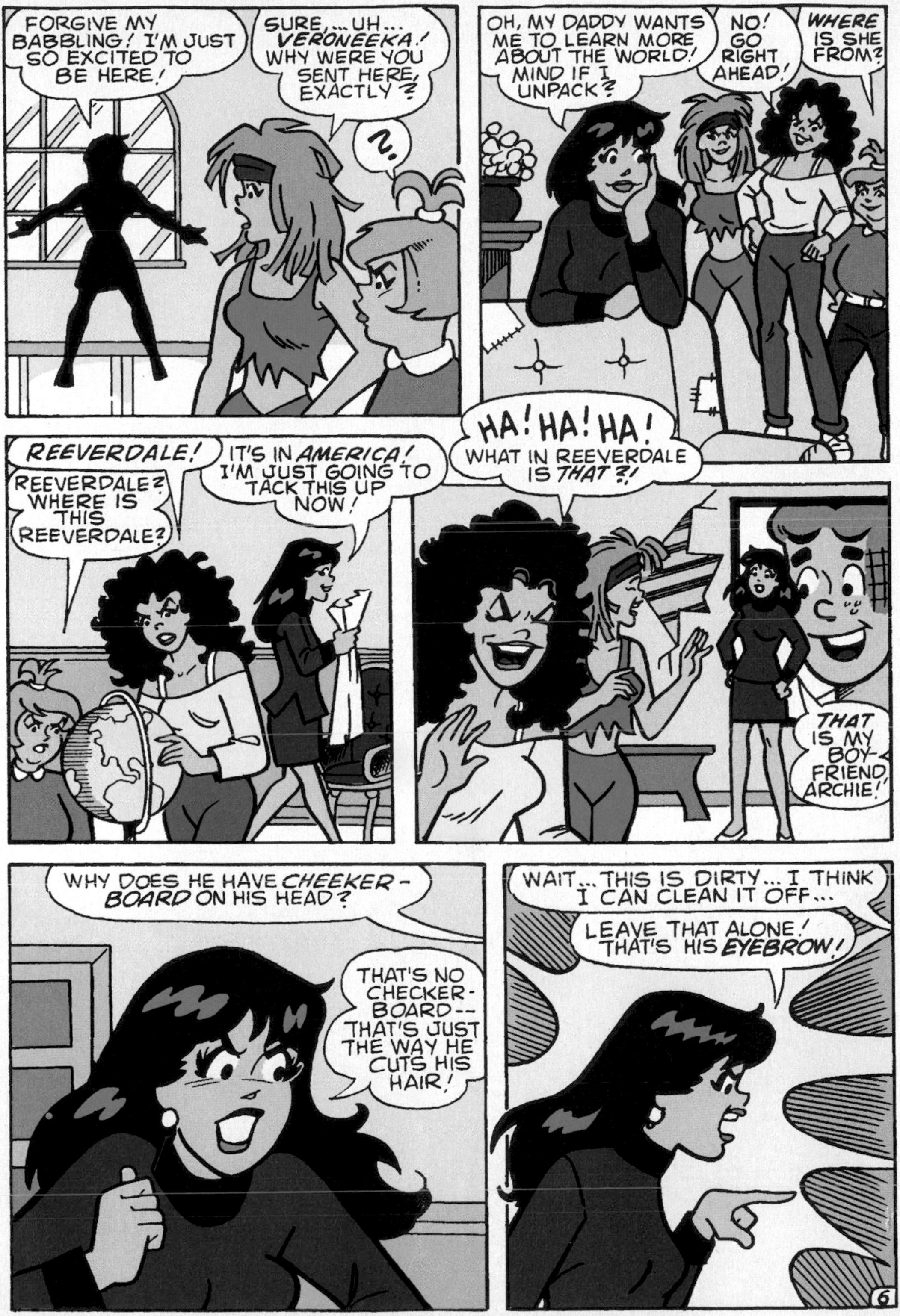
FORGIVE MY BABBLING! I'M JUST SO EXCITED TO BE HERE!
SURE, ... UH ... VERONEEKA! WHY WERE YOU SENT HERE, EXACTLY?
?
OH, MY DADDY WANTS ME TO LEARN MORE ABOUT THE WORLD! MIND IF I UNPACK?
NO! GO RIGHT AHEAD!
WHERE IS SHE FROM?
REEVERDALE!
REEVERDALE? WHERE IS THIS REEVERDALE?
IT'S IN AMERICA! I'M JUST GOING TO TACK THIS UP NOW!
HA! HA! HA! WHAT IN REEVERDALE IS THAT?!
THAT IS MY BOY-FRIEND ARCHIE!
WHY DOES HE HAVE CHEEKER-BOARD ON HIS HEAD?
THAT'S NO CHECKER-BOARD -- THAT'S JUST THE WAY HE CUTS HIS HAIR!
WAIT... THIS IS DIRTY... I THINK I CAN CLEAN IT OFF...
LEAVE THAT ALONE! THAT'S HIS EYEBROW!
6

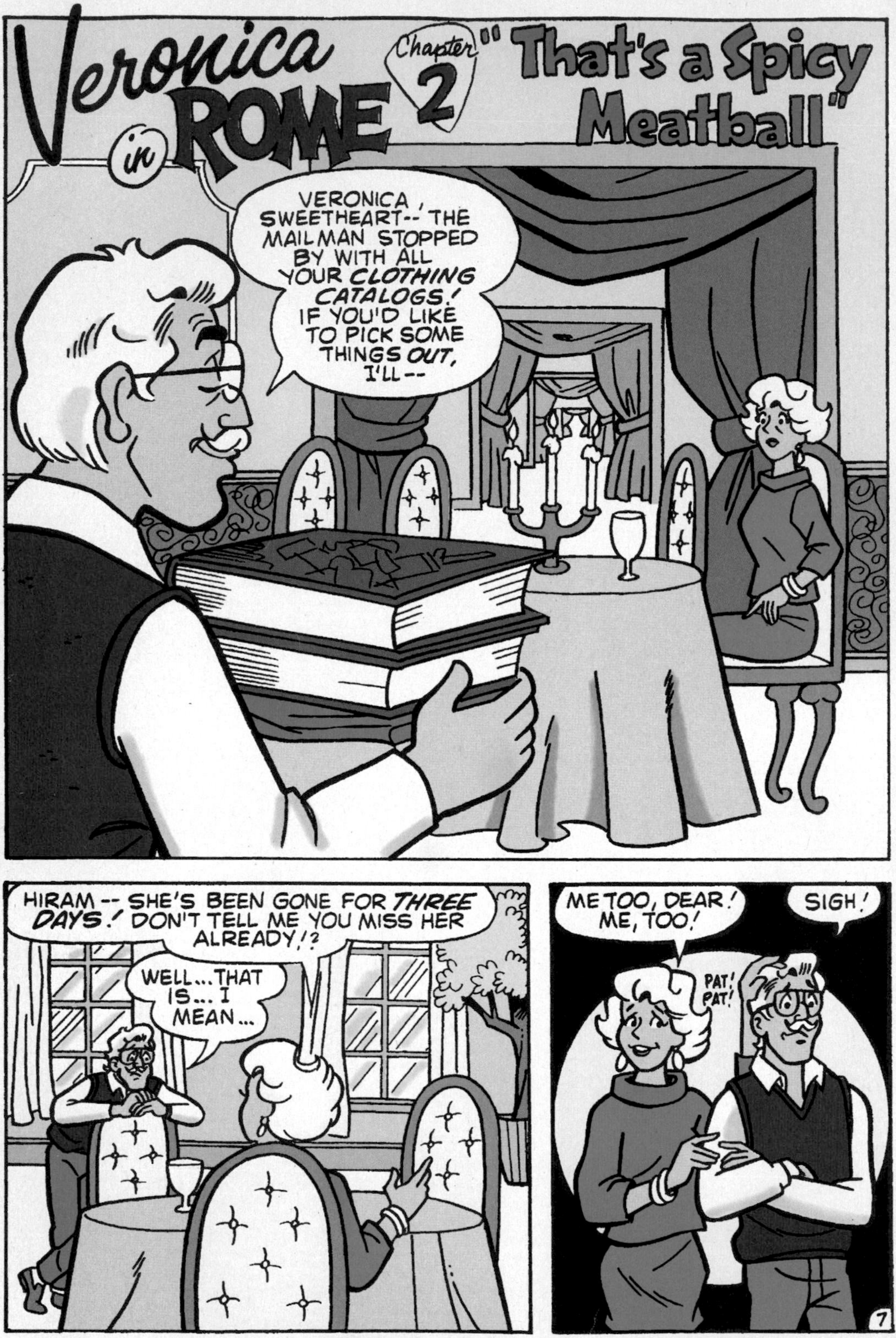
Veronica in ROME
Chapter 2 "That's a Spicy Meatball"
VERONICA, SWEETHEART-- THE MAILMAN STOPPED BY WITH ALL YOUR CLOTHING CATALOGS! IF YOU'D LIKE TO PICK SOME THINGS OUT, I'LL --
HIRAM -- SHE'S BEEN GONE FOR THREE DAYS! DON'T TELL ME YOU MISS HER ALREADY!?
WELL... THAT IS... I MEAN...
ME TOO, DEAR! ME, TOO!
PAT! PAT!
SIGH!
7

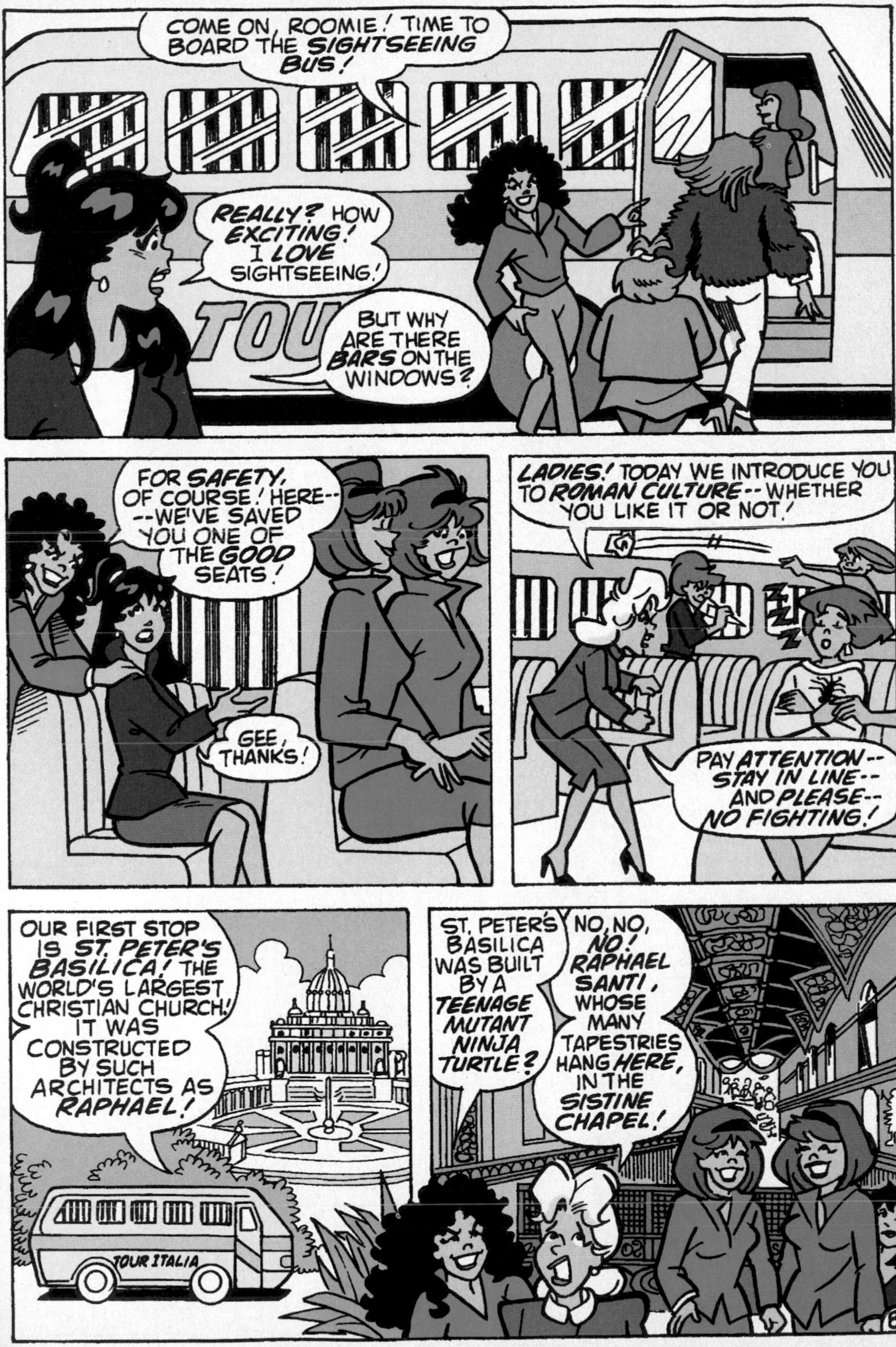
COME ON, ROOMIE! TIME TO BOARD THE SIGHTSEEING BUS!
REALLY? HOW EXCITING! I LOVE SIGHTSEEING!
TOU
BUT WHY ARE THERE BARS ON THE WINDOWS?
FOR SAFETY, OF COURSE! HERE-- --WE'VE SAVED YOU ONE OF THE GOOD SEATS!
GEE, THANKS!
LADIES! TODAY WE INTRODUCE YOU TO ROMAN CULTURE-- WHETHER YOU LIKE IT OR NOT!
PAY ATTENTION-- STAY IN LINE-- AND PLEASE-- NO FIGHTING!
OUR FIRST STOP IS ST. PETER'S BASILICA! THE WORLD'S LARGEST CHRISTIAN CHURCH! IT WAS CONSTRUCTED BY SUCH ARCHITECTS AS RAPHAEL!
TOUR ITALIA
ST. PETER'S BASILICA WAS BUILT BY A TEENAGE MUTANT NINJA TURTLE?
NO, NO, NO! RAPHAEL SANTI, WHOSE MANY TAPESTRIES HANG HERE, IN THE SISTINE CHAPEL!
8

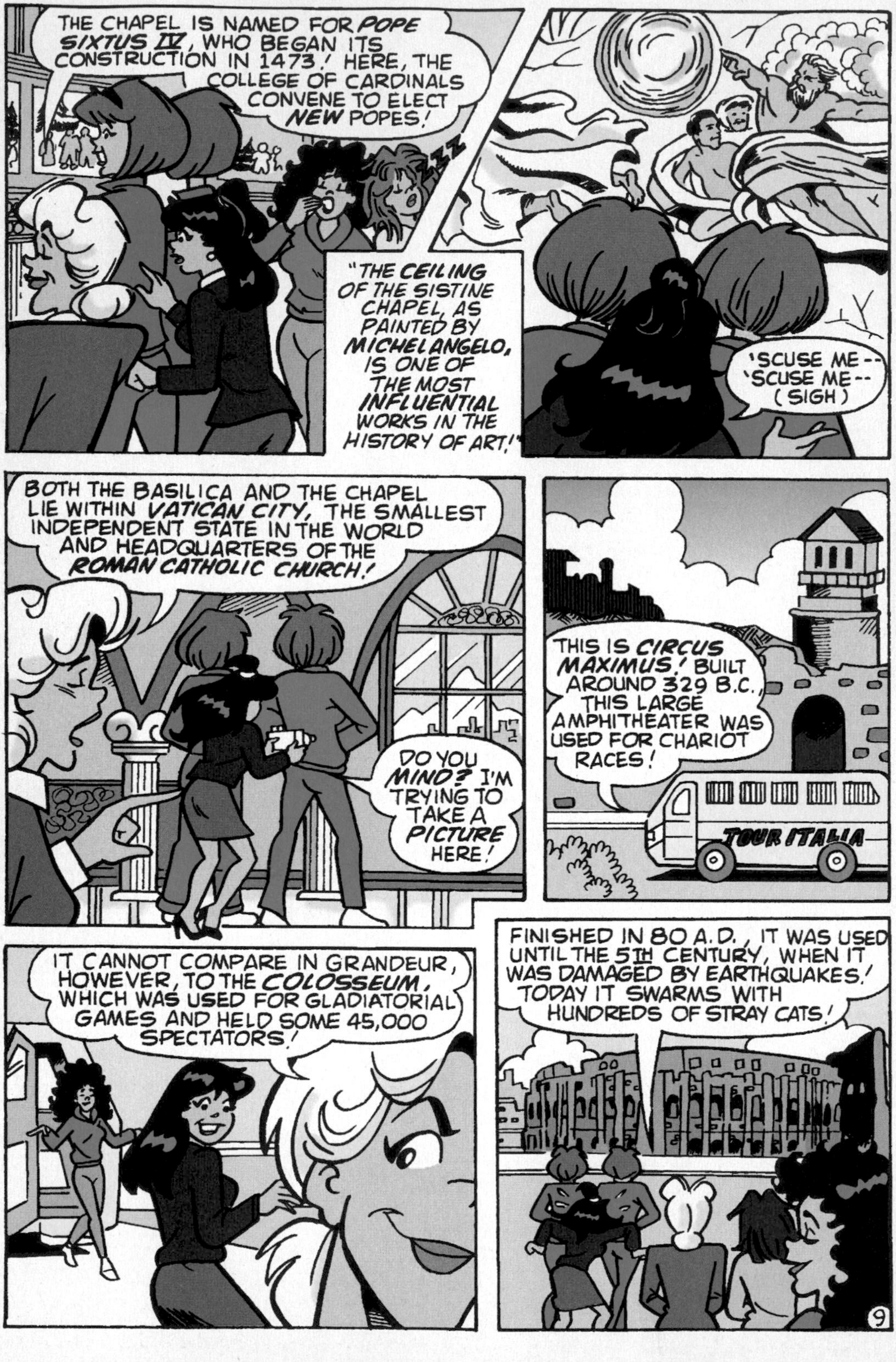
THE CHAPEL IS NAMED FOR POPE SIXTUS IV, WHO BEGAN ITS CONSTRUCTION IN 1473! HERE, THE COLLEGE OF CARDINALS CONVENE TO ELECT NEW POPES!
ZZZ
"THE CEILING OF THE SISTINE CHAPEL, AS PAINTED BY MICHELANGELO, IS ONE OF THE MOST INFLUENTIAL WORKS IN THE HISTORY OF ART!"
'SCUSE ME -- 'SCUSE ME -- (SIGH)
BOTH THE BASILICA AND THE CHAPEL LIE WITHIN VATICAN CITY, THE SMALLEST INDEPENDENT STATE IN THE WORLD AND HEADQUARTERS OF THE ROMAN CATHOLIC CHURCH!
DO YOU MIND? I'M TRYING TO TAKE A PICTURE HERE!
THIS IS CIRCUS MAXIMUS! BUILT AROUND 329 B.C., THIS LARGE AMPHITHEATER WAS USED FOR CHARIOT RACES!
TOUR ITALIA
IT CANNOT COMPARE IN GRANDEUR, HOWEVER, TO THE COLOSSEUM, WHICH WAS USED FOR GLADIATORIAL GAMES AND HELD SOME 45,000 SPECTATORS!
FINISHED IN 80 A.D., IT WAS USED UNTIL THE 5TH CENTURY, WHEN IT WAS DAMAGED BY EARTHQUAKES! TODAY IT SWARMS WITH HUNDREDS OF STRAY CATS!
9

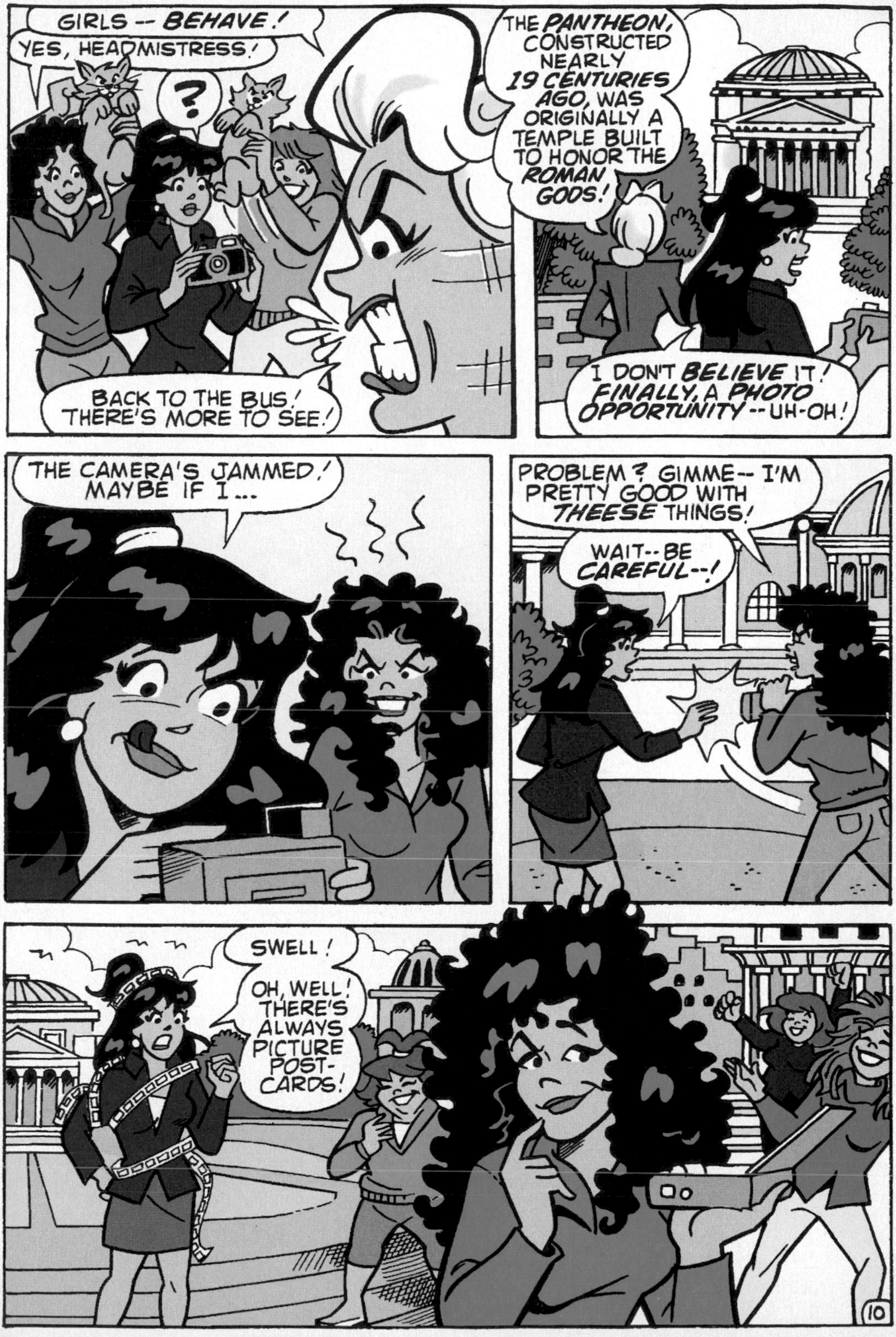
GIRLS -- BEHAVE!
YES, HEADMISTRESS!
?
BACK TO THE BUS! THERE'S MORE TO SEE!
THE PANTHEON, CONSTRUCTED NEARLY 19 CENTURIES AGO, WAS ORIGINALLY A TEMPLE BUILT TO HONOR THE ROMAN GODS!
I DON'T BELIEVE IT! FINALLY, A PHOTO OPPORTUNITY -- UH-OH!
THE CAMERA'S JAMMED! MAYBE IF I...
PROBLEM? GIMME-- I'M PRETTY GOOD WITH THEESE THINGS!
WAIT-- BE CAREFUL--!
SWELL!
OH, WELL! THERE'S ALWAYS PICTURE POST-CARDS!
10

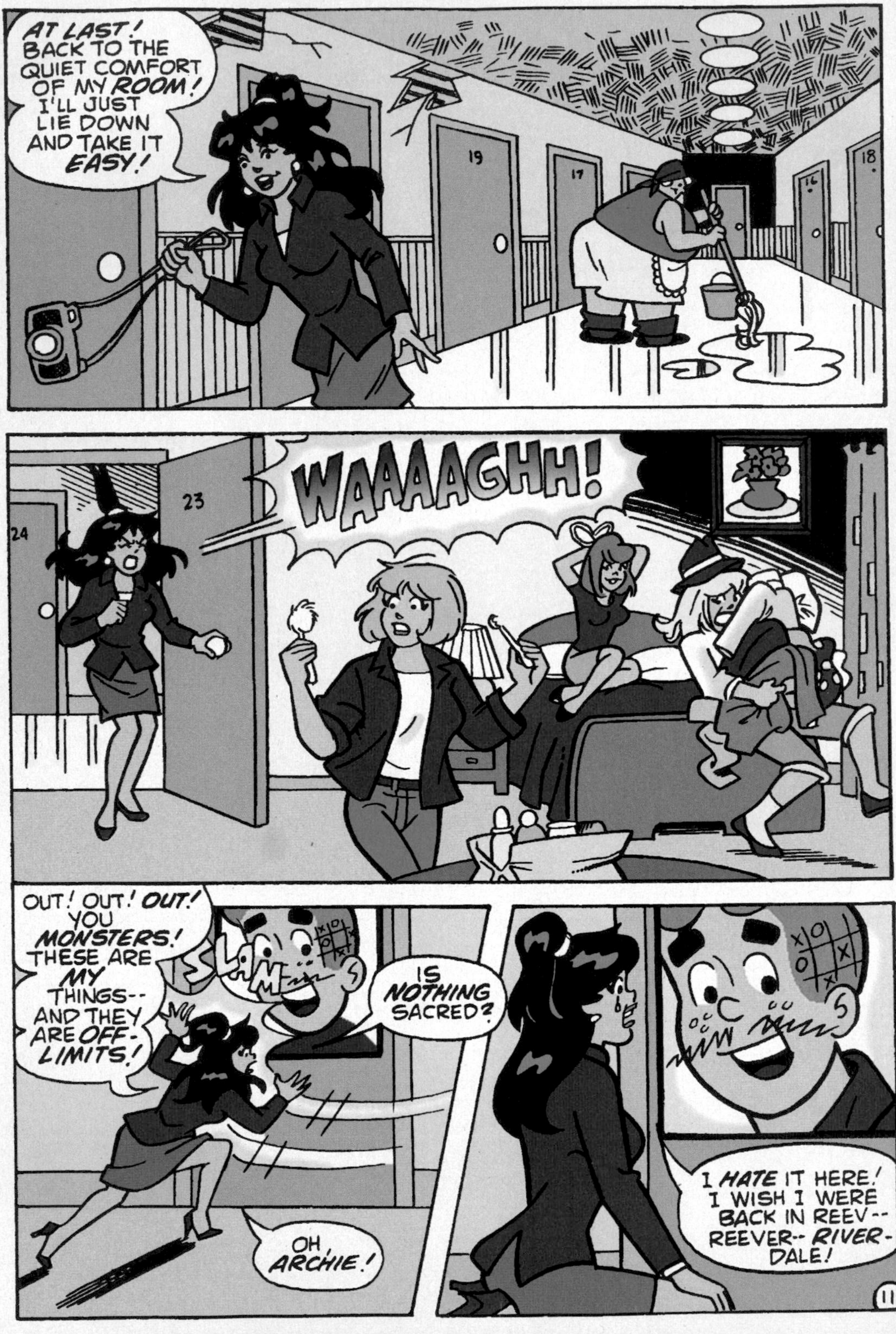
AT LAST! BACK TO THE QUIET COMFORT OF MY ROOM! I'LL JUST LIE DOWN AND TAKE IT EASY!
19
17
16
18
WAAAAGHH!
23
24
OUT! OUT! OUT! YOU MONSTERS! THESE ARE MY THINGS-- AND THEY ARE OFF-LIMITS!
SLAM
IS NOTHING SACRED?
OH, ARCHIE!
I HATE IT HERE! I WISH I WERE BACK IN REEV-- REEVER-- RIVER-DALE!
11

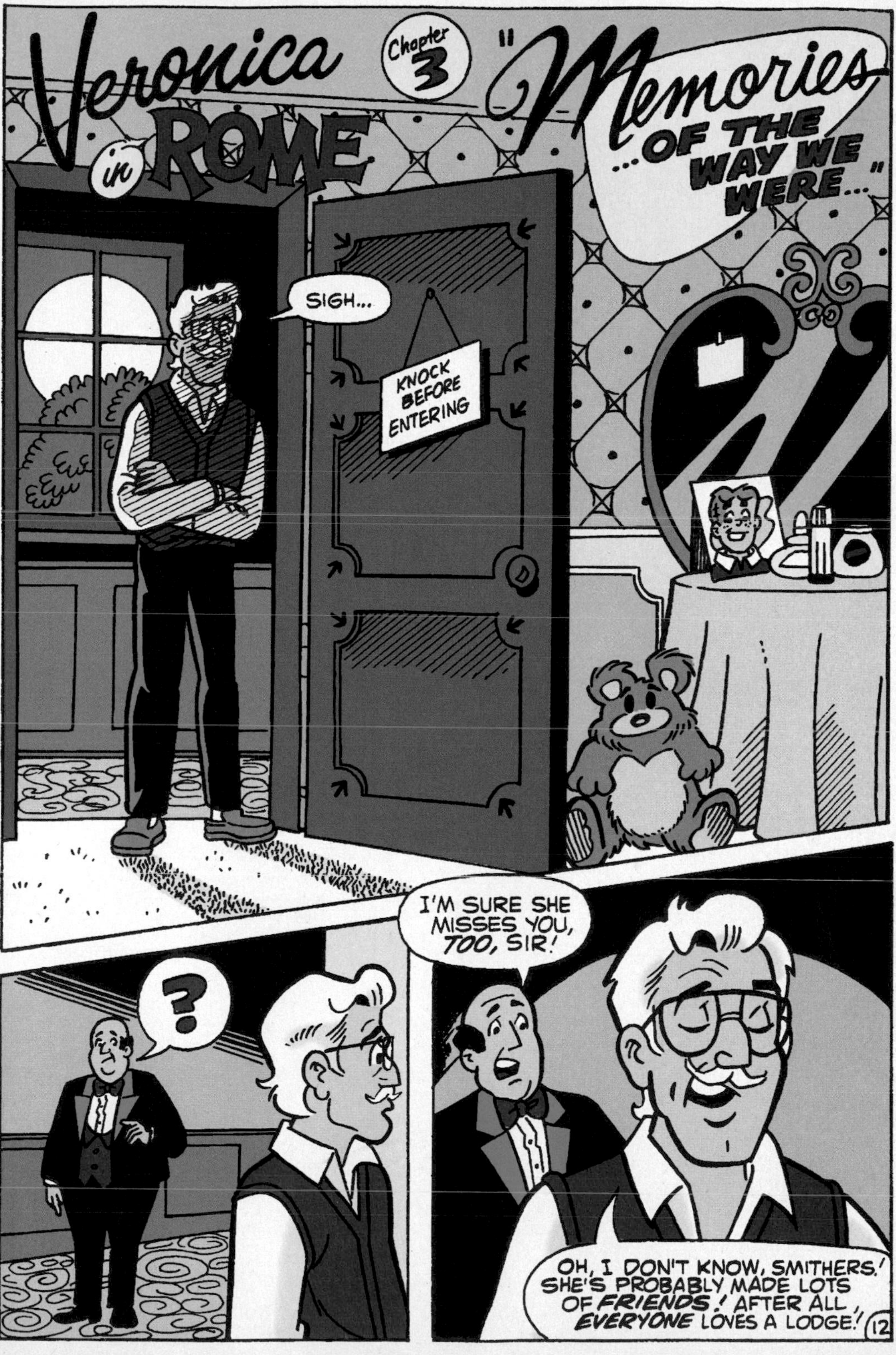
Veronica in ROME
Chapter 3
"Memories ...of the way we were..."
SIGH...
KNOCK BEFORE ENTERING
I'M SURE SHE MISSES YOU, TOO, SIR!
?
OH, I DON'T KNOW, SMITHERS! SHE'S PROBABLY MADE LOTS OF FRIENDS! AFTER ALL, EVERYONE LOVES A LODGE!
12

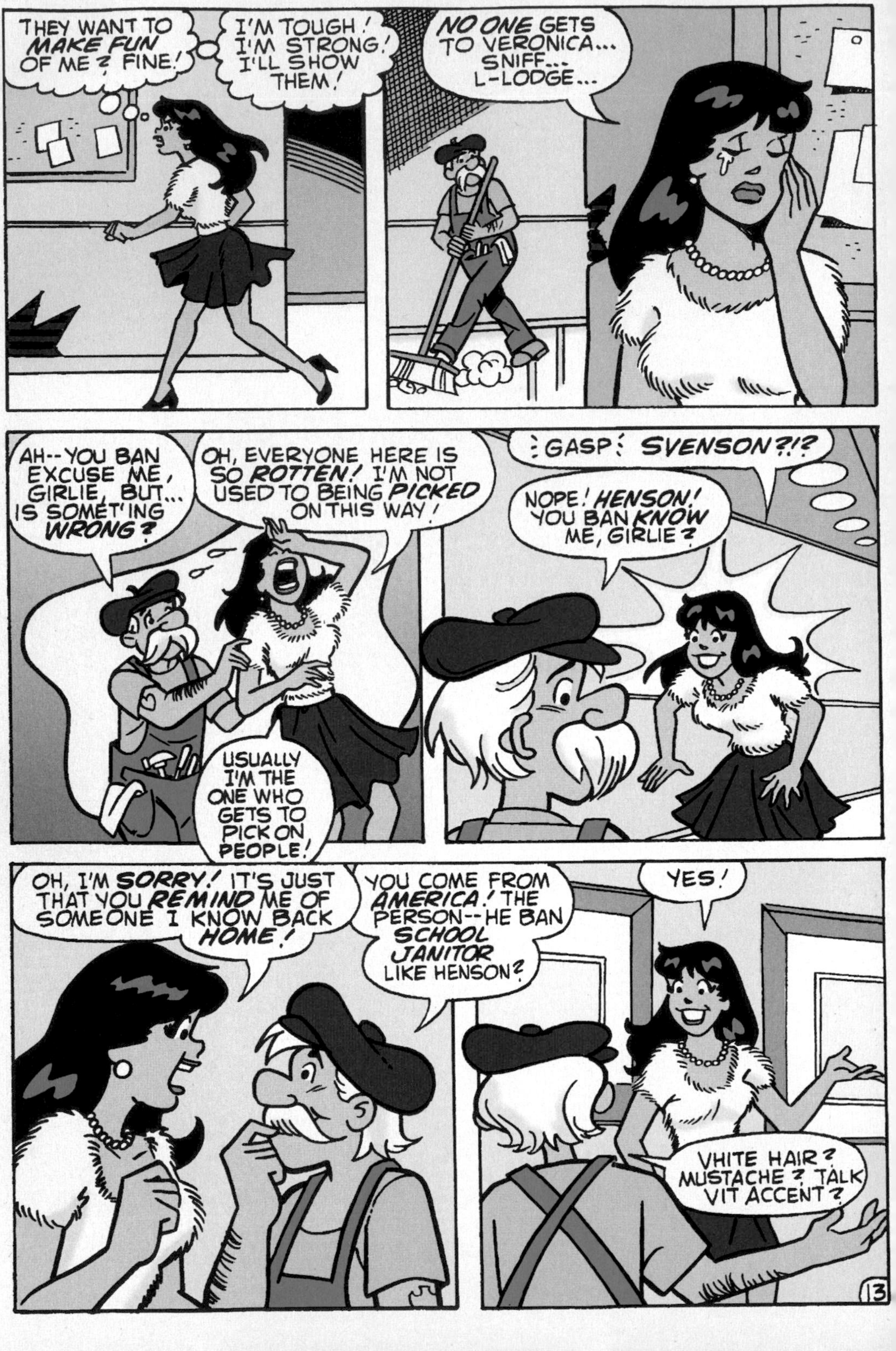
THEY WANT TO MAKE FUN OF ME? FINE!
I'M TOUGH! I'M STRONG! I'LL SHOW THEM!
NO ONE GETS TO VERONICA... SNIFF... L-LODGE...
AH--YOU BAN EXCUSE ME, GIRLIE, BUT... IS SOMET'ING WRONG?
OH, EVERYONE HERE IS SO ROTTEN! I'M NOT USED TO BEING PICKED ON THIS WAY!
USUALLY I'M THE ONE WHO GETS TO PICK ON PEOPLE!
:GASP: SVENSON?!?
NOPE! HENSON! YOU BAN KNOW ME, GIRLIE?
OH, I'M SORRY! IT'S JUST THAT YOU REMIND ME OF SOMEONE I KNOW BACK HOME!
YOU COME FROM AMERICA! THE PERSON--HE BAN SCHOOL JANITOR LIKE HENSON?
YES!
VHITE HAIR? MUSTACHE? TALK VIT ACCENT?
13

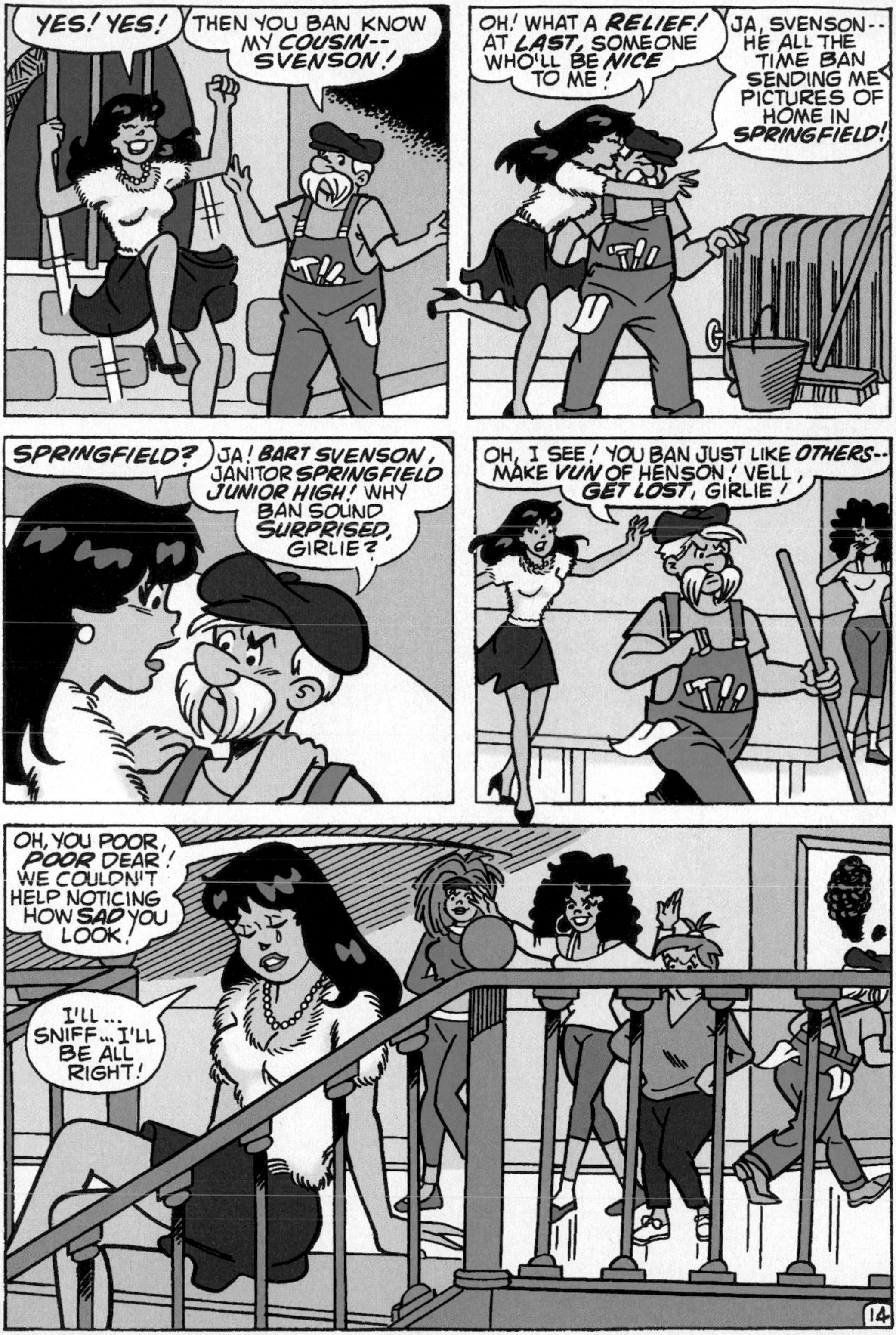
YES! YES!
THEN YOU BAN KNOW MY COUSIN-- SVENSON!
OH! WHAT A RELIEF! AT LAST, SOMEONE WHO'LL BE NICE TO ME!
JA, SVENSON-- HE ALL THE TIME BAN SENDING ME PICTURES OF HOME IN SPRINGFIELD!
SPRINGFIELD?
JA! BART SVENSON, JANITOR SPRINGFIELD JUNIOR HIGH! WHY BAN SOUND SURPRISED, GIRLIE?
OH, I SEE! YOU BAN JUST LIKE OTHERS-- MAKE VUN OF HENSON! VELL, GET LOST, GIRLIE!
OH, YOU POOR, POOR DEAR! WE COULDN'T HELP NOTICING HOW SAD YOU LOOK!
I'LL... SNIFF... I'LL BE ALL RIGHT!
14

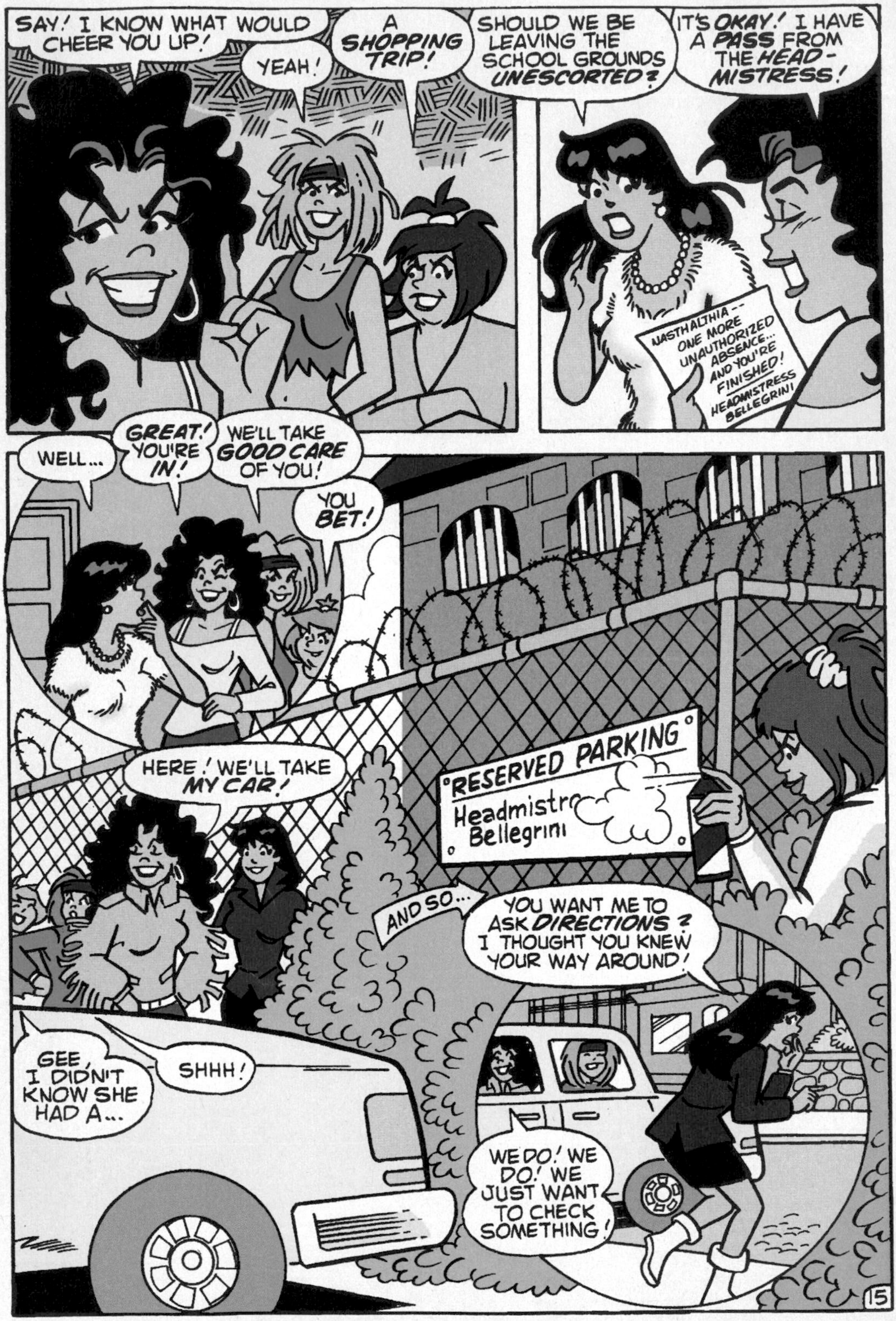
SAY! I KNOW WHAT WOULD CHEER YOU UP!
YEAH!
A SHOPPING TRIP!
SHOULD WE BE LEAVING THE SCHOOL GROUNDS UNESCORTED?
IT'S OKAY! I HAVE A PASS FROM THE HEAD-MISTRESS!
NASTHALTHIA -- ONE MORE UNAUTHORIZED ABSENCE... AND YOU'RE FINISHED! HEADMISTRESS BELLEGRINI
WELL...
GREAT! YOU'RE IN!
WE'LL TAKE GOOD CARE OF YOU!
YOU BET!
HERE! WE'LL TAKE MY CAR!
RESERVED PARKING
Headmistr
Bellegrini
GEE, I DIDN'T KNOW SHE HAD A...
SHHH!
AND SO...
YOU WANT ME TO ASK DIRECTIONS? I THOUGHT YOU KNEW YOUR WAY AROUND!
WE DO! WE DO! WE JUST WANT TO CHECK SOMETHING!
15

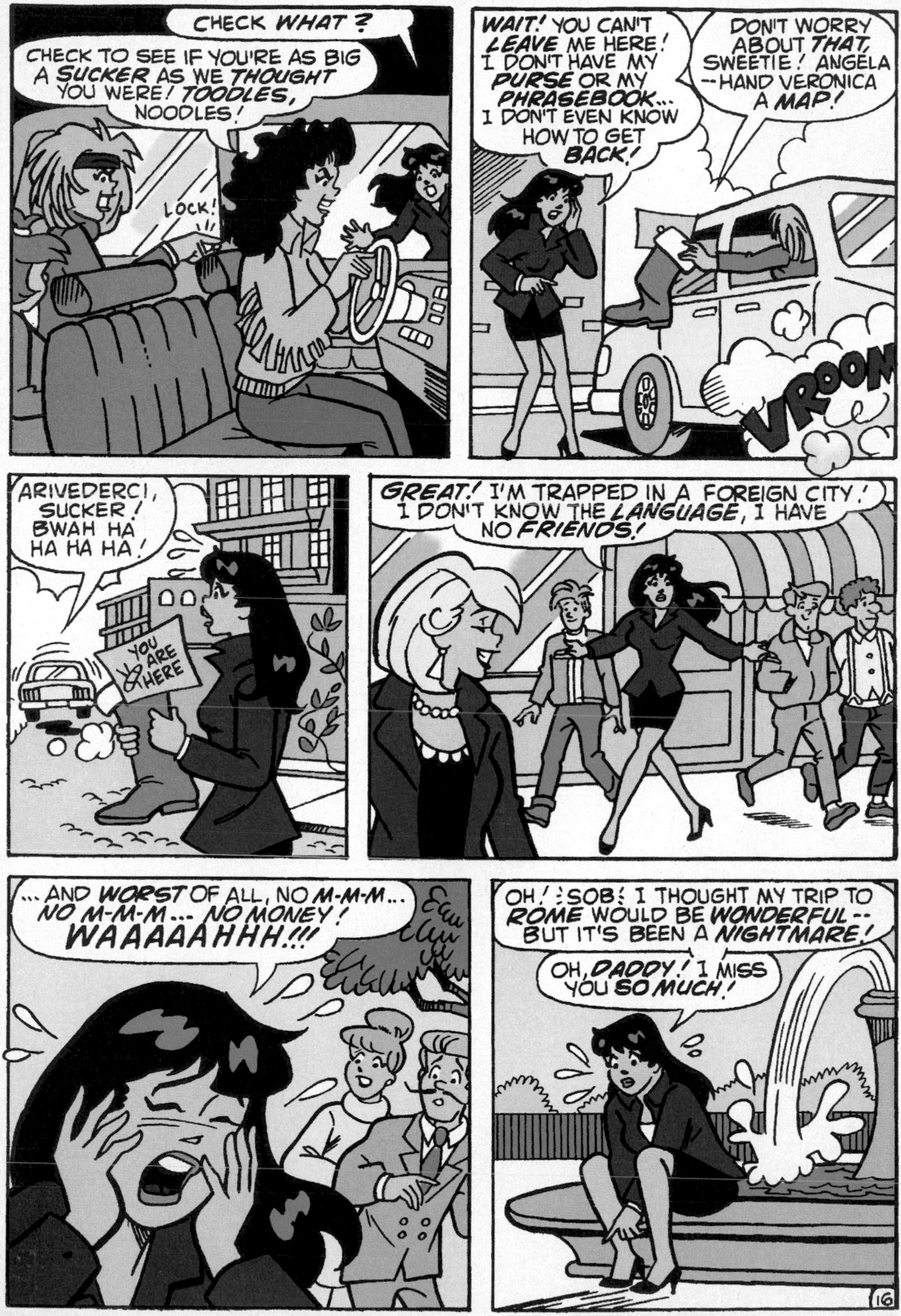
CHECK WHAT?
CHECK TO SEE IF YOU'RE AS BIG A SUCKER AS WE THOUGHT YOU WERE! TOODLES, NOODLES!
LOCK!
WAIT! YOU CAN'T LEAVE ME HERE! I DON'T HAVE MY PURSE OR MY PHRASEBOOK... I DON'T EVEN KNOW HOW TO GET BACK!
DON'T WORRY ABOUT THAT, SWEETIE! ANGELA --HAND VERONICA A MAP!
VROOM
ARIVEDERCI, SUCKER! BWAH HA HA HA HA!
YOU ARE HERE
GREAT! I'M TRAPPED IN A FOREIGN CITY! I DON'T KNOW THE LANGUAGE, I HAVE NO FRIENDS!
... AND WORST OF ALL, NO M-M-M... NO M-M-M... NO MONEY! WAAAAAHHH!!!
OH! SOB! I THOUGHT MY TRIP TO ROME WOULD BE WONDERFUL -- BUT IT'S BEEN A NIGHTMARE!
OH, DADDY! I MISS YOU SO MUCH!
16

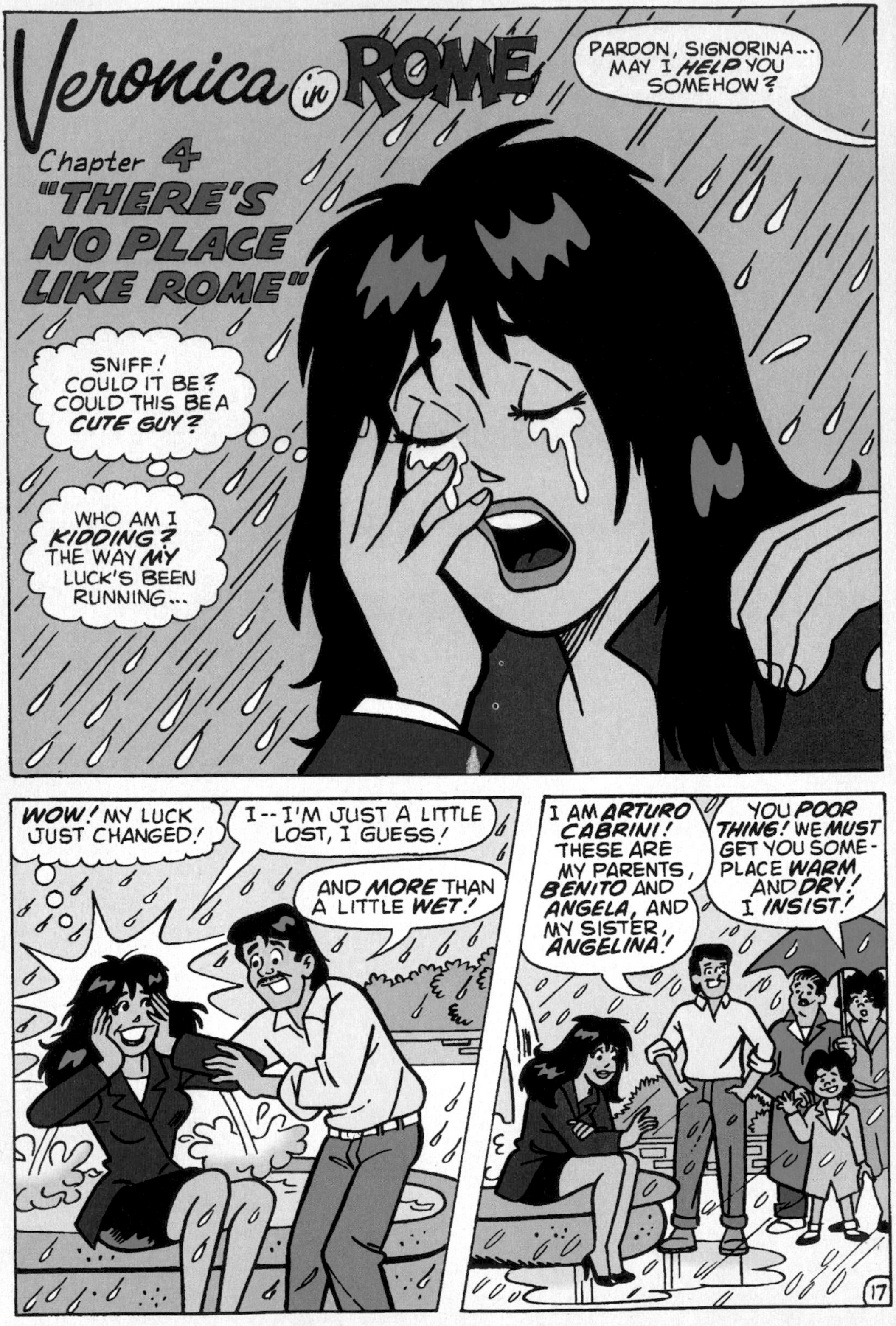
Veronica in ROME
Chapter 4
"THERE'S NO PLACE LIKE ROME"
PARDON, SIGNORINA... MAY I HELP YOU SOMEHOW?
SNIFF! COULD IT BE? COULD THIS BE A CUTE GUY?
WHO AM I KIDDING? THE WAY MY LUCK'S BEEN RUNNING...
WOW! MY LUCK JUST CHANGED!
I -- I'M JUST A LITTLE LOST, I GUESS!
AND MORE THAN A LITTLE WET!
I AM ARTURO CABRINI! THESE ARE MY PARENTS, BENITO AND ANGELA, AND MY SISTER, ANGELINA!
YOU POOR THING! WE MUST GET YOU SOME-PLACE WARM AND DRY! I INSIST!
17

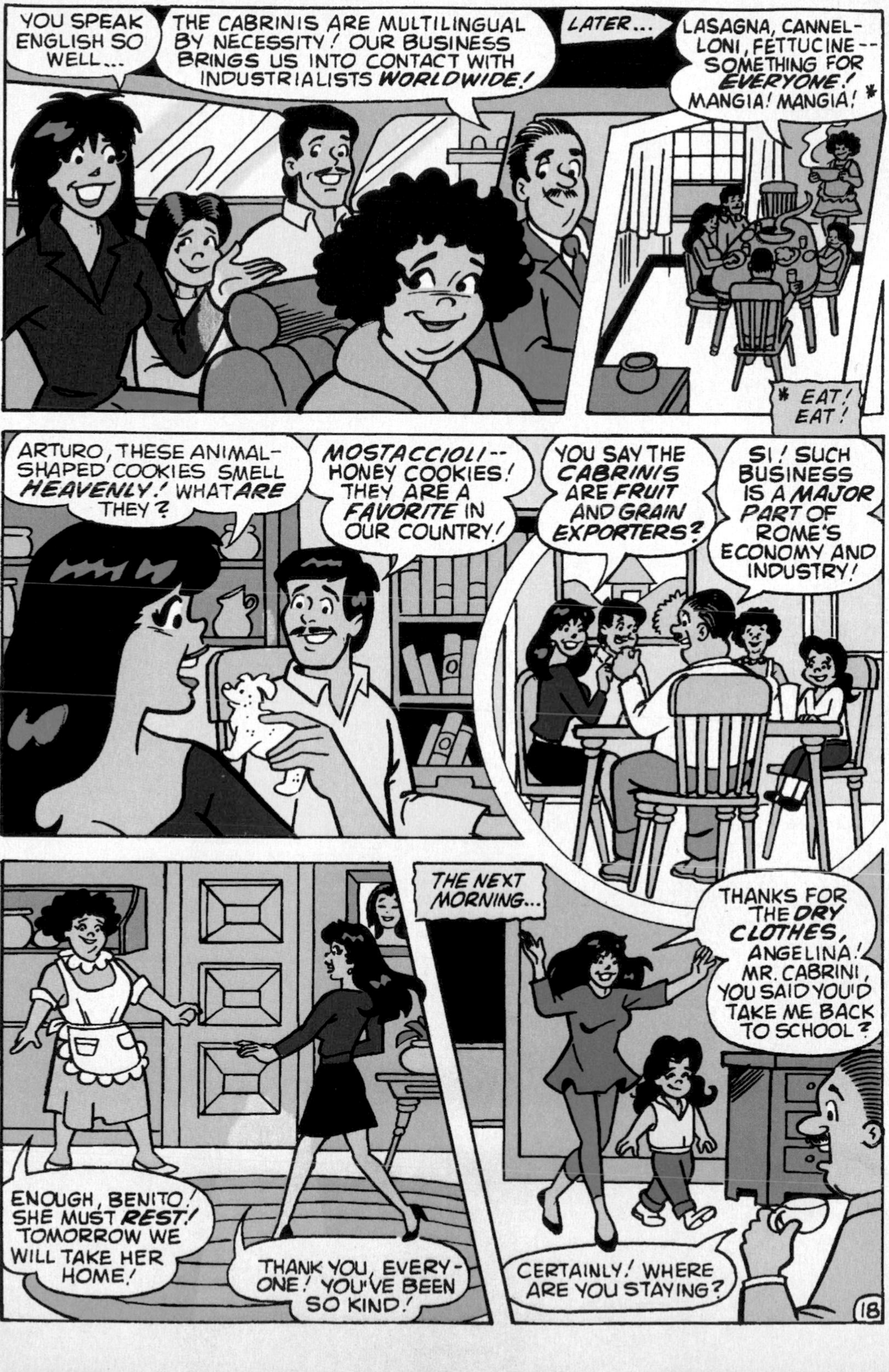
YOU SPEAK ENGLISH SO WELL...
THE CABRINIS ARE MULTILINGUAL BY NECESSITY! OUR BUSINESS BRINGS US INTO CONTACT WITH INDUSTRIALISTS WORLDWIDE!
LATER...
LASAGNA, CANNELLONI, FETTUCINE-- SOMETHING FOR EVERYONE! MANGIA! MANGIA! *
* EAT! EAT!
ARTURO, THESE ANIMAL-SHAPED COOKIES SMELL HEAVENLY! WHAT ARE THEY?
MOSTACCIOLI-- HONEY COOKIES! THEY ARE A FAVORITE IN OUR COUNTRY!
YOU SAY THE CABRINIS ARE FRUIT AND GRAIN EXPORTERS?
SI! SUCH BUSINESS IS A MAJOR PART OF ROME'S ECONOMY AND INDUSTRY!
ENOUGH, BENITO! SHE MUST REST! TOMORROW WE WILL TAKE HER HOME!
THANK YOU, EVERYONE! YOU'VE BEEN SO KIND!
THE NEXT MORNING...
THANKS FOR THE DRY CLOTHES, ANGELINA! MR. CABRINI, YOU SAID YOU'D TAKE ME BACK TO SCHOOL?
CERTAINLY! WHERE ARE YOU STAYING?
18

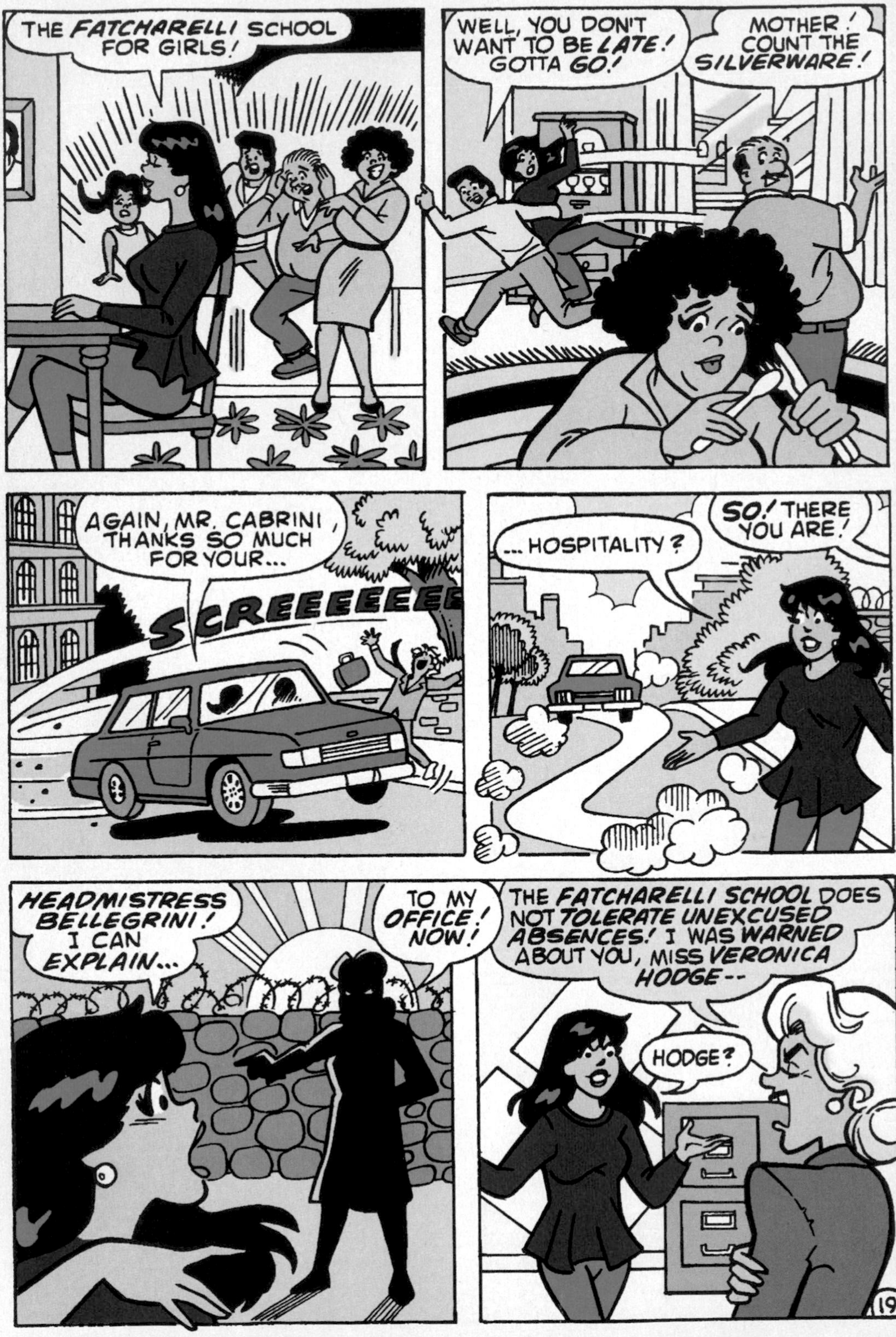
THE FATCHARELLI SCHOOL FOR GIRLS!
WELL, YOU DON'T WANT TO BE LATE! GOTTA GO!
MOTHER! COUNT THE SILVERWARE!
AGAIN, MR. CABRINI, THANKS SO MUCH FOR YOUR...
SCREEEEEEE
... HOSPITALITY?
SO! THERE YOU ARE!
HEADMISTRESS BELLEGRINI! I CAN EXPLAIN...
TO MY OFFICE! NOW!
THE FATCHARELLI SCHOOL DOES NOT TOLERATE UNEXCUSED ABSENCES! I WAS WARNED ABOUT YOU, MISS VERONICA HODGE--
HODGE?
19

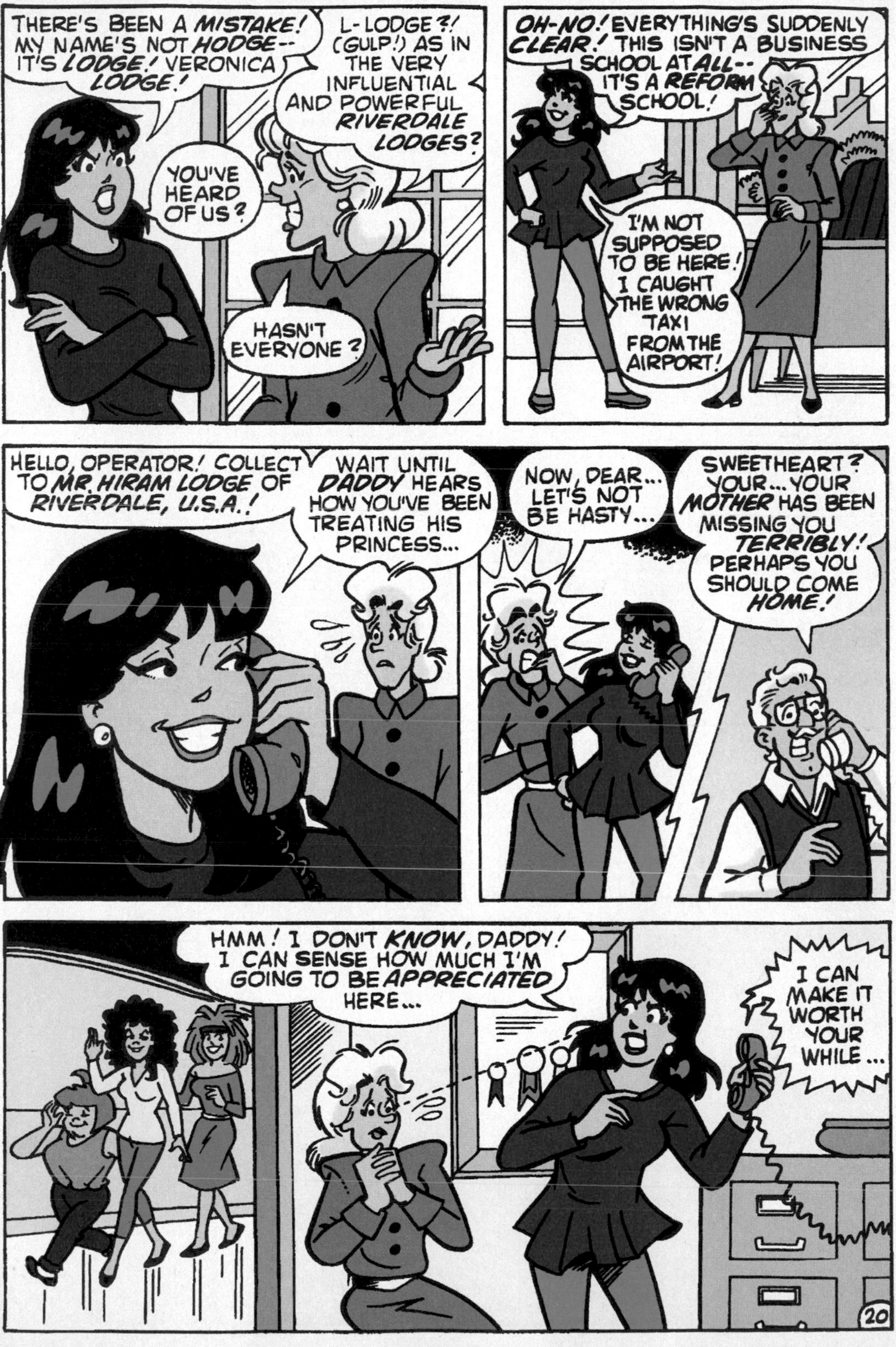
THERE'S BEEN A MISTAKE! MY NAME'S NOT HODGE-- IT'S LODGE! VERONICA LODGE!
L-LODGE?! (GULP!) AS IN THE VERY INFLUENTIAL AND POWERFUL RIVERDALE LODGES?
YOU'VE HEARD OF US?
HASN'T EVERYONE?
OH-NO! EVERYTHING'S SUDDENLY CLEAR! THIS ISN'T A BUSINESS SCHOOL AT ALL-- IT'S A REFORM SCHOOL!
I'M NOT SUPPOSED TO BE HERE! I CAUGHT THE WRONG TAXI FROM THE AIRPORT!
HELLO, OPERATOR! COLLECT TO MR. HIRAM LODGE OF RIVERDALE, U.S.A.!
WAIT UNTIL DADDY HEARS HOW YOU'VE BEEN TREATING HIS PRINCESS...
NOW, DEAR... LET'S NOT BE HASTY...
SWEETHEART? YOUR... YOUR MOTHER HAS BEEN MISSING YOU TERRIBLY! PERHAPS YOU SHOULD COME HOME!
HMM! I DON'T KNOW, DADDY! I CAN SENSE HOW MUCH I'M GOING TO BE APPRECIATED HERE...
I CAN MAKE IT WORTH YOUR WHILE...
20

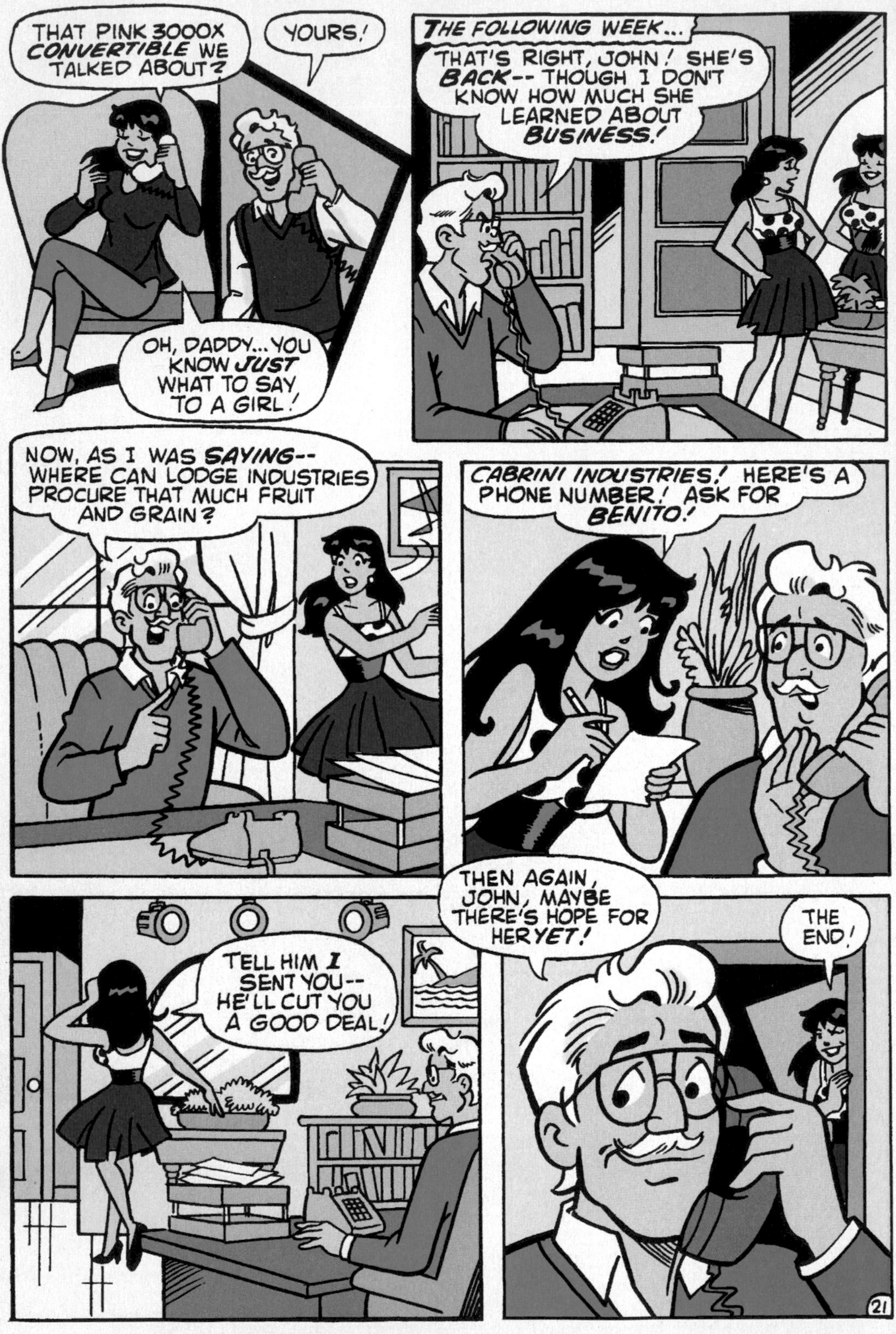
THAT PINK 3000X CONVERTIBLE WE TALKED ABOUT?
YOURS!
OH, DADDY... YOU KNOW JUST WHAT TO SAY TO A GIRL!
THE FOLLOWING WEEK...
THAT'S RIGHT, JOHN! SHE'S BACK-- THOUGH I DON'T KNOW HOW MUCH SHE LEARNED ABOUT BUSINESS!
NOW, AS I WAS SAYING-- WHERE CAN LODGE INDUSTRIES PROCURE THAT MUCH FRUIT AND GRAIN?
CABRINI INDUSTRIES! HERE'S A PHONE NUMBER! ASK FOR BENITO!
TELL HIM I SENT YOU-- HE'LL CUT YOU A GOOD DEAL!
THEN AGAIN, JOHN, MAYBE THERE'S HOPE FOR HER YET!
THE END!
21

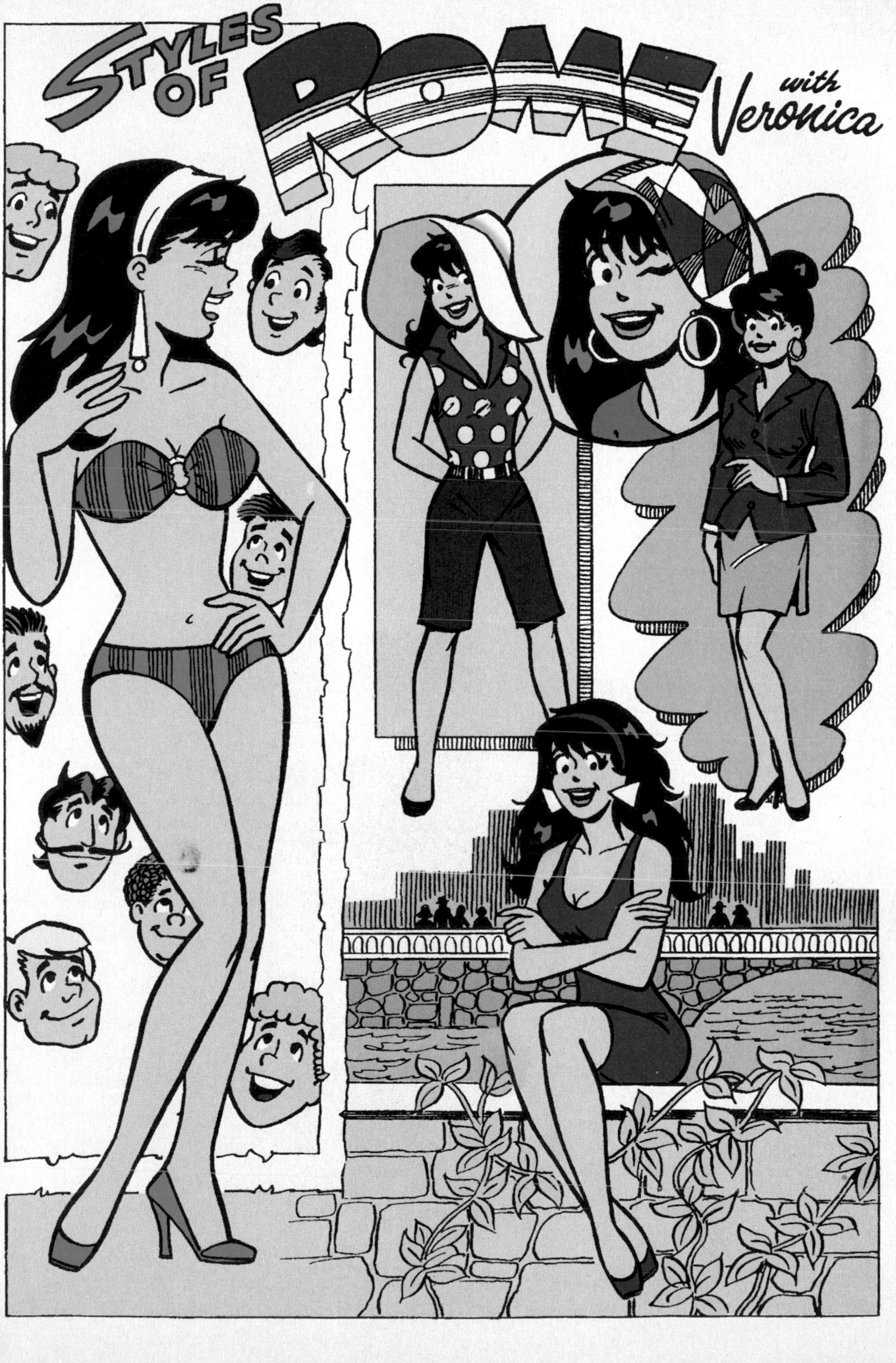
STYLES OF ROME
with Veronica

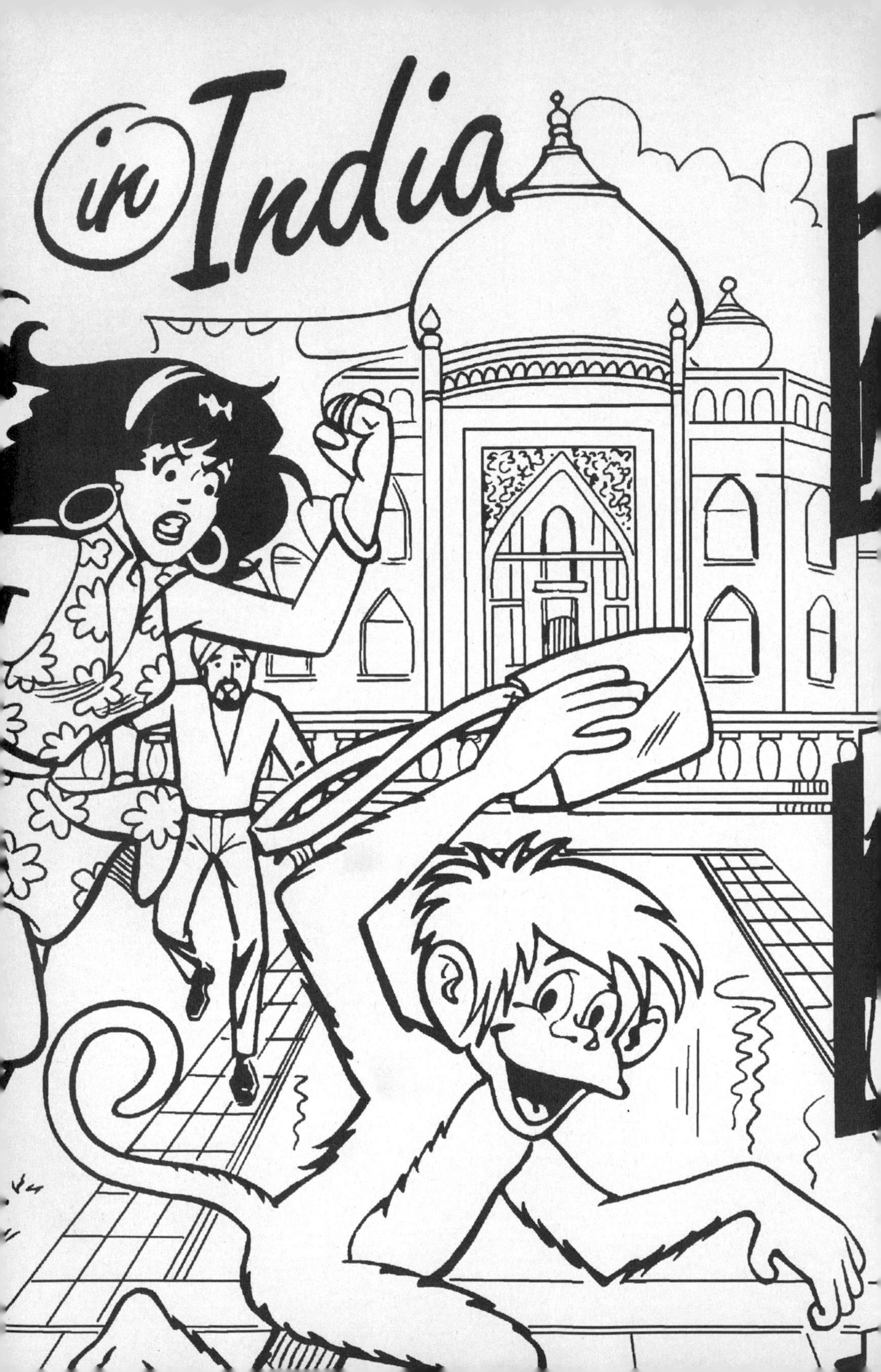
in India

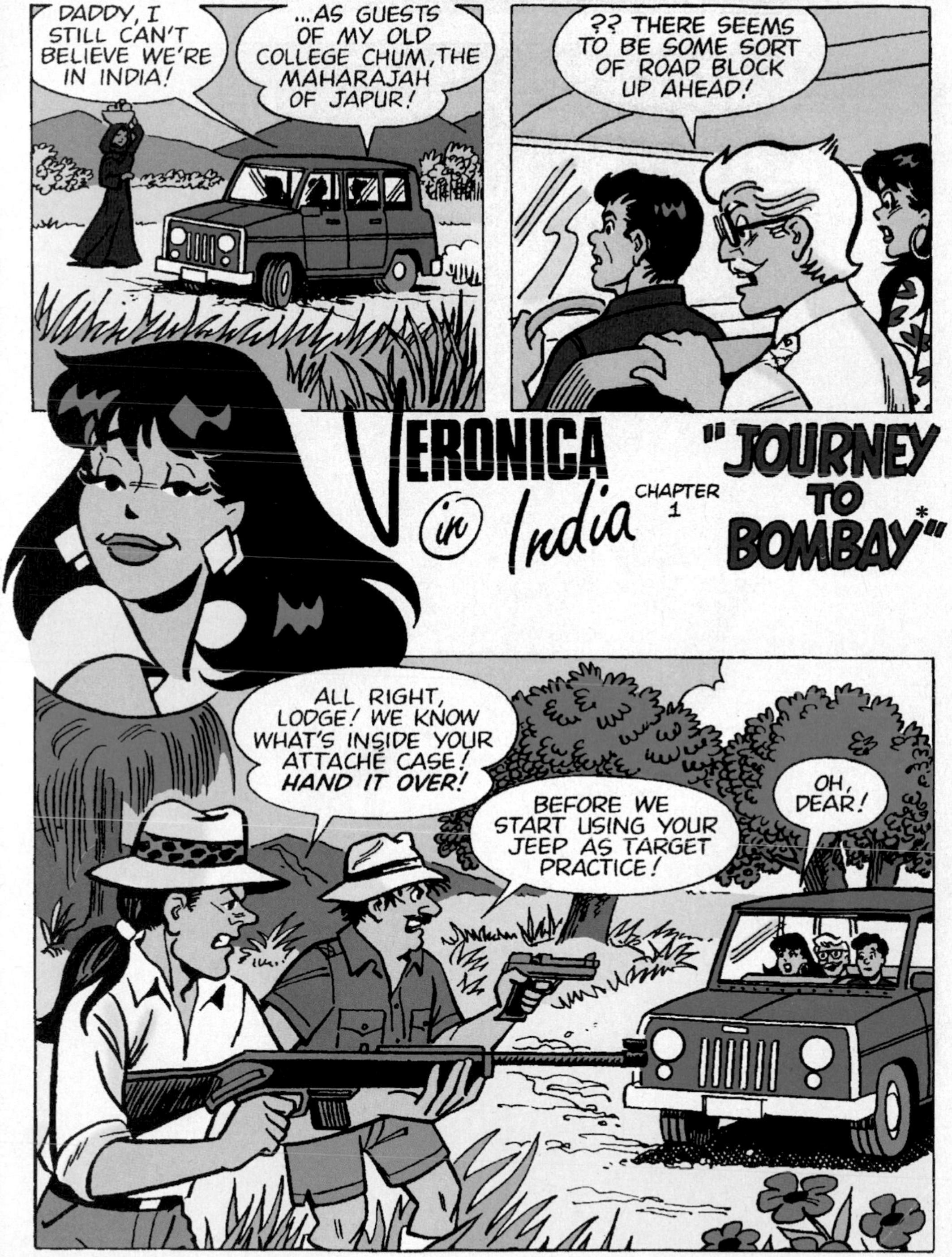
DADDY, I STILL CAN'T BELIEVE WE'RE IN INDIA!
...AS GUESTS OF MY OLD COLLEGE CHUM, THE MAHARAJAH OF JAPUR!
?? THERE SEEMS TO BE SOME SORT OF ROAD BLOCK UP AHEAD!
VERONICA in India
CHAPTER 1
"JOURNEY TO BOMBAY*"
ALL RIGHT, LODGE! WE KNOW WHAT'S INSIDE YOUR ATTACHE CASE! HAND IT OVER!
BEFORE WE START USING YOUR JEEP AS TARGET PRACTICE!
OH, DEAR!

* Bombay is now known as Mumbai

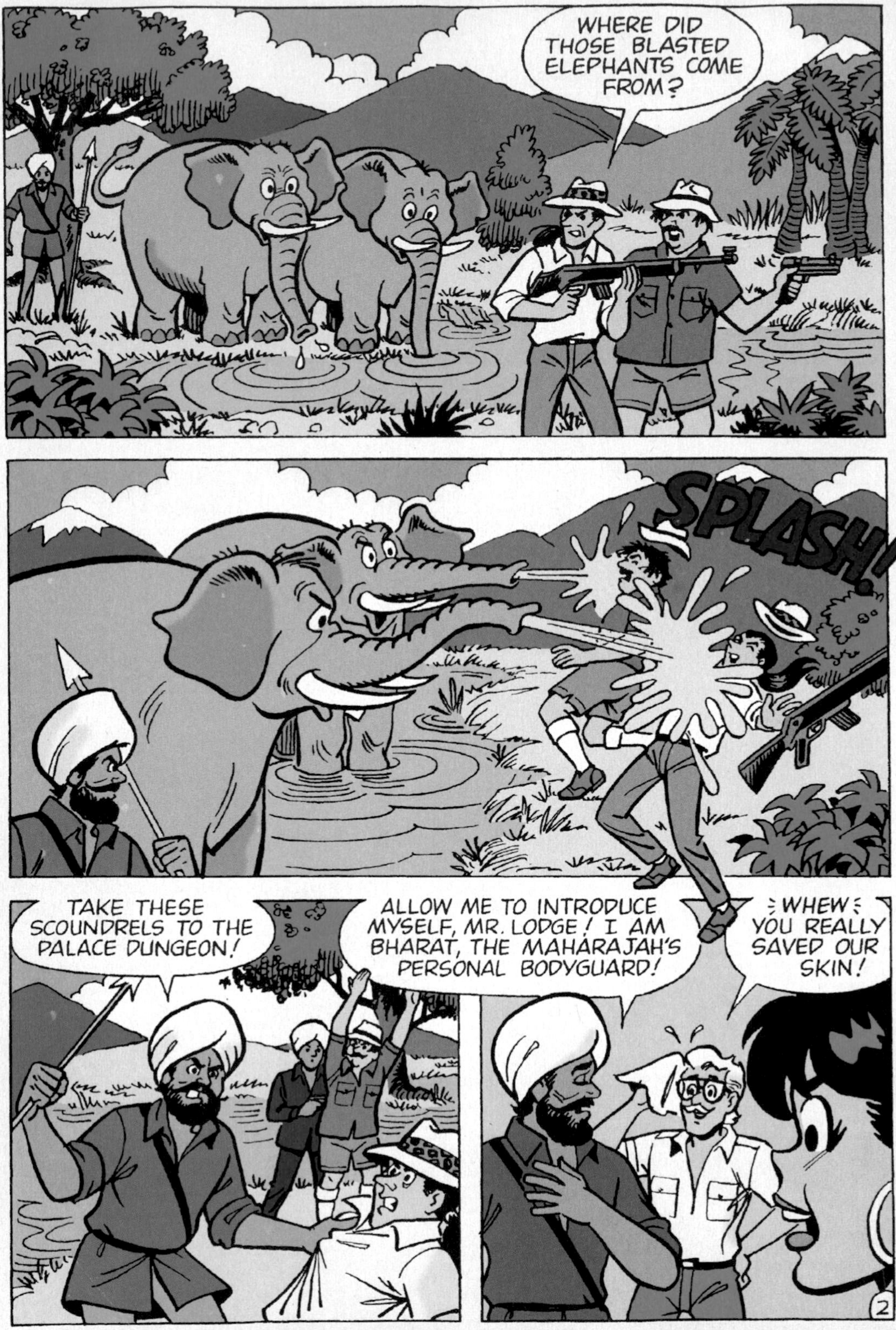
WHERE DID THOSE BLASTED ELEPHANTS COME FROM?
SPLASH!
TAKE THESE SCOUNDRELS TO THE PALACE DUNGEON!
ALLOW ME TO INTRODUCE MYSELF, MR. LODGE! I AM BHARAT, THE MAHARAJAH'S PERSONAL BODYGUARD!
WHEW! YOU REALLY SAVED OUR SKIN!
2

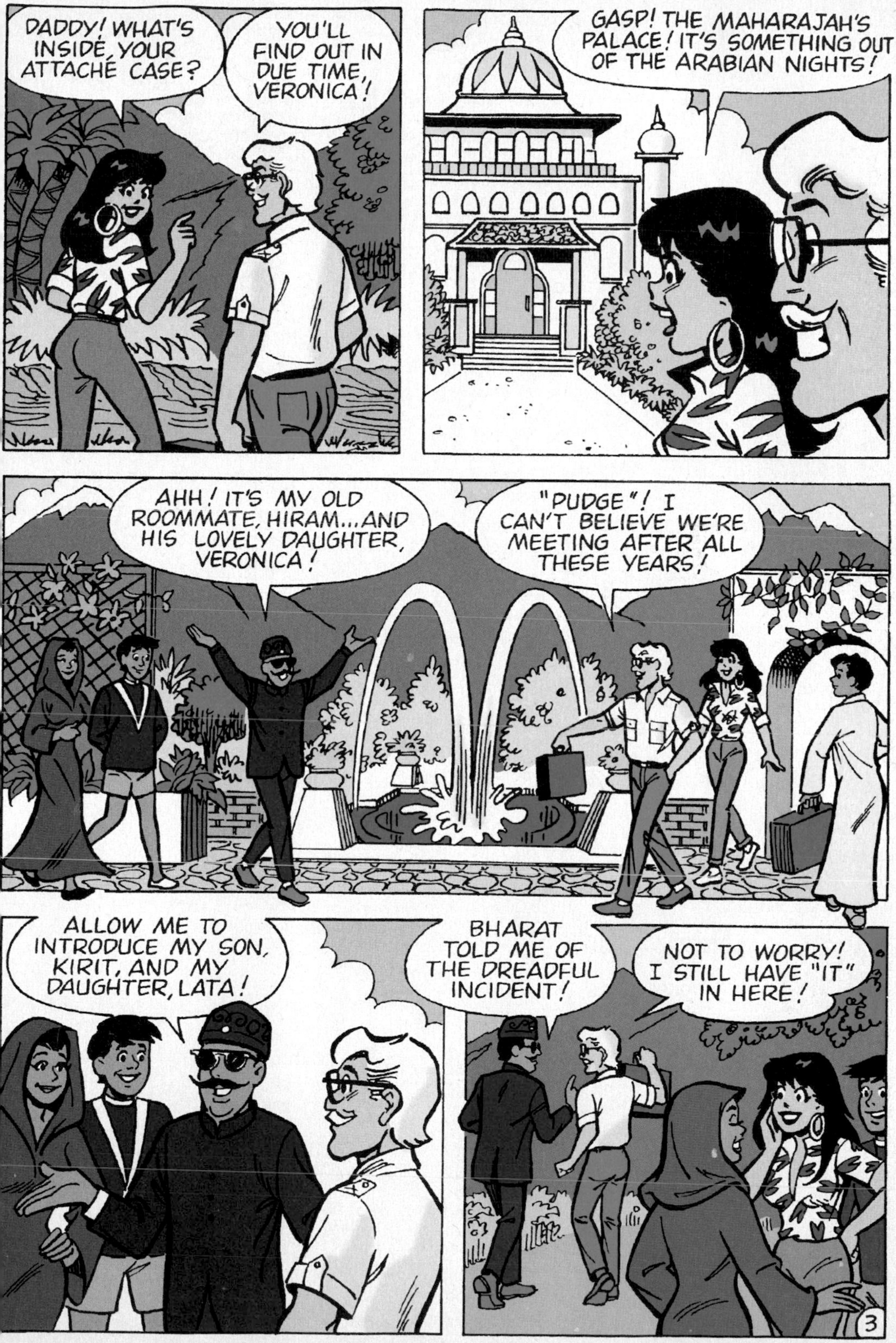
DADDY! WHAT'S INSIDE YOUR ATTACHÉ CASE?
YOU'LL FIND OUT IN DUE TIME, VERONICA!
GASP! THE MAHARAJAH'S PALACE! IT'S SOMETHING OUT OF THE ARABIAN NIGHTS!
AHH! IT'S MY OLD ROOMMATE, HIRAM...AND HIS LOVELY DAUGHTER, VERONICA!
"PUDGE"! I CAN'T BELIEVE WE'RE MEETING AFTER ALL THESE YEARS!
ALLOW ME TO INTRODUCE MY SON, KIRIT, AND MY DAUGHTER, LATA!
BHARAT TOLD ME OF THE DREADFUL INCIDENT!
NOT TO WORRY! I STILL HAVE "IT" IN HERE!
3

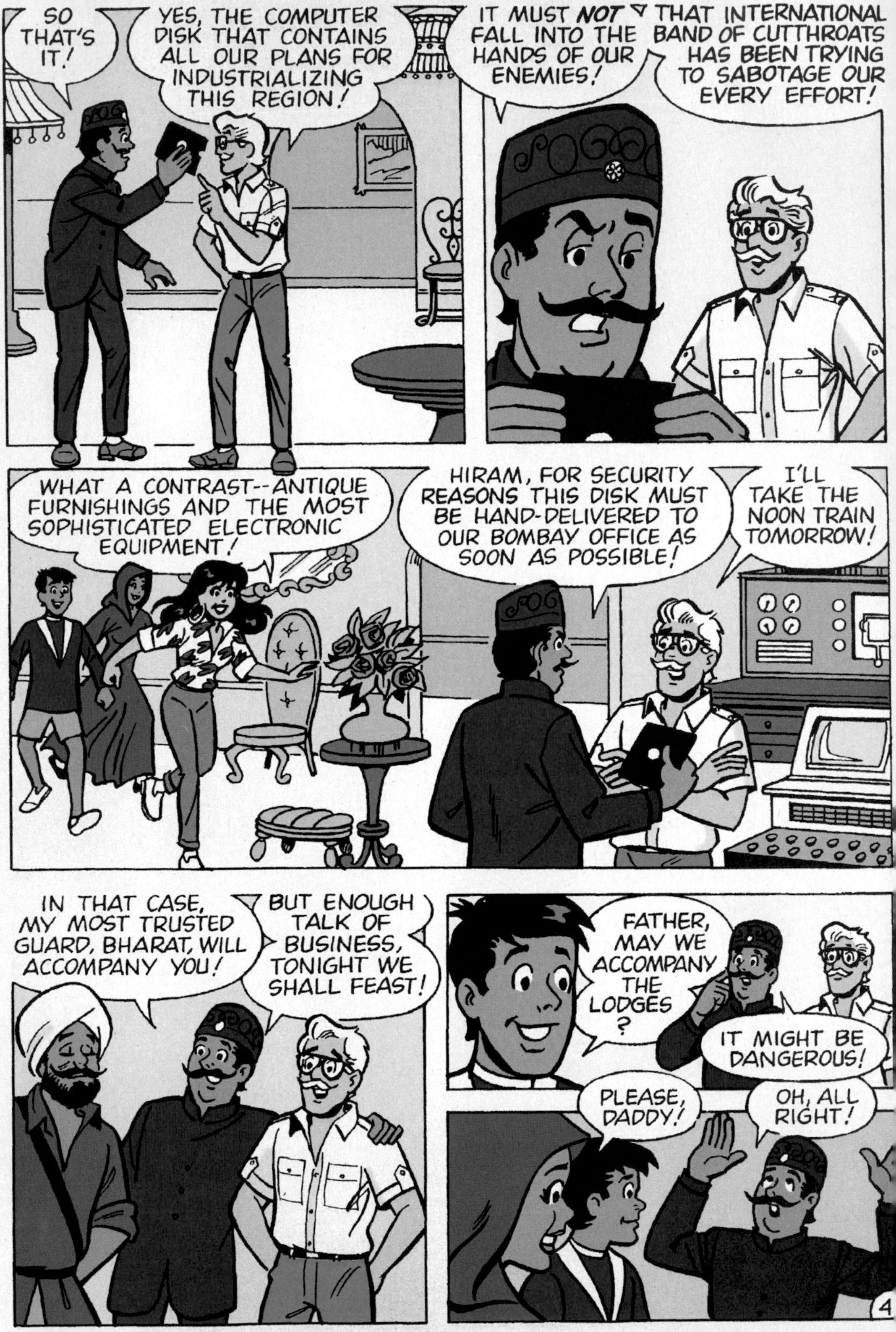
SO THAT'S IT!
YES, THE COMPUTER DISK THAT CONTAINS ALL OUR PLANS FOR INDUSTRIALIZING THIS REGION!
IT MUST NOT FALL INTO THE HANDS OF OUR ENEMIES!
THAT INTERNATIONAL BAND OF CUTTHROATS HAS BEEN TRYING TO SABOTAGE OUR EVERY EFFORT!
WHAT A CONTRAST--ANTIQUE FURNISHINGS AND THE MOST SOPHISTICATED ELECTRONIC EQUIPMENT!
HIRAM, FOR SECURITY REASONS THIS DISK MUST BE HAND-DELIVERED TO OUR BOMBAY OFFICE AS SOON AS POSSIBLE!
I'LL TAKE THE NOON TRAIN TOMORROW!
IN THAT CASE, MY MOST TRUSTED GUARD, BHARAT, WILL ACCOMPANY YOU!
BUT ENOUGH TALK OF BUSINESS, TONIGHT WE SHALL FEAST!
FATHER, MAY WE ACCOMPANY THE LODGES?
IT MIGHT BE DANGEROUS!
PLEASE, DADDY!
OH, ALL RIGHT!
4

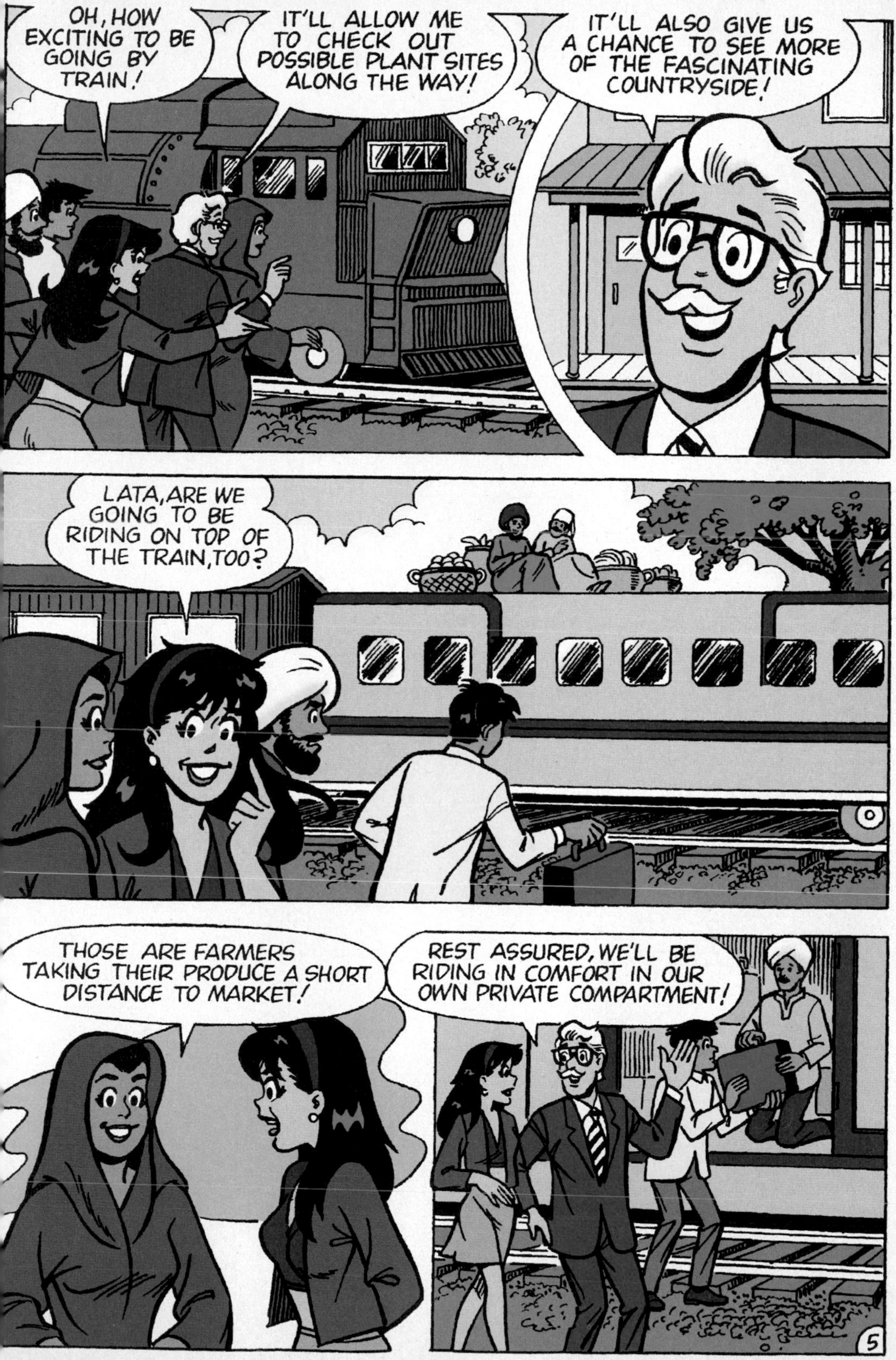
OH, HOW EXCITING TO BE GOING BY TRAIN!
IT'LL ALLOW ME TO CHECK OUT POSSIBLE PLANT SITES ALONG THE WAY!
IT'LL ALSO GIVE US A CHANCE TO SEE MORE OF THE FASCINATING COUNTRYSIDE!
LATA, ARE WE GOING TO BE RIDING ON TOP OF THE TRAIN, TOO?
THOSE ARE FARMERS TAKING THEIR PRODUCE A SHORT DISTANCE TO MARKET!
REST ASSURED, WE'LL BE RIDING IN COMFORT IN OUR OWN PRIVATE COMPARTMENT!
5

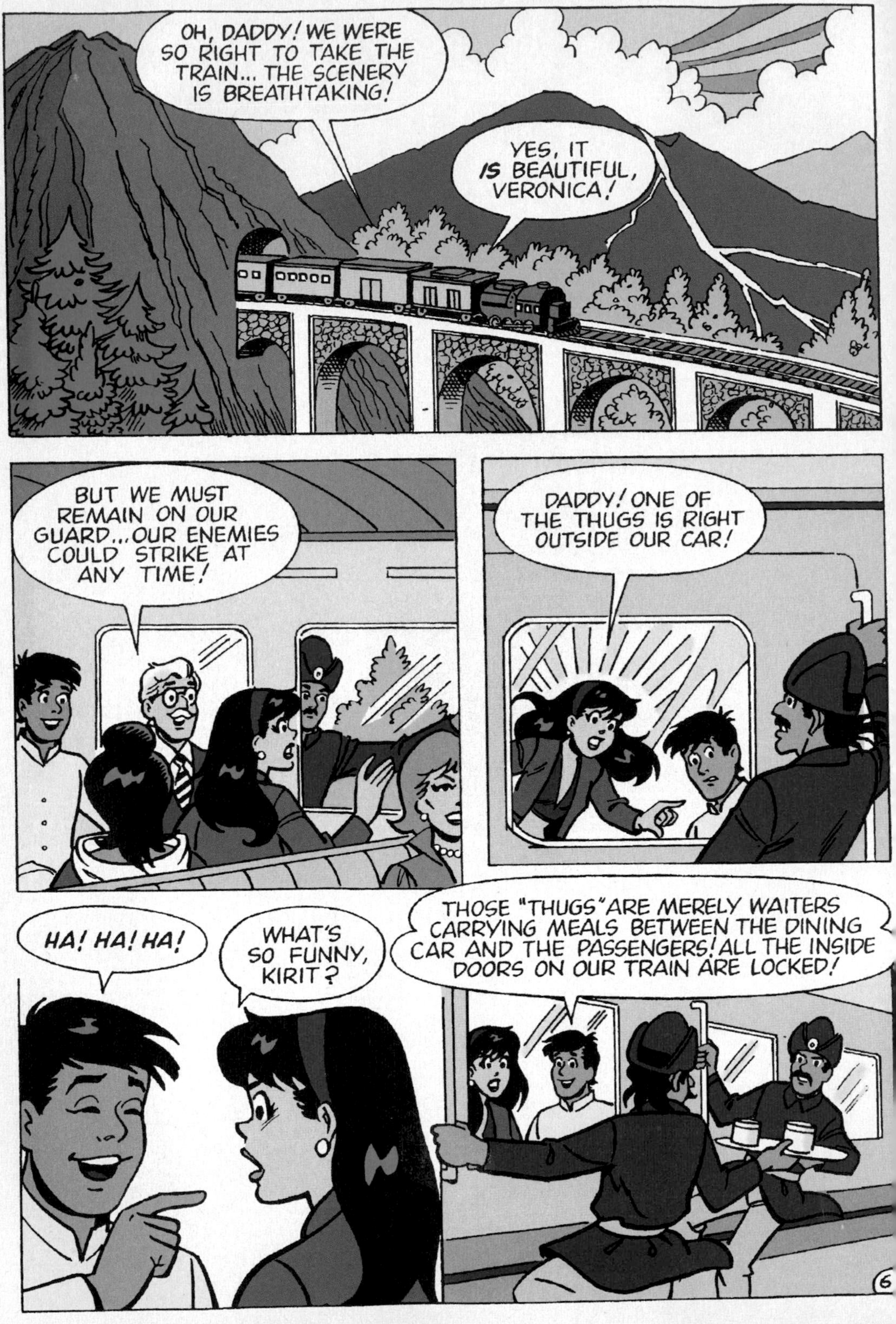
OH, DADDY! WE WERE SO RIGHT TO TAKE THE TRAIN... THE SCENERY IS BREATHTAKING!
YES, IT *IS* BEAUTIFUL, VERONICA!
BUT WE MUST REMAIN ON OUR GUARD...OUR ENEMIES COULD STRIKE AT ANY TIME!
DADDY! ONE OF THE THUGS IS RIGHT OUTSIDE OUR CAR!
HA! HA! HA!
WHAT'S SO FUNNY, KIRIT?
THOSE "THUGS" ARE MERELY WAITERS CARRYING MEALS BETWEEN THE DINING CAR AND THE PASSENGERS! ALL THE INSIDE DOORS ON OUR TRAIN ARE LOCKED!
6

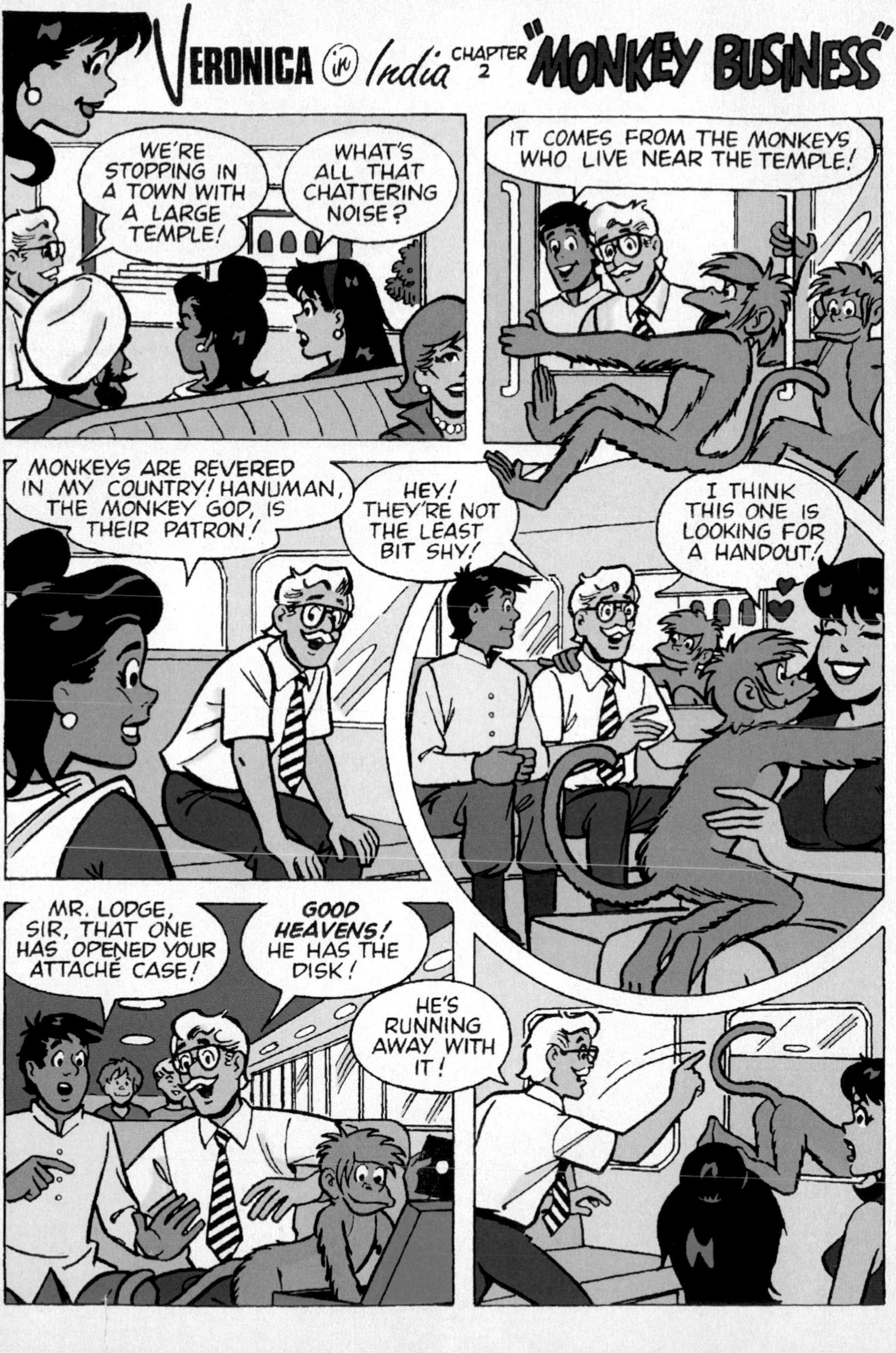

VERONICA in India CHAPTER 2 "MONKEY BUSINESS"
WE'RE STOPPING IN A TOWN WITH A LARGE TEMPLE!
WHAT'S ALL THAT CHATTERING NOISE?
IT COMES FROM THE MONKEYS WHO LIVE NEAR THE TEMPLE!
MONKEYS ARE REVERED IN MY COUNTRY! HANUMAN, THE MONKEY GOD, IS THEIR PATRON!
HEY! THEY'RE NOT THE LEAST BIT SHY!
I THINK THIS ONE IS LOOKING FOR A HANDOUT!
MR. LODGE, SIR, THAT ONE HAS OPENED YOUR ATTACHÉ CASE!
GOOD HEAVENS! HE HAS THE DISK!
HE'S RUNNING AWAY WITH IT!

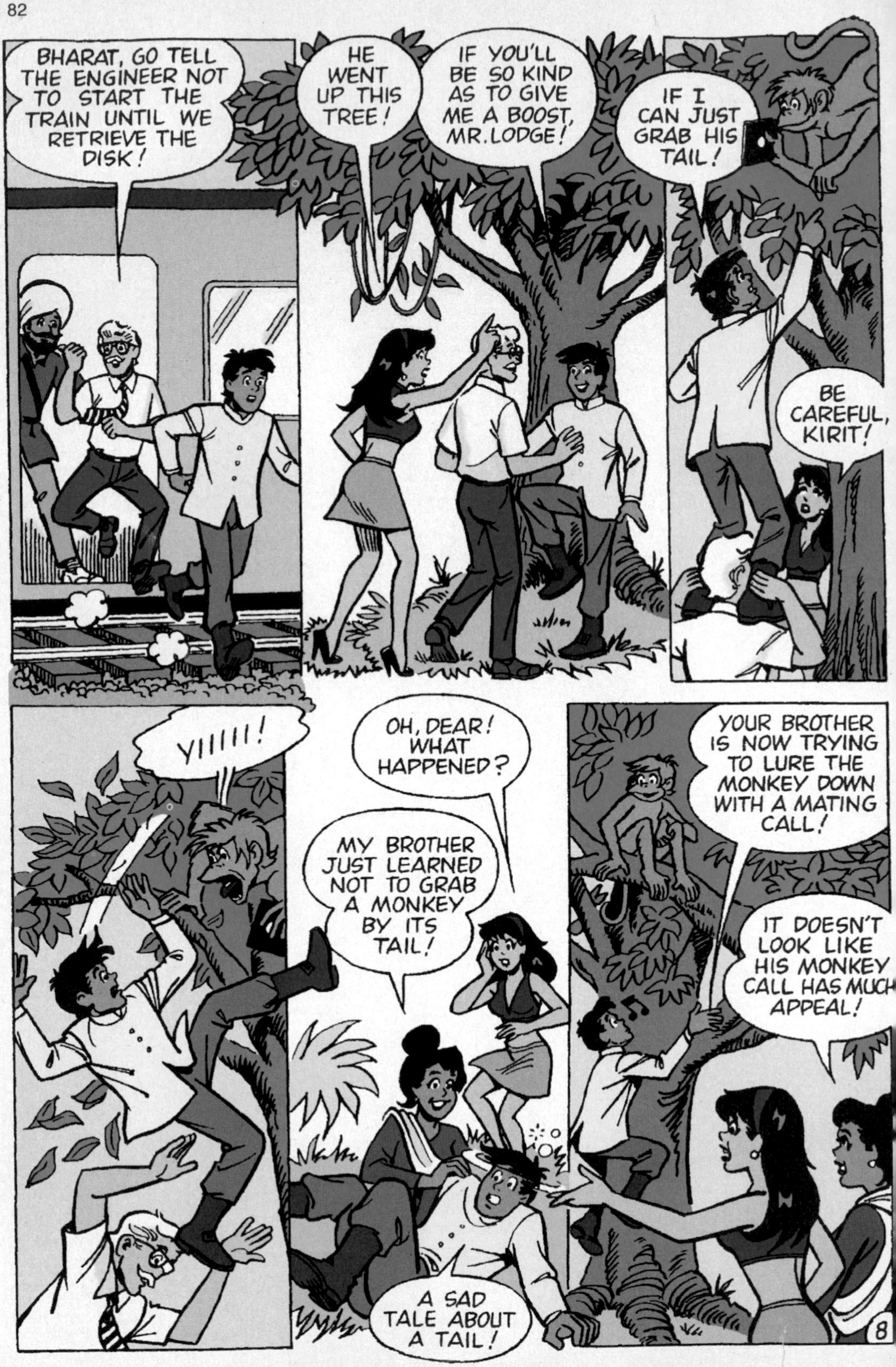
BHARAT, GO TELL THE ENGINEER NOT TO START THE TRAIN UNTIL WE RETRIEVE THE DISK!
HE WENT UP THIS TREE!
IF YOU'LL BE SO KIND AS TO GIVE ME A BOOST, MR. LODGE!
IF I CAN JUST GRAB HIS TAIL!
BE CAREFUL, KIRIT!
YIIIII!
OH, DEAR! WHAT HAPPENED?
MY BROTHER JUST LEARNED NOT TO GRAB A MONKEY BY ITS TAIL!
A SAD TALE ABOUT A TAIL!
YOUR BROTHER IS NOW TRYING TO LURE THE MONKEY DOWN WITH A MATING CALL!
IT DOESN'T LOOK LIKE HIS MONKEY CALL HAS MUCH APPEAL!
8

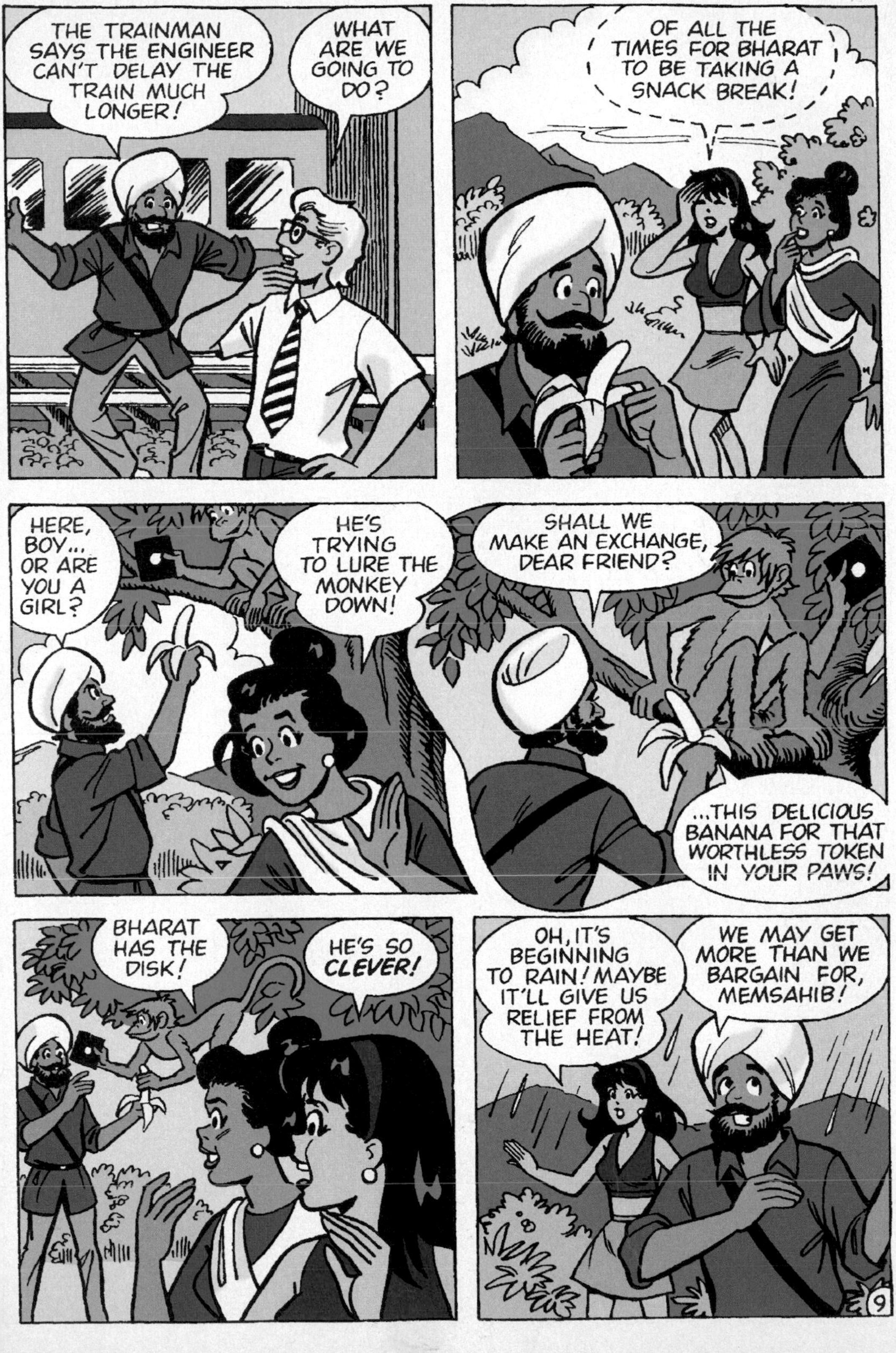
THE TRAINMAN SAYS THE ENGINEER CAN'T DELAY THE TRAIN MUCH LONGER!
WHAT ARE WE GOING TO DO?
OF ALL THE TIMES FOR BHARAT TO BE TAKING A SNACK BREAK!
HERE, BOY... OR ARE YOU A GIRL?
HE'S TRYING TO LURE THE MONKEY DOWN!
SHALL WE MAKE AN EXCHANGE, DEAR FRIEND?
...THIS DELICIOUS BANANA FOR THAT WORTHLESS TOKEN IN YOUR PAWS!
BHARAT HAS THE DISK!
HE'S SO CLEVER!
OH, IT'S BEGINNING TO RAIN! MAYBE IT'LL GIVE US RELIEF FROM THE HEAT!
WE MAY GET MORE THAN WE BARGAIN FOR, MEMSAHIB!
9

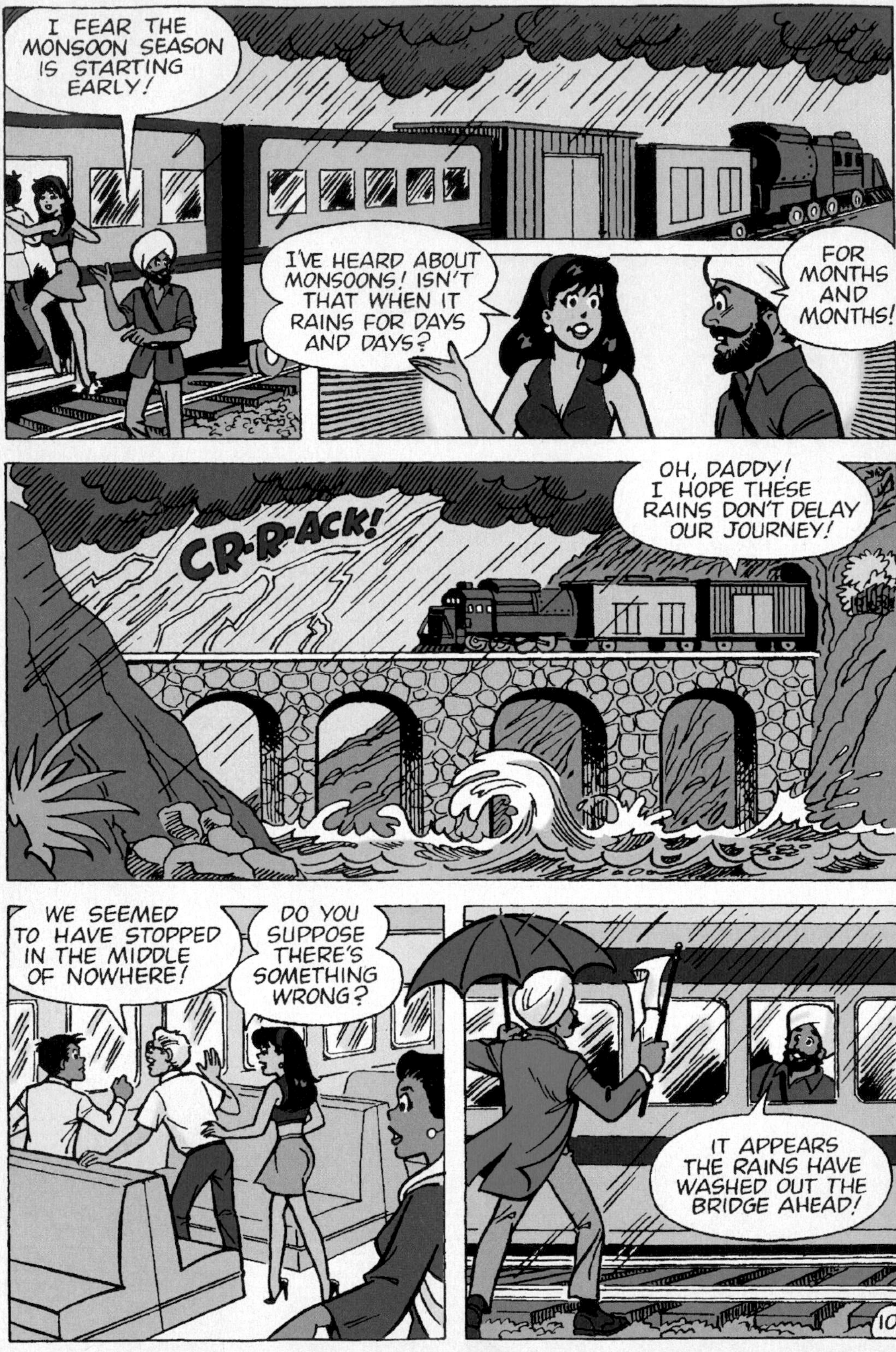
I FEAR THE MONSOON SEASON IS STARTING EARLY!
I'VE HEARD ABOUT MONSOONS! ISN'T THAT WHEN IT RAINS FOR DAYS AND DAYS?
FOR MONTHS AND MONTHS!
CR-R-ACK!
OH, DADDY! I HOPE THESE RAINS DON'T DELAY OUR JOURNEY!
WE SEEMED TO HAVE STOPPED IN THE MIDDLE OF NOWHERE!
DO YOU SUPPOSE THERE'S SOMETHING WRONG?
IT APPEARS THE RAINS HAVE WASHED OUT THE BRIDGE AHEAD!
10

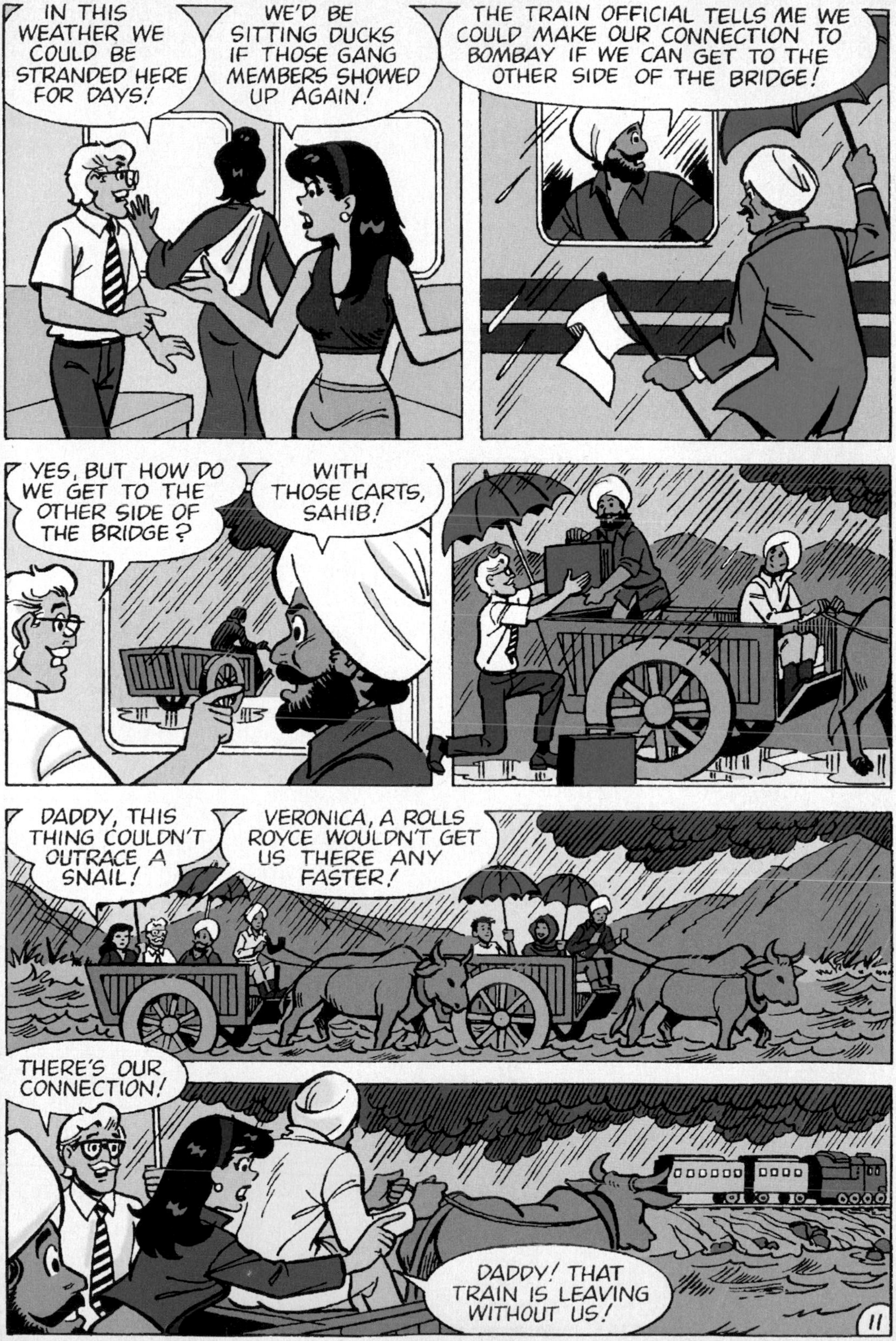
IN THIS WEATHER WE COULD BE STRANDED HERE FOR DAYS!
WE'D BE SITTING DUCKS IF THOSE GANG MEMBERS SHOWED UP AGAIN!
THE TRAIN OFFICIAL TELLS ME WE COULD MAKE OUR CONNECTION TO BOMBAY IF WE CAN GET TO THE OTHER SIDE OF THE BRIDGE!
YES, BUT HOW DO WE GET TO THE OTHER SIDE OF THE BRIDGE?
WITH THOSE CARTS, SAHIB!
DADDY, THIS THING COULDN'T OUTRACE A SNAIL!
VERONICA, A ROLLS ROYCE WOULDN'T GET US THERE ANY FASTER!
THERE'S OUR CONNECTION!
DADDY! THAT TRAIN IS LEAVING WITHOUT US!
11

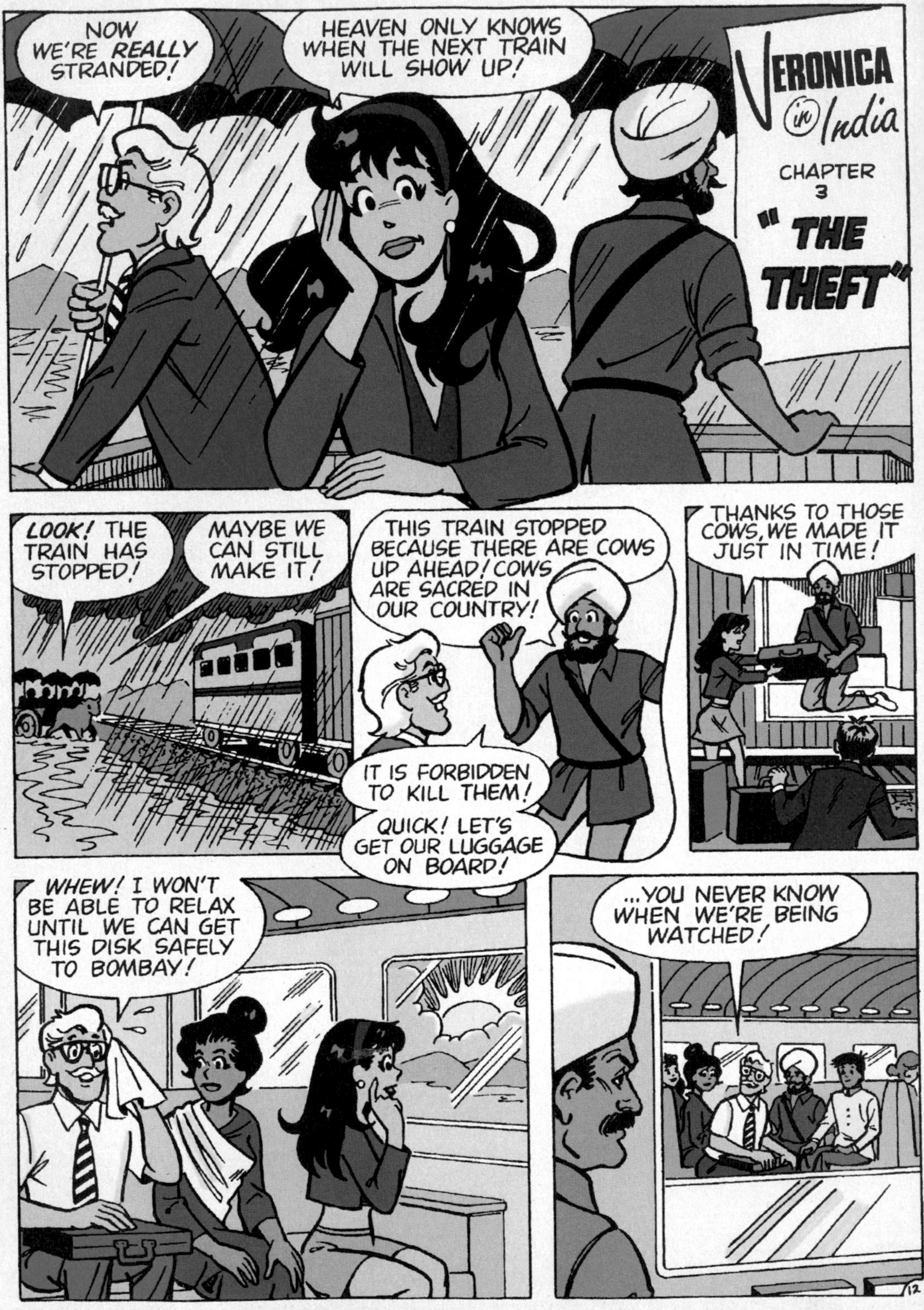
NOW WE'RE REALLY STRANDED!
HEAVEN ONLY KNOWS WHEN THE NEXT TRAIN WILL SHOW UP!
VERONICA in India
CHAPTER 3
"THE THEFT"
LOOK! THE TRAIN HAS STOPPED!
MAYBE WE CAN STILL MAKE IT!
THIS TRAIN STOPPED BECAUSE THERE ARE COWS UP AHEAD! COWS ARE SACRED IN OUR COUNTRY!
IT IS FORBIDDEN TO KILL THEM!
QUICK! LET'S GET OUR LUGGAGE ON BOARD!
THANKS TO THOSE COWS, WE MADE IT JUST IN TIME!
WHEW! I WON'T BE ABLE TO RELAX UNTIL WE CAN GET THIS DISK SAFELY TO BOMBAY!
...YOU NEVER KNOW WHEN WE'RE BEING WATCHED!
12

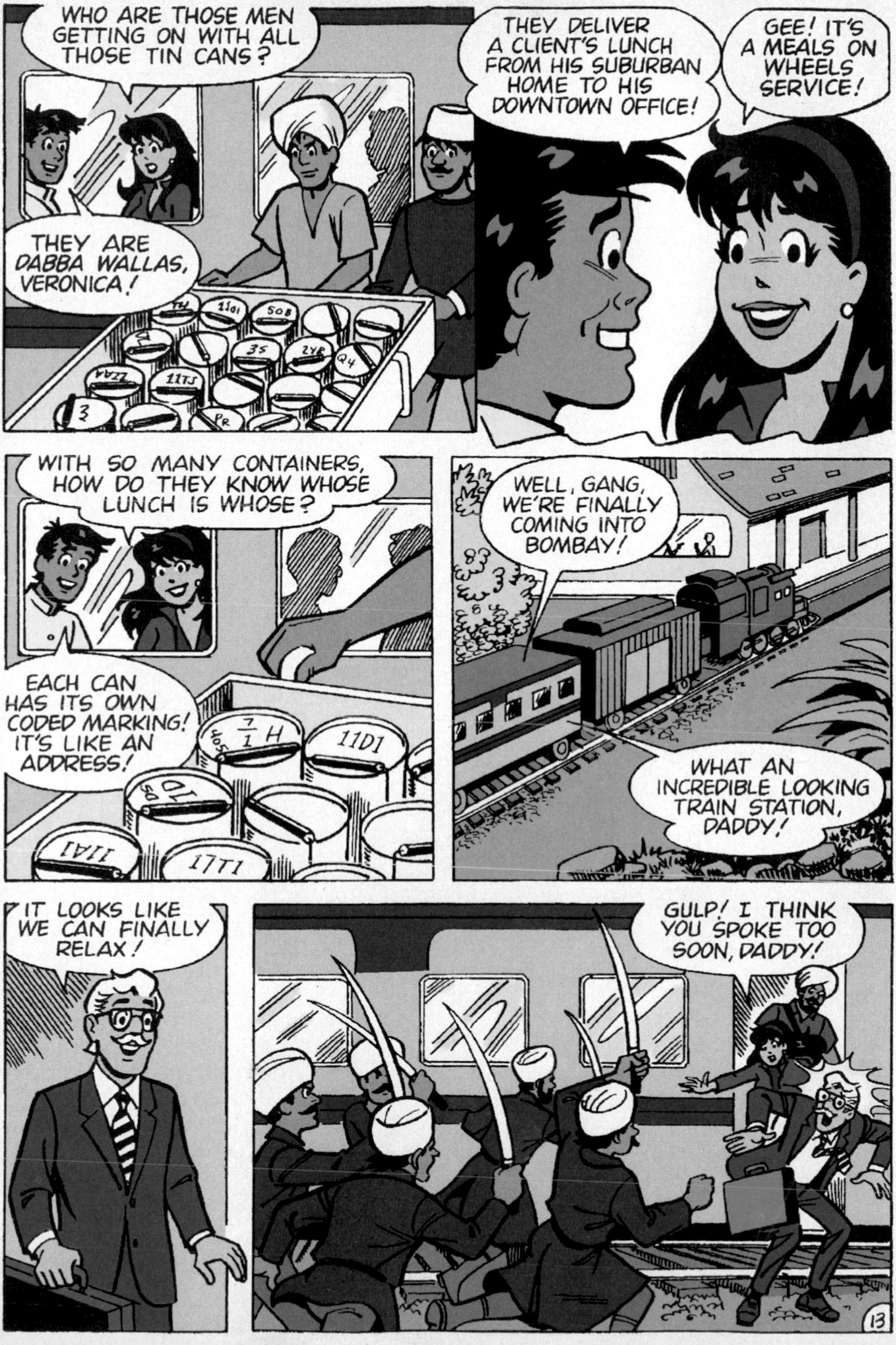
WHO ARE THOSE MEN GETTING ON WITH ALL THOSE TIN CANS?
THEY ARE DABBA WALLAS, VERONICA!
THEY DELIVER A CLIENT'S LUNCH FROM HIS SUBURBAN HOME TO HIS DOWNTOWN OFFICE!
GEE! IT'S A MEALS ON WHEELS SERVICE!
WITH SO MANY CONTAINERS, HOW DO THEY KNOW WHOSE LUNCH IS WHOSE?
EACH CAN HAS ITS OWN CODED MARKING! IT'S LIKE AN ADDRESS!
WELL, GANG, WE'RE FINALLY COMING INTO BOMBAY!
WHAT AN INCREDIBLE LOOKING TRAIN STATION, DADDY!
IT LOOKS LIKE WE CAN FINALLY RELAX!
GULP! I THINK YOU SPOKE TOO SOON, DADDY!
13

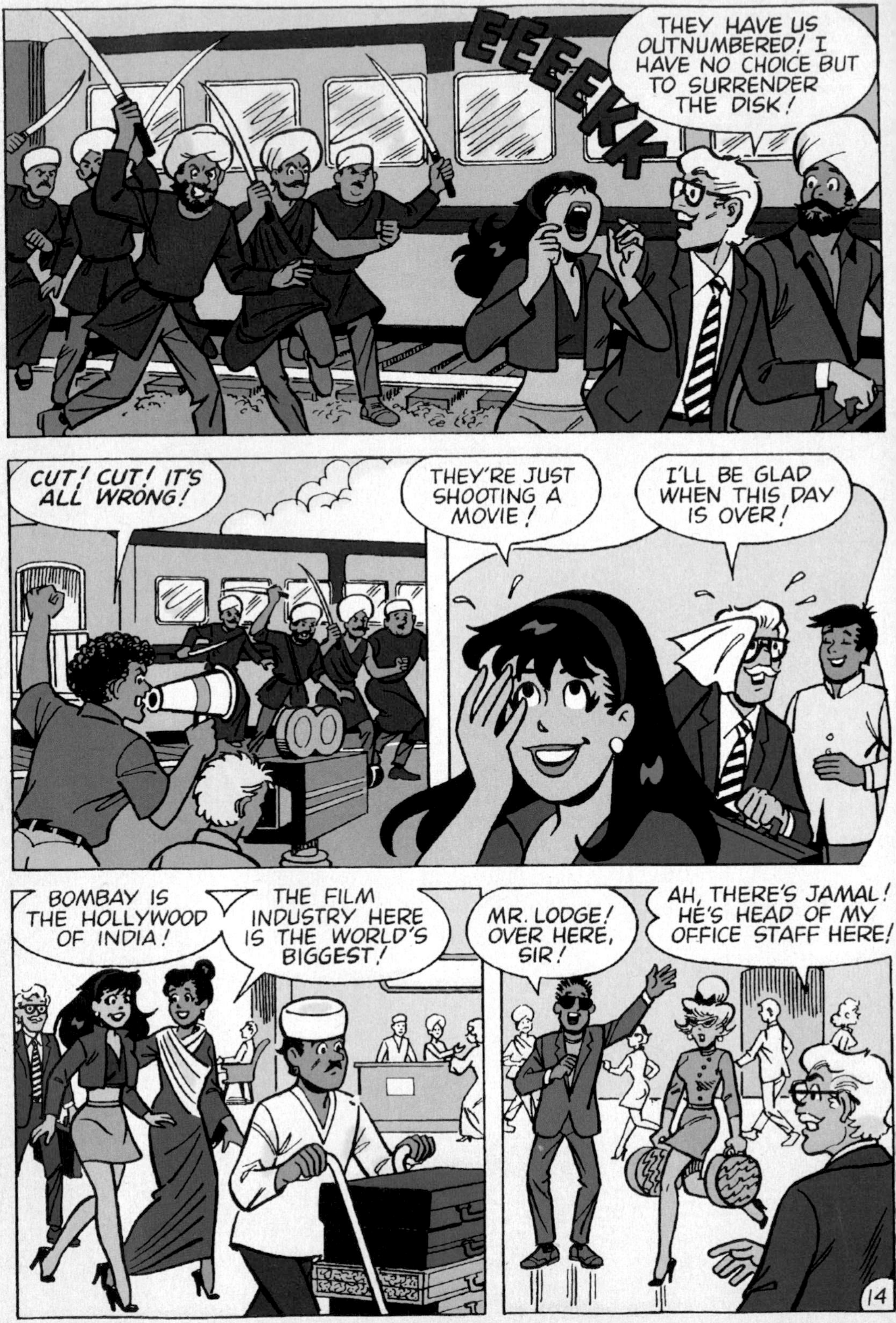
EEEEKK
THEY HAVE US OUTNUMBERED! I HAVE NO CHOICE BUT TO SURRENDER THE DISK!
CUT! CUT! IT'S ALL WRONG!
THEY'RE JUST SHOOTING A MOVIE!
I'LL BE GLAD WHEN THIS DAY IS OVER!
BOMBAY IS THE HOLLYWOOD OF INDIA!
THE FILM INDUSTRY HERE IS THE WORLD'S BIGGEST!
MR. LODGE! OVER HERE, SIR!
AH, THERE'S JAMAL! HE'S HEAD OF MY OFFICE STAFF HERE!
14

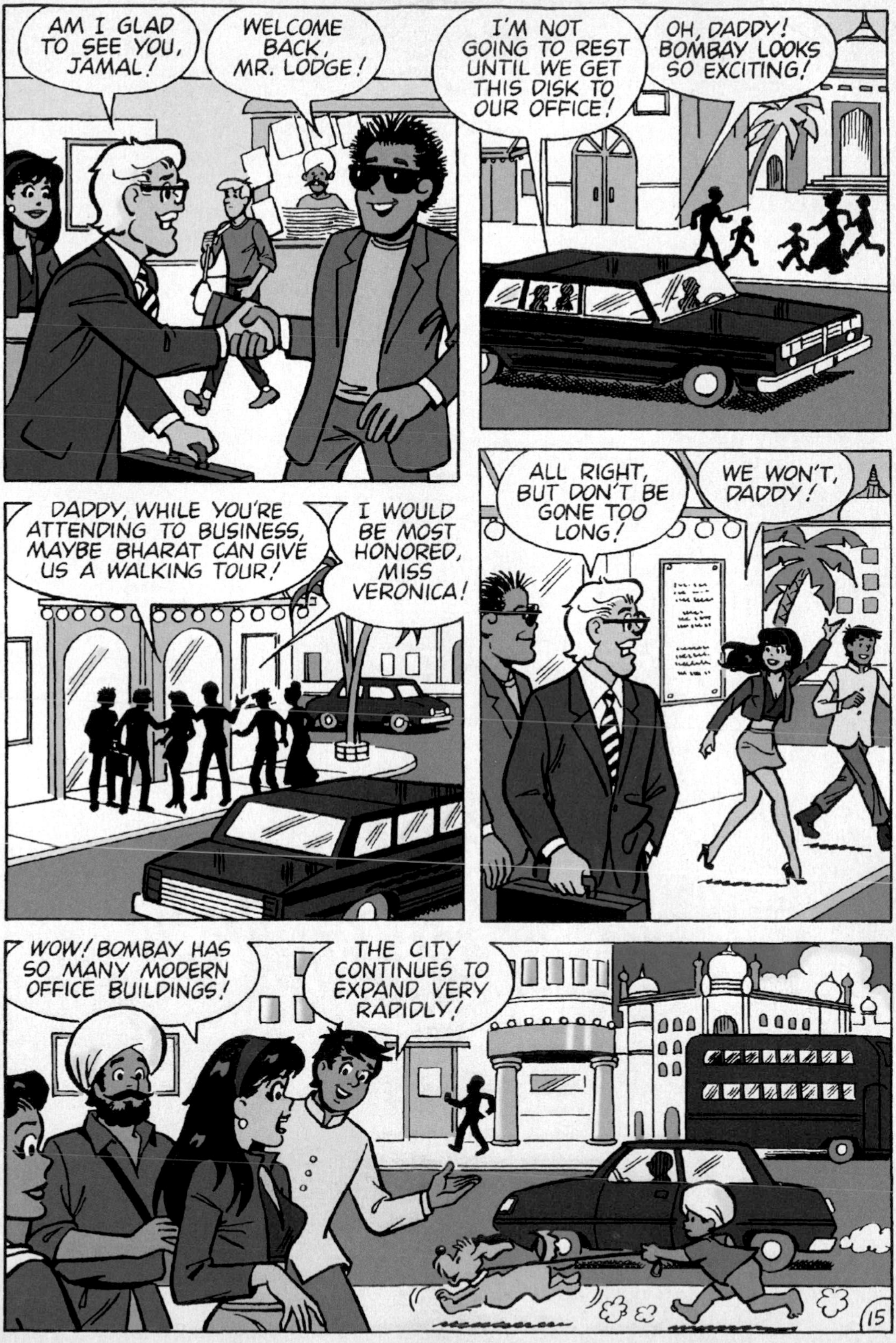
AM I GLAD TO SEE YOU, JAMAL!
WELCOME BACK, MR. LODGE!
I'M NOT GOING TO REST UNTIL WE GET THIS DISK TO OUR OFFICE!
OH, DADDY! BOMBAY LOOKS SO EXCITING!
DADDY, WHILE YOU'RE ATTENDING TO BUSINESS, MAYBE BHARAT CAN GIVE US A WALKING TOUR!
I WOULD BE MOST HONORED, MISS VERONICA!
ALL RIGHT, BUT DON'T BE GONE TOO LONG!
WE WON'T, DADDY!
WOW! BOMBAY HAS SO MANY MODERN OFFICE BUILDINGS!
THE CITY CONTINUES TO EXPAND VERY RAPIDLY!
15

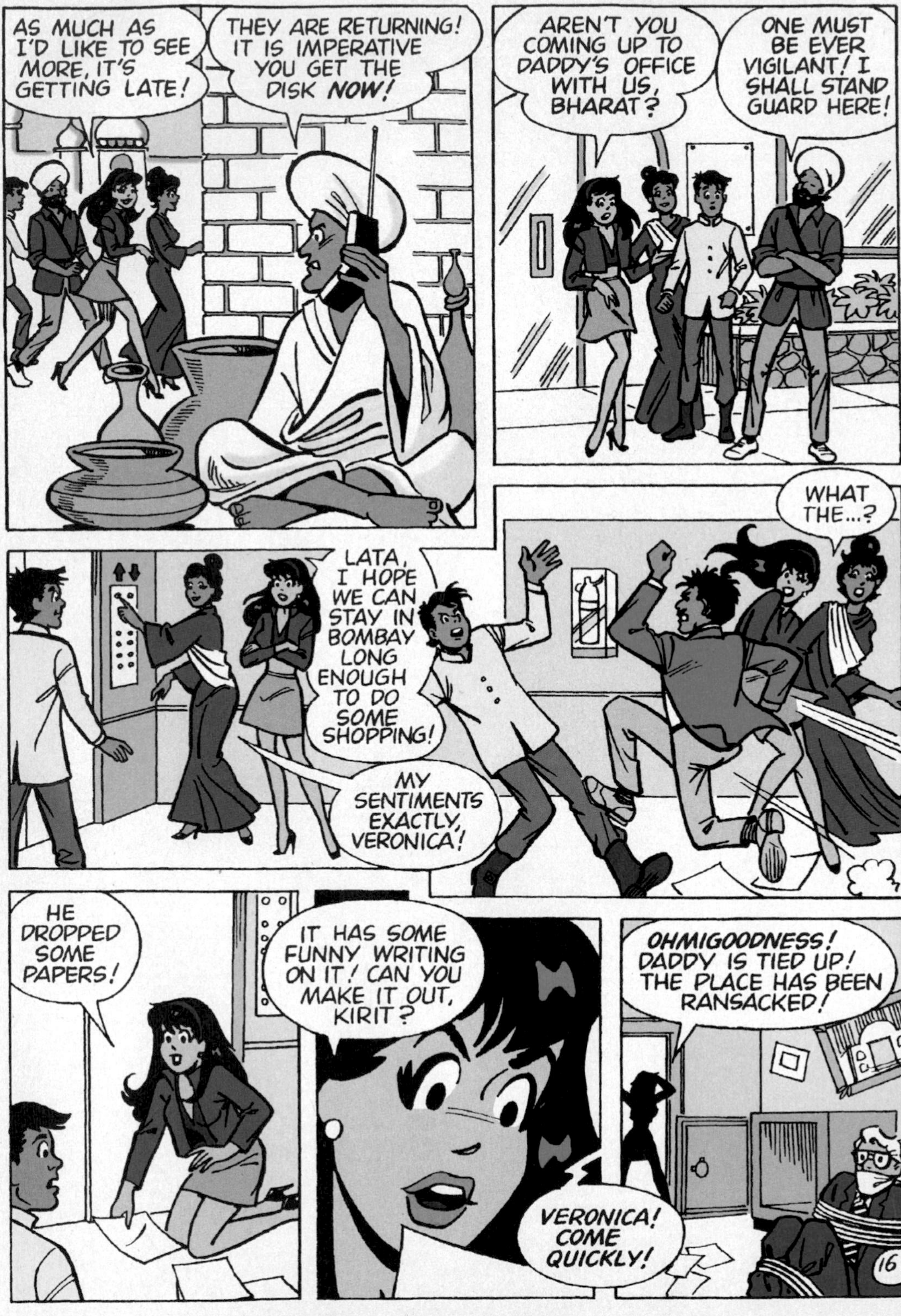
AS MUCH AS I'D LIKE TO SEE MORE, IT'S GETTING LATE!
THEY ARE RETURNING! IT IS IMPERATIVE YOU GET THE DISK NOW!
AREN'T YOU COMING UP TO DADDY'S OFFICE WITH US, BHARAT?
ONE MUST BE EVER VIGILANT! I SHALL STAND GUARD HERE!
LATA, I HOPE WE CAN STAY IN BOMBAY LONG ENOUGH TO DO SOME SHOPPING!
MY SENTIMENTS EXACTLY, VERONICA!
WHAT THE...?
HE DROPPED SOME PAPERS!
IT HAS SOME FUNNY WRITING ON IT! CAN YOU MAKE IT OUT, KIRIT?
OHMIGOODNESS! DADDY IS TIED UP! THE PLACE HAS BEEN RANSACKED!
VERONICA! COME QUICKLY!
16

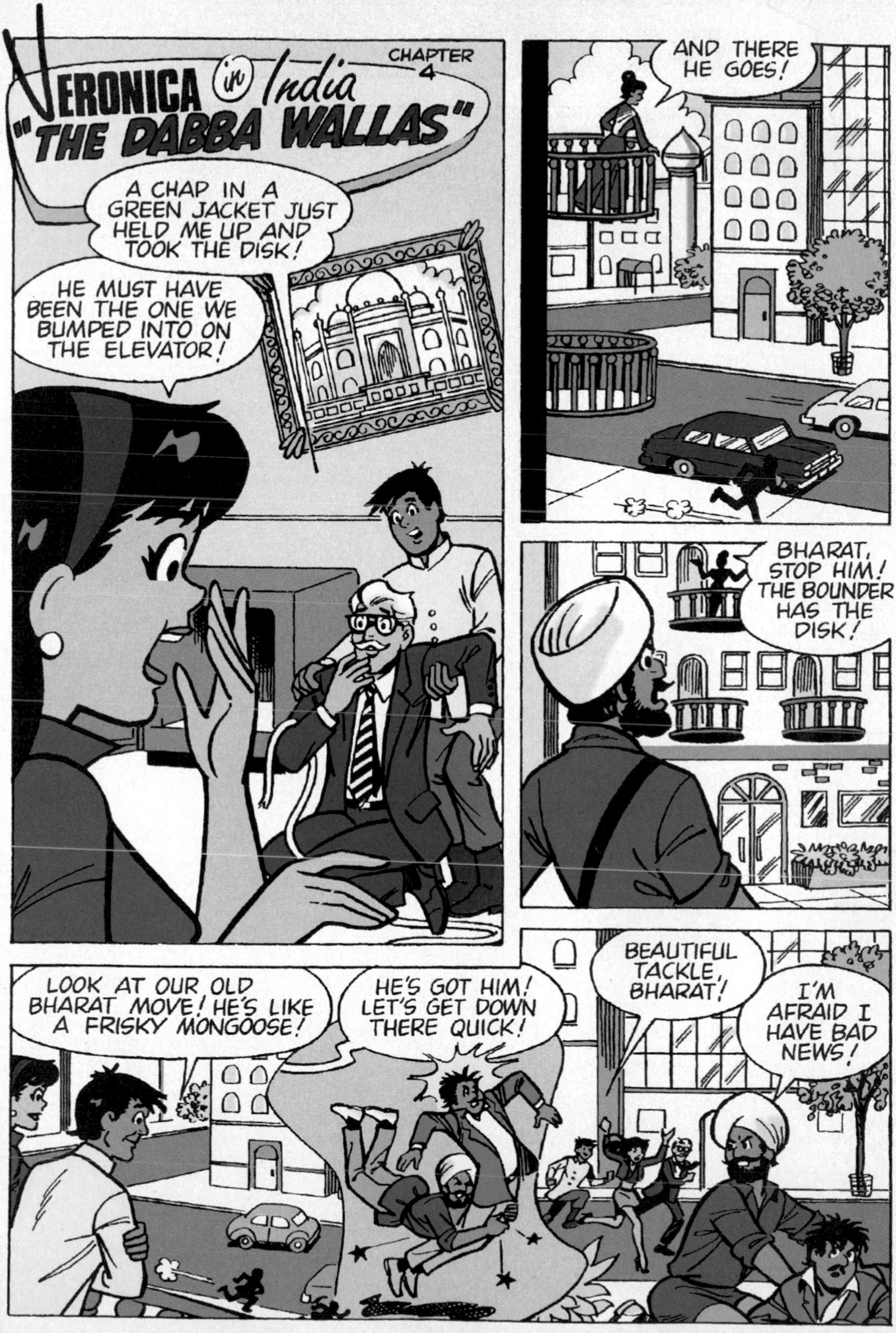
VERONICA in India
CHAPTER 4
"THE DABBA WALLAS"
A CHAP IN A GREEN JACKET JUST HELD ME UP AND TOOK THE DISK!
HE MUST HAVE BEEN THE ONE WE BUMPED INTO ON THE ELEVATOR!
AND THERE HE GOES!
BHARAT, STOP HIM! THE BOUNDER HAS THE DISK!
LOOK AT OUR OLD BHARAT MOVE! HE'S LIKE A FRISKY MONGOOSE!
HE'S GOT HIM! LET'S GET DOWN THERE QUICK!
BEAUTIFUL TACKLE, BHARAT!
I'M AFRAID I HAVE BAD NEWS!

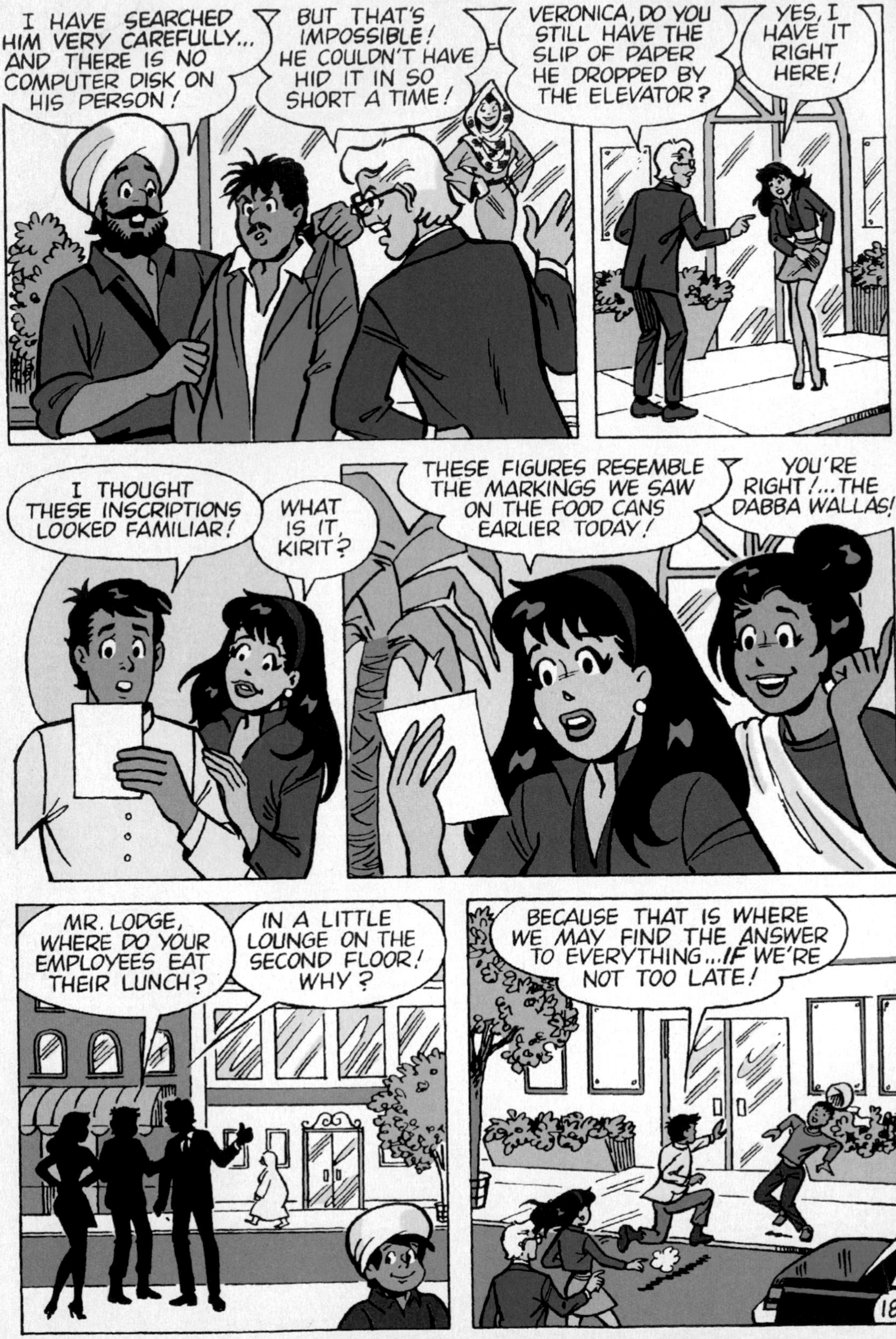
I HAVE SEARCHED HIM VERY CAREFULLY... AND THERE IS NO COMPUTER DISK ON HIS PERSON!
BUT THAT'S IMPOSSIBLE! HE COULDN'T HAVE HID IT IN SO SHORT A TIME!
VERONICA, DO YOU STILL HAVE THE SLIP OF PAPER HE DROPPED BY THE ELEVATOR?
YES, I HAVE IT RIGHT HERE!
I THOUGHT THESE INSCRIPTIONS LOOKED FAMILIAR!
WHAT IS IT, KIRIT?
THESE FIGURES RESEMBLE THE MARKINGS WE SAW ON THE FOOD CANS EARLIER TODAY!
YOU'RE RIGHT!...THE DABBA WALLAS!
MR. LODGE, WHERE DO YOUR EMPLOYEES EAT THEIR LUNCH?
IN A LITTLE LOUNGE ON THE SECOND FLOOR! WHY?
BECAUSE THAT IS WHERE WE MAY FIND THE ANSWER TO EVERYTHING...IF WE'RE NOT TOO LATE!
18

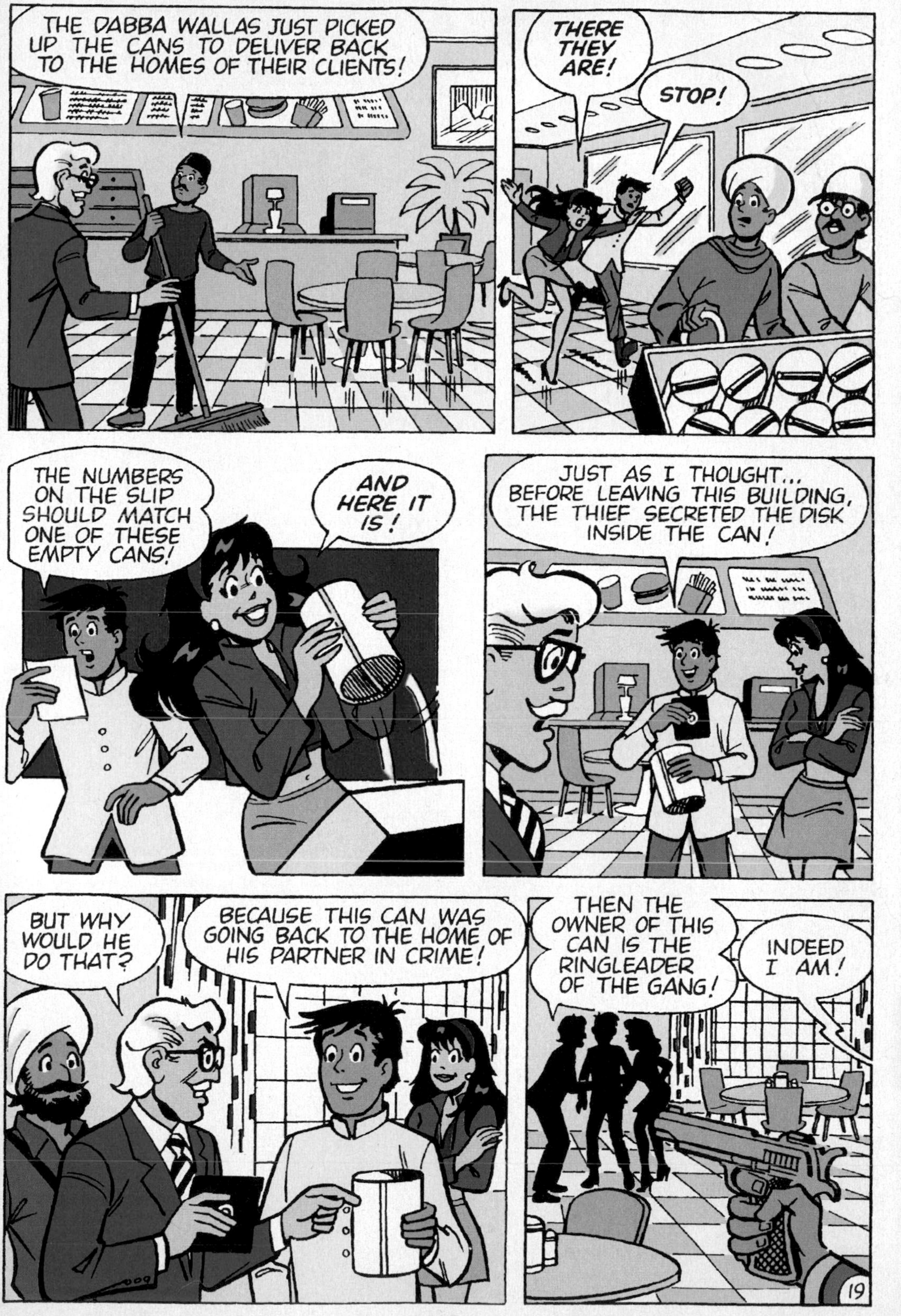
THE DABBA WALLAS JUST PICKED UP THE CANS TO DELIVER BACK TO THE HOMES OF THEIR CLIENTS!
THERE THEY ARE!
STOP!
THE NUMBERS ON THE SLIP SHOULD MATCH ONE OF THESE EMPTY CANS!
AND HERE IT IS!
JUST AS I THOUGHT... BEFORE LEAVING THIS BUILDING, THE THIEF SECRETED THE DISK INSIDE THE CAN!
BUT WHY WOULD HE DO THAT?
BECAUSE THIS CAN WAS GOING BACK TO THE HOME OF HIS PARTNER IN CRIME!
THEN THE OWNER OF THIS CAN IS THE RINGLEADER OF THE GANG!
INDEED I AM!
19

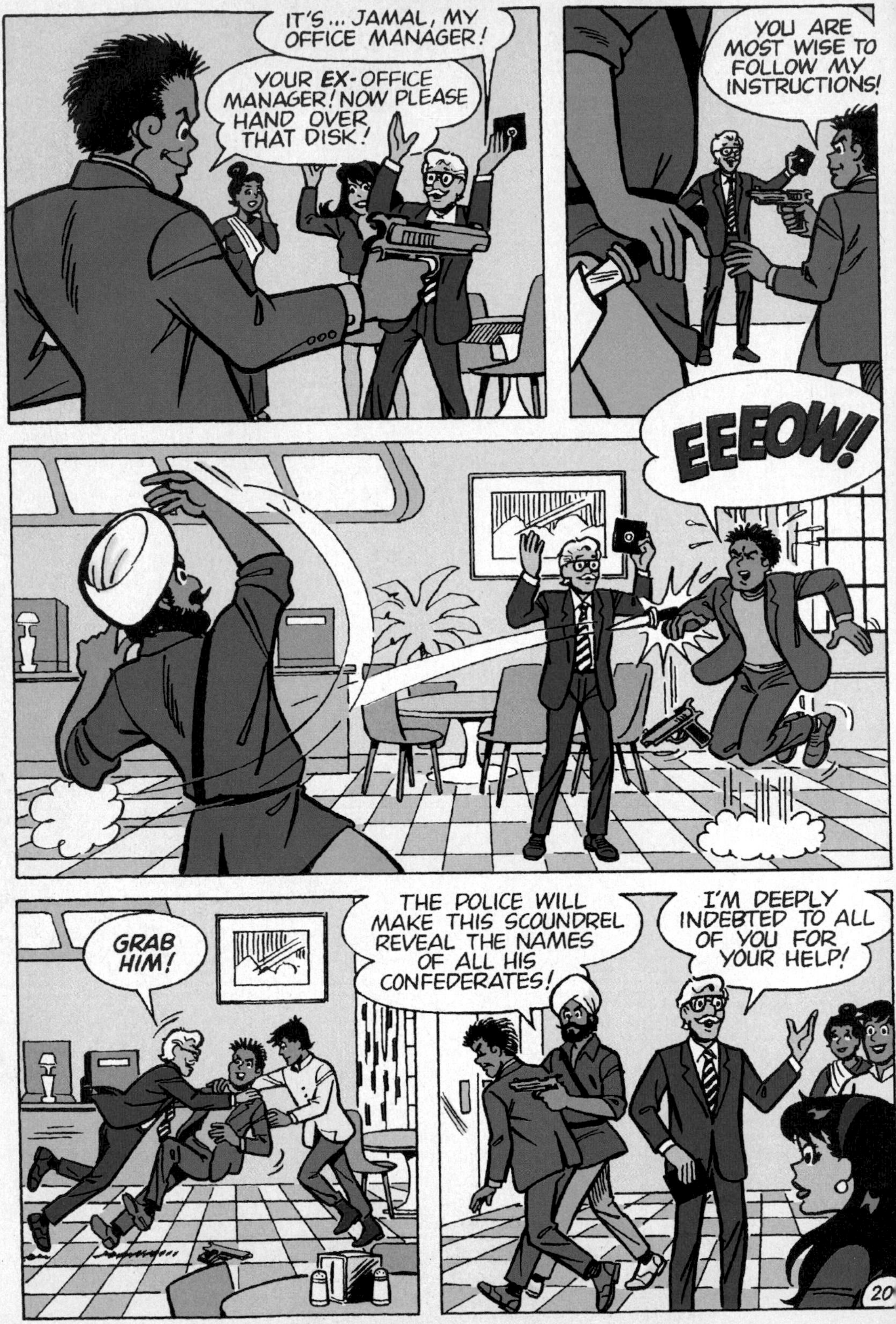
IT'S... JAMAL, MY OFFICE MANAGER!
YOUR EX-OFFICE MANAGER! NOW PLEASE HAND OVER THAT DISK!
YOU ARE MOST WISE TO FOLLOW MY INSTRUCTIONS!
EEEOW!
GRAB HIM!
THE POLICE WILL MAKE THIS SCOUNDREL REVEAL THE NAMES OF ALL HIS CONFEDERATES!
I'M DEEPLY INDEBTED TO ALL OF YOU FOR YOUR HELP!
20

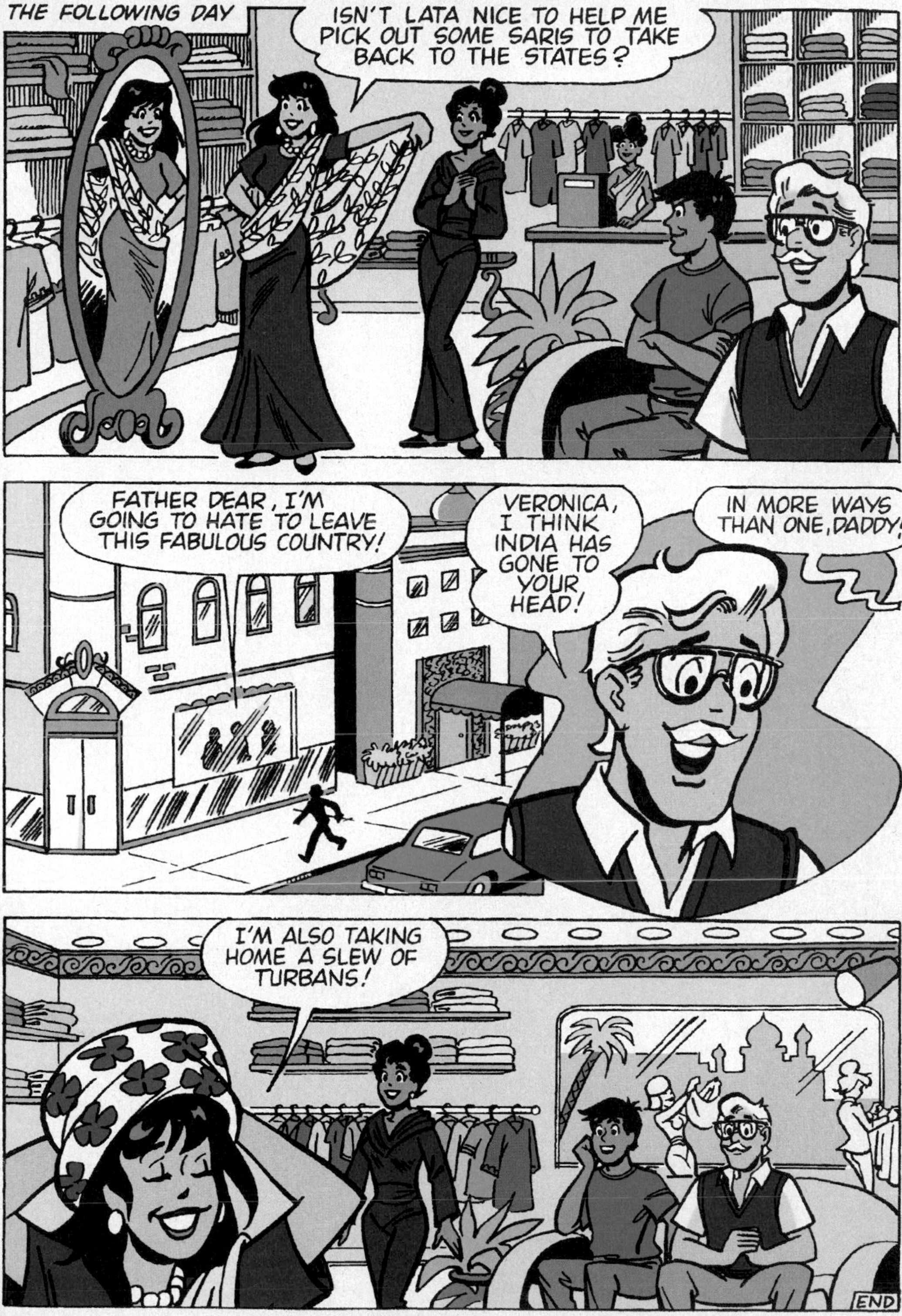
THE FOLLOWING DAY
ISN'T LATA NICE TO HELP ME PICK OUT SOME SARIS TO TAKE BACK TO THE STATES?
FATHER DEAR, I'M GOING TO HATE TO LEAVE THIS FABULOUS COUNTRY!
VERONICA, I THINK INDIA HAS GONE TO YOUR HEAD!
IN MORE WAYS THAN ONE, DADDY!
I'M ALSO TAKING HOME A SLEW OF TURBANS!
END

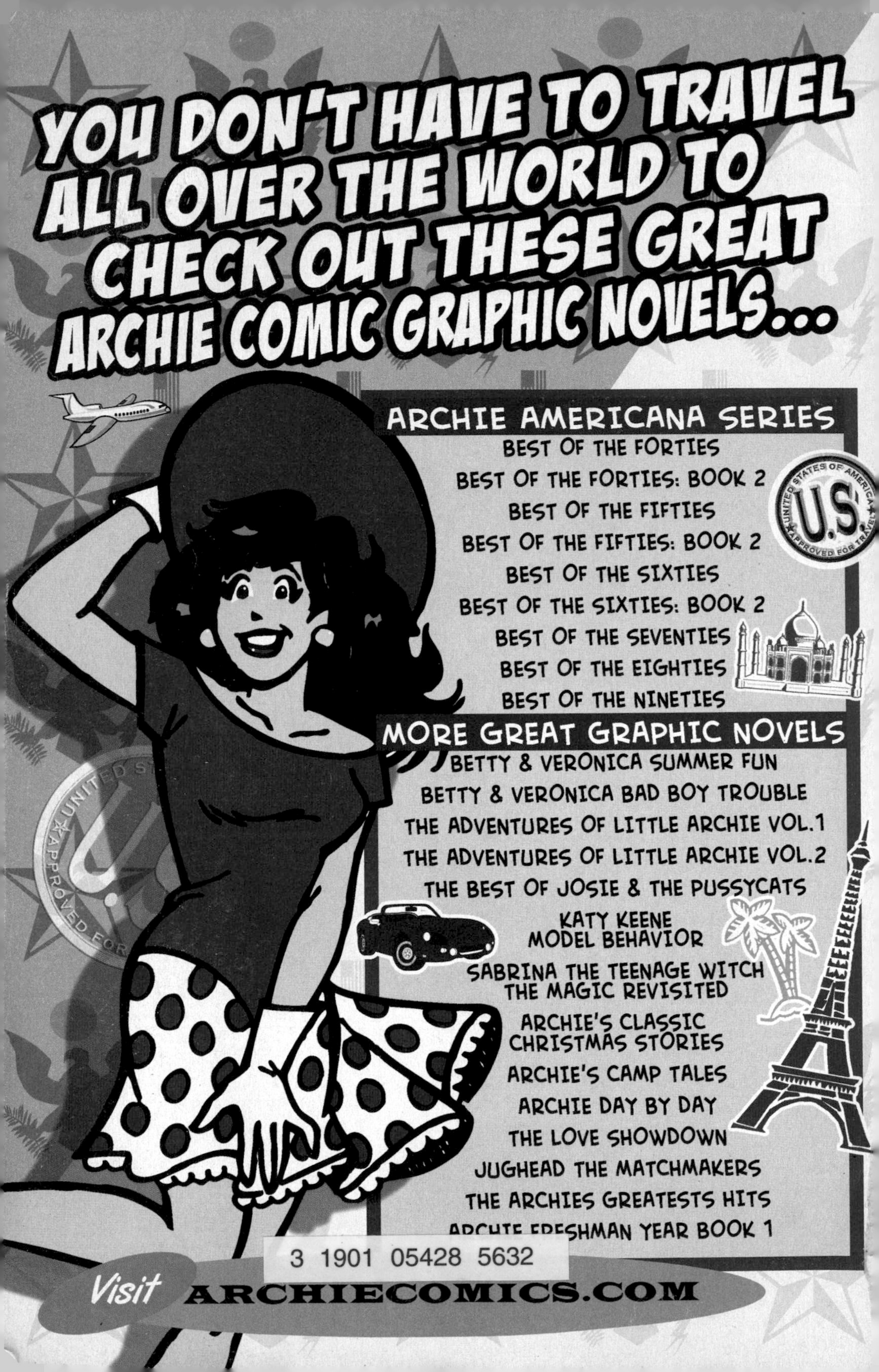
YOU DON'T HAVE TO TRAVEL ALL OVER THE WORLD TO CHECK OUT THESE GREAT ARCHIE COMIC GRAPHIC NOVELS...
ARCHIE AMERICANA SERIES
BEST OF THE FORTIES
BEST OF THE FORTIES: BOOK 2
BEST OF THE FIFTIES
BEST OF THE FIFTIES: BOOK 2
BEST OF THE SIXTIES
BEST OF THE SIXTIES: BOOK 2
BEST OF THE SEVENTIES
BEST OF THE EIGHTIES
BEST OF THE NINETIES
MORE GREAT GRAPHIC NOVELS
BETTY & VERONICA SUMMER FUN
BETTY & VERONICA BAD BOY TROUBLE
THE ADVENTURES OF LITTLE ARCHIE VOL.1
THE ADVENTURES OF LITTLE ARCHIE VOL.2
THE BEST OF JOSIE & THE PUSSYCATS
KATY KEENE MODEL BEHAVIOR
SABRINA THE TEENAGE WITCH THE MAGIC REVISITED
ARCHIE'S CLASSIC CHRISTMAS STORIES
ARCHIE'S CAMP TALES
ARCHIE DAY BY DAY
THE LOVE SHOWDOWN
JUGHEAD THE MATCHMAKERS
THE ARCHIES GREATESTS HITS
ARCHIE FRESHMAN YEAR BOOK 1
U.S.
UNITED STATES OF AMERICA
APPROVED FOR TRAVEL
Visit ARCHIECOMICS.COM